Leonard C. Smithers

The Transmigrations of the Mandarin Fum-Hoam

Chinese Tales

Leonard C. Smithers

The Transmigrations of the Mandarin Fum-Hoam
Chinese Tales

ISBN/EAN: 9783337072193

Printed in Europe, USA, Canada, Australia, Japan

Cover: Foto ©Andreas Hilbeck / pixelio.de

More available books at **www.hansebooks.com**

THE

TRANSMIGRATIONS

OF THE

MANDARIN FUM-HOAM

(CHINESE TALES)

EDITED BY

LEONARD C. SMITHERS

LONDON

. H. S. NICHOLS AND CO.

3 SOHO SQUARE W

MDCCCXCIIII

PREFACE

THE success which the edition of "The Thousand and One Quarters of an Hour (Tartarian Tales)" issued last year by the present publishers met with, has induced them to print in similar style its companion work, "The Transmigrations of the Mandarin Fum-Hoam (Chinese Tales)," written by the same author, Thomas Simon Gueulette, of whom a brief biographical sketch was given in the prefatory note to the *Quarters of an Hour*.

Commenting on these collections of stories, Mr. W. A. Clouston, a well-known "storiologist," remarks : "Much of the groundwork of these clever imitations of the Arabian Nights has been, directly or indirectly, derived from Eastern sources ; for instance, in the so-called Tartar tales, the adventures of the Young Calender find parallels, (1) in the well-known Bidpai tale of the Bráhman, the Sharpers and the Goat (Kalila and Dimna, Pánchatantra, Hitopadesa, &c.) and (2) in the world-wide story of the Farmer who outwitted the Six

Men (Indian Antiquary, vol. 3) of which there are many versions current in Europe, such as the Norse tale of Big Peter and Little Peter, the Danish tale of Great Claus and Little Claus; the German tale (Grimm) of the Little Farmer ; the Irish tale of Little Fairly (Samuel Lover's collection of Irish Fairy Legends and Stories) ; four Gaelic versions in Campbell's Popular Tales of the West Highlands; a Kaba'il version in Rivière's French collection (Contes populaires Kabylies) ; Uncle Capriano in Crane's recently published Italian Popular Tales ; and a Latin mediæval version (written probably in the 11th century) in which the hero is called ' Unibos,' because he had only one cow."

CONTENTS

INTRODUCTION

HOLONJAH, the nephew of Tahi-Kia, who was prime wazir to Tongluck, King of Gannan, was sent by his uncle into Circassia, to buy up the most beautiful damsels he could meet with in that country, designing them for a present to the Sultan of China; and the young man discharged his commission with so much exactness that never was there a seraglio stored with such variety of beauties as was the vessel wherein he embarked these Circassian women from Bassorah.

In travelling through part of Persia, Holonjah fell into the company of two darwayshes, and contracted an intimate friendship with them. The one was about sixty years old, and had such an air of majesty in his looks as shewed the greatness of his quality and condition before he embraced that kind of life; the other, who passed for his nephew, was not above sixteen, but had features so just and regular that nothing could be compared to him, except one of those pages who, according to Mohammed's doctrine, present the poncire to good and virtuous Mohammedans after their death. These darwayshes quitted their convent, as they pretended, with a design to travel over all the East; and when Holonjah proposed to carry them into China, they readily accepted his offer, and the ship was under full sail, just off the Gulf of Cambay, when it happened to be attacked by two corsairs of Adel. Their vessels were a great deal superior in strength to that wherein Holonjah was; but he and his whole crew did such wonders, and behaved with so much bravery, that the corsairs, having lost a great number of their best soldiers, were forced to sheer off.

The two darwayshes bore likewise their part in the engagement, and the elder more especially shewed such courage and magnanimity that Holonjah in a great measure imputed the victory to him. He thought himself very happy in having so brave a man on board, and was making his compliments to him to that purpose, when, perceiving his nephew all on a sudden turn pale, and the blood appear on his clothes, he was so startled at the sight that he ran to him and tore his vest hastily open with a design to help him; but was not a little surprised to find that this young person was a lady of most incomparable beauty. As good luck would have it, the wound was but slight, and had gone no farther than the flesh, a little below her breast; but the old darwaysh, perceiving that he could no longer conceal a secret which he had never disclosed to any creature before, addressed himself to Holonjah in this manner. I take you, sir, to be too much a gentleman to make any bad use of this discovery; and since an accident has let you into the sex of this young darwaysh, I shall take the freedom to relate to you what our condition is, and who we are, being well satisfied that a mind possessed with your generous sentiments will take pleasure in relieving a prince who, from the height of all worldly grandeur, is plunged, as you see, into the abyss of nothing.

HISTORY OF MALIK AL-SALIM, KING OF GEORGIA

I AM the King of Georgia; my name is Malik al-Salim, and my ordinary residence was at a castle in the province of Guriyal, that borders upon the Black Sea. By all the sultanas I kept in my seraglio I never had but two children, a boy and a girl, both born of the same mother. But my joy for her fruitfulness was soon abated by the loss of young Al-Rohamat (that was my son's name), who, together with his nurse, was stolen away by pirates when he was about two years old. I gave orders, but it was to no purpose, for my people to pursue them; they never could come up with them; and a violent tempest, which soon after arose and sunk most of the vessels that I sent out, gave me cause to think that he likewise was swallowed up in the waves. After I had sufficiently bewailed the loss of my son, I was resolved to retire with my daughter into the city of Tiflis, which is the capital of my kingdom.

This princess, whom you now see in the habit of a darwaysh, was named Gulchinraz Gundogdi (*i.e.*, morning), because at her birth she gave us great hopes of becoming in time a perfect beauty. I was then grown into years myself; and therefore, leaving the government of my kingdom in the hands of my wazirs, and spending most of my days with my daughter, I saw with infinite pleasure by the time she was arrived at fifteen that there was not a woman comparable to her. In short, I began to think seriously of choosing a son-in-law to succeed in my kingdom, when, by a sudden and unexpected turn of fate, the Sultan of Bitlis invaded my territories with a numerous army. That prince, who was commonly called Dilsinghin (*i.e.*, stony-hearted), had no cause to be angry with me ; but as the fame of my daughter's perfections was spread over all the East, and himself was too conscious that the information I had of his cruelty and vile character would hinder me from ever consenting that she should have him, he took methods to compel me to it, and entered into a resolution to seize upon my throne and to take away Gulchinraz from me ; and by the force and violence of war he in a great measure executed his design.

It was no small grief to me to see Dilsinghin lay all in fire and sword before him ; the few troops I was able to raise, after a peace of ten years' continuance, were not sufficient to make any head against him. He carried every place sword in hand, and threatened at last to put ·me to death in the most cruel manner, unless I would deliver up Gulchinraz to him. I must needs own, sir, that the despair wherein I beheld my daughter augmented my grief ; and therefore, thinking it not advisable to stay at Tiflis with an army unable to make resistance until this outrageous king should come upon me, I took with me what gold and jewels I could carry, and putting myself and Gulchinraz in the habits you see, left my palace and dominions in the night ; and travelling

through part of Persia in your company came at last
to the Gulf of Bassorah, where we embarked in your
vessel. Since then we are resolved to go with you as
far as China. You yourself, sir, may very well judge
whether we have any hopes of returning to Georgia,
and whether our misfortunes might not have sunk us
had we not set bounds to the violence of our grief when
at first we became wanderers and fugitives upon the
earth.

*   *   *   *   *   *

Holonjah was astonished to hear the misfortunes
of the Sultan of Georgia; and having asked pardon of
the princess for his indiscretion, he offered them all the
assistance that was in his power, and promised them
both never to reveal the secret. And to assuage your
grief, added he, suffer me to remind you, sir, that the
greatest evils live always in the neighbourhood of the
greatest blessings, as our august sultan not above four
years ago experienced; who from the most unfortunate
condition was advanced to the throne of China, as if
the one had been a footstep to the other. And if a
history so singular will be any alleviation of your sorrow
to hear, I will do myself the pleasure to relate it.—By
all means, replied Gulchinraz; you cannot oblige us
more.—Well then, continued Holonjah, I am ready
to do it.

HISTORY OF SULTAN TONGLUCK

Upon the death of the Sultan Yum-Vu, King of Gannan, who left no son behind him, a certain bonze, insinuating to the people that he was the nearest relation to the deceased king, came and demanded the crown, which (notwithstanding the opposition that it met with in council, and the wise remonstrances which several mandarins made to it, that a man who from his youth upwards had abandoned the care of all worldly concerns was very improper to govern a kingdom, and a head that had been accustomed to dust and ashes unable to bear the weight of a crown with decency) he obtained, and was, with the general acclamation of the people, chosen King of Gannan. But as soon as he had taken possession of his throne, the Governor of the Isle of Kiumchin made preparations to contest it with him. He certainly was the nearer relation to Yum-Vu, and proved it very plainly; but the new king, being now accustomed to the splendour of a throne, was so far from relinquishing it that he issued out his proclamations with such diligence, that having seized his rival about twenty miles from Tonquin, as he was advancing with a small army to maintain his right, he was resolved to keep him prisoner, according to the manner of the Chinese in cases of the like nature.

When any rebel is apprehended, the king goes to meet him and orders a basin and golden ewer to be presented him, which he is obliged to carry on his head, walking on foot to the place of his imprisonment. This prison is a cave dug under the throne where the king sits; they open it every day to give the prisoners victuals, and without ever troubling themselves whether they are dead or alive, do it for six months, and then wall it up for good and all. Our king, according to this custom, was going one day to meet his rival, with a purpose to treat him in this manner, when, falling into hunting, and continuing his sport till noon, the heat of the day made him flee to a shade to rest himself a little; he accordingly lay down upon the grass in the middle of a small wood to take a nap, and, to secure his face against the insects, covered it with a red silk handkerchief. His principal officers out of respect withdrew some twenty or thirty paces; and the king was in a sound sleep, when he was suddenly awakened by a very odd accident, for a bird of prey that had its nest in the tree under which the king slept, taking the red handkerchief for a piece of raw flesh, made a stoop at it with such violence that with its beak and talons, which were extremely sharp and strong, it struck out both his eyes. The officers, hearing the sultan cry out, ran to him in a great fright; but this accident, which should have raised compassion in their breasts, had a quite contrary effect upon them; for, thinking him now no longer fit to reign over them by reason of the loss of his eyes, they immediately resolved to give the crown to him who was made prisoner, since he was of the royal line; and therefore, taking the basin and golden ewer, they set it upon this poor prince's head, and so carried him to Tongluck (for that was his rival's name) whom they made choice of for their king.

This new monarch, struck with the sudden change of his fortune, and the great danger he had so lately escaped, made wise reflections, and such as well became the occasion. Heavens! said he, that ever in so short a time I should be in such different circumstances. But one of our poets has rightly observed, " Who for another makes a pit, digs for himself a grave." Unhappy bonze! continued he, your fortune grieves me exceedingly. But be in no concern for your life; you shall not be put into that frightful dungeon you had prepared for me; your sorrows I will alleviate as much as possible, and leave it to your choice, either to stay in my court, or retire into what place of my dominions you please, with a pension of a hundred thousand pieces of gold, which I will pay you yearly.—Ah, generous Tongluck! cried the bonze, throwing himself at the new sultan's feet: you shew by this how much better you deserve the throne than I. Seduced by the splendour of a crown, which I deprived you of, I intended to have put you to a most cruel and unjust death; whereas you give me a life I have not deserved; and not only so, but heap your benefits upon me likewise. Ah, sir! these are sentiments becoming a worthy monarch! Tongluck that moment embracing the bonze assured him of his perfect friendship, and so, ascending a throne which was his right, both upon the account of his birth and this singular instance of his moderation, he hath reigned about four years to the perfect satisfaction of all China.

       *   *   *   *   *   *

How happy is this prince! cried Malik al-Salim; and how wonderful is his clemency!—Nay, he is his people's darling, replied Holonjah; and if there is anything that can afflict us, it is his insensibility of love, and the apprehensions we are under of not having his posterity to reign over our children; for, of all the sultanas that he has yet received into his seraglio, none has been able to touch his heart. For this reason it was that my uncle, who is his prime wazir, sent me into Circassia; but what merit soever there may be in the rare beauties I have brought with me into China, I fear I shall have no better success than others who have been employed in the like commission before me.—This prediction proved true; for, notwithstanding all the arts that Holonjah could use to brighten the beauties of nature, and to set off the women he brought with him to Tonquin to the best advantage, Tongluck looked upon them with such an indifference as gave the other a vast uneasiness.

Malik al-Salim and the Princess of Georgia had accepted apartments in Holonjah's house in Tonquin, who took all the methods imaginable to divert the melancholy that had seized them, but himself could find no remedy for his own. And as he was one day expressing his concern to the king and Gulchinraz, on his having succeeded no better than others, in very moving terms, the princess addressed him in these words. You need not wonder in the least at the sultan your master's coldness; were I in his place, I should do the self-same thing, for his indifference, as I take it, proceeds from a heart truly noble, and not attached to the pleasures of sense. There is not one of these young women whom you present to him but thinks his favours an honour to her, and makes more account of the monarch than she does of Tongluck. Divest him of his grandeur for a moment, and it is ten to one but they will despise his person, and he by that means find out the bottom of their hearts, and that it is their ambition only which makes them desirous to partake of his bed; but find him out a person who overlooks the throne which captivates others, that rejects the addresses of a monarch, and considers him only as a private person, and then you will raise in him all those emotions and tender passions which he is not yet acquainted with.—Nothing can be juster, madam, than these reflections, replied Holonjah, but where shall we find this rare person?—You have her before your eyes, continued Gulchinraz; the throne on which I was brought up accustomed me to such respect and submission as the women you buy at Circassia know nothing of; and if I have but beauty enough to engage your sultan's eye, be his merit ever so great, I will let him know the difference between a princess and a slave, and how far the notions of the one surpass the other. There is a kind of reserve and a greatness of spirit in our sex that make us esteemed; but the ease and forwardness of almost all the Eastern women draw upon them the contempt they deserve. I may seem perhaps a little too discerning for my age, but the queen, my mother, whose royal blood raised her above the rest of her sex, took care in my tender age to inculcate these lessons into my memory so that they will for ever be engraven there.

Malik al-Salim heard this speech of his daughter with admiration. Of all the sultanas I had in my seraglio, said he, none ever found the secret of approaching my heart but the charming Abadan-Scirux, the mother of Al-Rohamat and Gulchinraz; her reservedness, her modesty, everything enchanted me in that adorable princess, and my life has been a burden to me since the moment I lost her for ever.—No more of these melancholy reflections, sir, replied Holonjah ; I very well understand the solidity of your daughter's argument ; but the way to put it in execution, that's the difficulty. Few princesses here are so beautiful as those of Georgia, and as it is no easy matter to gain admittance into their apartments, our monarchs choose, rather than marry a woman whose merit may not possibly come up to the idea they have of her beauty, to entertain themselves with slaves, where they meet with an entire submission, and from the principle of self-esteem are induced to believe that they perfectly love them. After some more discourse of the like nature, Holonjah retired into his own apartment ; where, if anything could comfort him under his want of success, it was that two merchants of slaves had presented the Sultan of China with a great number of very beautiful damsels with whom he was no more moved than at the sight of the Circassian women, who had cost Holonjah so much care and pains.

The King of Georgia and the princess had been about a month at Holonjah's house, where he endeavoured to entertain them with all possible respect and assiduity, when one day he requested the favour of introducing a brother of his, who had returned from a long voyage and had brought considerable riches with him. Malik al-Salim had too much obligation to Holonjah to deny him any favour ; and notwithstanding the aversion Gulchinraz had to be seen in the proper habit of her sex (which since her arrival in China she had put on again), she consented to receive him. After the first civilities usual among persons of their distinction were over, they sat down at table, and Uzumquay (for that was Holonjah's brother's name) seemed

to have so much wit and vivacity in conversation as
drew upon him the princess's eye more than once ; but
if Gulchinraz beheld him with some attention, he for
his part was so taken with the charms of her face and
the delicacy of her wit that he was that very moment
going to make a declaration of his passion ; but that the
presence of Malik al-Salim (who had now quitted the
habit of a darwaysh, and was known to be the young
lady's father), as well as a certain greatness of mind
that regulated all his actions, restrained him for that
time until a more favourable opportunity should
happen, and his respect and observance should inform
her of what his heart felt for her. He never failed,
however, to be at his brother's house at meal-time,
and discovered every moment new graces in the object
of his wishes. Oh! how happy are we, dear brother,
said he one day in a transport he could not refrain, that
the Sultan of China knows nothing of the treasure we
have in this house! His frozen heart would soon be
melted with the rays of the eyes of your charming guest,
and I should die with grief. But I forget myself, continued he ; you will pardon, most beautiful Gulchinraz,
this involuntary transport, and not be offended at a
declaration I am constrained to make. My respect,
however, shall at all times set bounds to my passion,
be it ever so strong and violent. The princess immediately blushed. She had for some time a struggle
within herself, between the secret inclination she felt
for Uzum-quay, and that greatness of spirit which
was the rule of all her actions. But hastily rising
up: Uzum-quay, said she, with her eyes sparkling
with anger, you know not who I am, and there-

fore I think it proper to let you know the distance that is between us ! The King of Georgia, who is here before your eyes, is my father ; judge, therefore, whether our conditions be equal: examine yourself, in short, and fail not in the respect which is due to me for the future, unless you are desirous that I should quit your brother's house.—You the Princess of Georgia ! cried out Uzum-quay instantly. Heavens ! what do I hear, and what must I be ! Oh, beauteous Gulchinraz, that I were this moment the Sultan Tongluck, to offer you a heart worthy of your acceptance !—That would not make you more amiable in my eyes, answered the princess, with great modesty. The lustre of a throne blinds not me ; and the monarch of China, with all his power and greatness, could have no more right over my heart than another person, unless I felt a secret sympathy for him, without which my father has promised me never to dispose of my hand. Nay, I will own something more to you, to ease the sorrow I see painted in your eyes, and I will own it without a blush. From the first day I saw you, I conceived an esteem for you ; I wished you had been born a prince, and that you had sufficient power to restore my father to his kingdom of Georgia, which the traitor Dilsinghin, King of Bitlis, has robbed him of by surprise. I should then have preferred you before all the monarchs in the world ; and my father who loves you too would have confirmed my choice with his consent. But this is superfluous talk ; I was born to a throne, nor will I dispose of my heart without one.

Uzum-quay threw himself down that moment at Gulchinraz's feet. I am sensible, madam, said he, of the rashness of my love, and I will do what I can to subdue it, nor will I ever more mention a passion to you which I finds offends you; and saying these words he withdrew full of confusion. Holonjah asked a thousand pardons of Malik al-Salim and the princess for his brother's indiscretion. For above eight days together the afflicted lover durst not appear in Gulchinraz's presence; and when upon express order he ventured to come, there appeared so many tokens of fear and sorrow in his looks that the king pitied him, and ordered his daughter to comfort him with some indications of her forgiveness. Re-assume, Uzum-quay, said she, your former gaiety. I forget the offence you have committed, and therefore beg you will let us live in the same familiarity as before it was disturbed by your profession of a passion which I never can or ought to accept. Uzum-quay obeyed the princess's commands; he returned to his former manner of living, and with infinite satisfaction perceived that she was no longer offended with him.

He had already lived five months every day in the princess's company, when, going one night into his own apartment: You are avenged, sir, said he to Malik al-Salim, for Dilsinghin is dead, and your faithful subjects expect your return with the utmost impatience. Here is a letter that your wazirs have sent you; and, to convince you farther, behold the head of the King of Bitlis, which I here give you in this basket. It is impossible to express the surprise that Malik al-Salim and Gulchinraz were in at this sight. The head of their enemy, which was still bloody, and the letter signed by all the wazirs of Georgia, made them not question the truth of what they saw. But by what enchantment, said they, could you perform things that seem impossible ?   Nothing, replied he, with looks full of modesty, but my passionate desire to be serviceable to the most beautiful princess in the world. You may now return with the king your father when you please, madam, into Georgia, and I will conduct you thither in less than four hours. In less than four hours, answered the princess. Ah, sir ! how desirous soever I may be of returning to Tiflis, I am not for that kind of voyage ; it seems a little too supernatural and dangerous. My father and I had better go the common road than hazard our lives in that. There is no danger at all in it, continued Uzum-quay ; and when I have told you in what manner you came to be avenged of your adversary, you will not be afraid of the conveyance wherein I offer to conduct you to Tiflis. But supper is ready. My brother, to testify his joy for your re-establishment, is desirous to regale you this night ; and I after supper will recount to you the manner in which so many wonders were wrought.

Malik al-Salim and the princess went into the apartment where they were to sup. There was exquisite meat of every kind ; but above all, a fine young pig with a pudding in the belly of it. The whole entertainment, indeed, was served up with great elegance, and being all sat down at table there was perfect joy in everyone's countenance. How great is the obligation I have to you ! was the King of Georgia every now and then exclaiming. No, my dear Uzum-quay, I can never sufficiently acknowledge it, and my daughter Gulchinraz is the only thing wherewith I can repay it. You are not born a prince, indeed, but does birth depend upon ourselves ? True nobility lies in virtue and glorious actions, and not in a train of ancestors, whose deeds are too often our disgrace ; what a joy will it be to me, if my daughter will accept you for a husband ! ˉAh ! if she must needs have a crown, I will relinquish mine, and think myself happy to be your first subject. Uzum-quay, seeing that Gulchinraz ḍid not oppose the king's intentions, threw himself at her feet. Confirm, said he, adorable princess, confirm your father's desire, but let it not cost him his throne. I had rather renounce the possession of my queen than deprive him of his rights. The princess raised her lover up, not knowing well how to act. She suffered him to hang about her knees and kiss her hand, and Malik al-Salim embraced them both in the most affectionate manner, when all on a sudden they heard a noise in the ante-chamber. The doors were forced open, and immediately entered thirty black slaves, with their sabres drawn ; and at the head of them a young man about thirty years old, but beautiful beyond imagination. Perfidious Holonjah ! cried he ; is it so you deal with your master ? To me you have presented a set of slaves, the very refuse of Circassia, and kept for yourself a beauty, whose charms are superior even to those of the houri. But I will soon shew you the consequence of such treacherous behaviour.

These words, spoken in great wrath, and the confusion which Holonjah and Uzum-quay appeared to be in, made Gulchinraz suppose that he who spoke in such an absolute tone must needs be Tongluck. King of China, said she, with a fierce undaunted air, persons of my rank and quality are not wont to be presented to such as you, like slaves, but are sued to by way of

ambassadors. I am the Princess of Georgia, and this
is my father, the Sultan Malik al-Salim. A base usurper
banished us from our kingdom ; and Fortune, who from
that time was all along our cruel enemy, seems now to
have declared herself in our favour. The lovely Uzum-
quay has made a reparation for all her mistakes by
reinstating us in a throne which Dilsinghin, King of
Bitlis, had unjustly invaded. You are not ignorant in
what manner a prince like you should behave to those
who are his equals. Treat us, then, with the dignity that
becomes our character, and Holonjah for not informing
you we resided at his house. I forbade him, because I
was unwilling that your sight of me should increase the
aversion you had for our sex.—Ah, madam ! replied the
Sultan of China, how unjust are you to your eyes ! Are
you ignorant of their power, and think you that they are
incapable to touch my heart ? Yes, adorable princess,
you were the only person who could dissipate the coldness that surrounded it ; you were born for no other
purpose but to work miracles. But you change colour,
I perceive, and my love makes you uneasy. Uzum-quay,
the lovely Uzum-quay (for so you called him) whom I
saw at your feet, has found out the way to please you.—
Sir, says Malik al-Salim, immediately interrupting him,
I am concerned to see your love ; but our obligations to
Uzum-quay are so exceeding great there is no way of
paying him but by giving him my daughter in marriage.
—Oh, Heaven ! cried Tongluck ; does the charming
Gulchinraz prefer a private person to the monarch of
China ?—Yes, sir, replied the princess with an air of
constancy ; I loved Uzum-quay without his knowing it,
and even before he restored us to our throne ; since that

time he has put the head of our enemy under our feet, and this service has gained him the empire of my heart, which my father's consent has confirmed. From that moment I looked upon him as my husband; nor are all the powers upon earth able to make me change my resolution. However, sir, continued the princess, in a little softer tone, I know myself but poorly qualified to dissolve the coldness of your temper. There are others enough to fill the place that I am not at all ambitious of; for, in short, your hour is come; and if it be true, that you could love me, as your majesty is pleased to assure me, it will not be long before you will contract yourself to some beautiful sultana, who will answer your passion more favourably than I can do.

What says the happy Uzum-quay, continued the Sultan of China, to such noble and endearing sentiments as these?—I say, replied the tender lover, throwing himself at the princess's feet, that my happiness exceeds my hope, and I have at last found what I have been looking for—a disinterested heart, and one who, in loving me, loves my person only. But it is time, adorable Gulchinraz, that I discover to you who I am; and you will pardon this innocent artifice, which I only made use of to gain assurance of your heart. You see in Uzum-quay, then, the true King of China; whereof the other, who acted his part so well, is no more than a phantom. I know now the bottom of your heart; I owe not your love to my quality. It was love alone that gained your declaration of a passion, where the monarch would have no preference. I have the consent of the king your father; you are avenged of Dilsinghin by the help of one of my mandarins, before whom Nature herself is naked; and being master of the elements he commands the jinnis who inhabit there with such absolute authority that they even tremble at his voice. What have I, then, more to desire, after such a declaration as you have made in my favour? Come, my dear princess, come and ascend a throne, where you will become the happiness of the King of Gannan and the admiration of all China.

Malik al-Salim and Gulchinraz were so surprised at this strange discovery that they stood immovable as statues; but Tongluck having ordered the pretended king with his attendants to retire, and Holonjah confirming the truth of what had passed by throwing himself at the princess's feet to ask pardon for having made use of this artifice, she raised him up, and giving her hand to kiss: Do I then find, said she, in the person of Uzum-quay, the sultan who reigns here? Is this an illusion? and are these transactions anything but a dream?—No, madam, nothing is more true, than that it depends upon you alone to make the King of China happy. Holonjah raised my curiosity speaking of a beautiful stranger he had at his house, and whose heart, as he told me, was as insensible as mine. I have seen you several times under different disguises; but at last I thought proper to personate Holonjah's brother, more particularly to know those sentiments which have raised my esteem of you. You could not yourself but perceive the love I conceived for you at first view, and how great my astonishment was when I understood that you were the Princess of Georgia, a secret which Holonjah had concealed from me till then, with a design to have you revenged on the traitor Dilsinghin. Upon this occasion

2—2

I had recourse to the famous Fum-Hoam, the mandarin of the law, whom I was mentioning to you. He carried me to Tiflis in less than three hours ; by this means I got into the usurper's chamber. I awoke him with my sabre in my hand, and challenged him to fight me; but the poor poltroon betook himself to nothing but abject prayers. I thought it not worth while to trifle with the wretch any longer, and therefore I took away his life ; and Fum-Hoam having assembled your chief wazirs, I shewed them your enemy's head (at the sight of which there were a thousand acclamations of joy) and upbraided them with their weakness in owning a traitor for their sovereign. I then ordered his favourites to be seized, and all who would not acknowledge their lawful king; and being, in short, become absolute master of the city of Tiflis I appointed two of the principal wazirs to govern your dominions until your father's return ; and having received from them the letter I delivered into his hands, I and Fum-Hoam came back again as quick as lightning, and in as short a time as we went brought your enemy's head to Tonquin. Thus you see, madam, what my love has made me enterprise for your sake ; and shall not this love be recompensed with the present of your heart ? Or can you delay giving yourself up to the tender instances of a prince who adores you ?

Every circumstance of this account which the Sultan of China gave increased the astonishment of Malik al-Salim and Gulchinraz. Sir, replied she, with a blush, I love you; and having made that declaration so lately, it is no time now to dissemble; but still my religion is above my love ; you are an idolator, I am a true believer. You adore several monsters, whose very figure is enough to terrify one, and make one renounce their worship; I know but one God, whose ambassador and great prophet is Mohammed. You believe in the passage of the soul from one body to another, which is a principal point with your Doctor Shakabut; and I hold it to be absurd and ridiculous. This, sir, is my opinion; and I leave you to judge whether we can be joined together in eternal bonds without your swearing to me in the most solemn manner that you will allow me the free exercise of my religion in Tonquin. Oh, madam, cried Tongluck, may my head be a mark for my bitterest enemies to shoot at, if ever I pretend to molest you in your religion! but I hope you will not always be so fixed in your resolution, but that the famous Fum-Hoam may in time convince you of your error. He assures me that the Chinese and the Georgians are both to be subject to the same Divinity; but if he does not succeed in what he has promised me, I swear by the same oath that I will not only be a proselyte to your religion, and own Mohammed to be the true messenger sent from God, but will destroy likewise all the pagodas in my empire, and tread under foot the statues which at present we adore. Upon this assurance, replied Gulchinraz, I am yours, sir, and here is my hand. Whereupon Tongluck, transported with joy, took his bride by the hand, and led her to his palace through a line of soldiers, who held every one a flambeau of odoriferous wax in his hand. Fum-Hoam and the other mandarins soon dispatched the marriage ceremonies; and this charming couple having first conducted Malik al-Salim into a noble apartment retired afterwards to their own.

After some days spent in those pleasures which usually attend a marriage that is founded upon love, the queen bethought herself of the mandarin. You promised, sir, said she to the sultan, to bring Fum-Hoam into my company; but I hear you say no more of him. He shall attend your orders, my beautiful queen, answered Tongluck; let somebody go for him. The mandarin came in about a quarter of an hour; and after he had paid his due observance to the two sultans and the queen, he was ordered to sit down upon a velvet cushion. The learned and illustrious Fum-Hoam, said Gulchinraz to him, to whom I have so great an obligation, and who has restored my father to his throne in a manner so extraordinary, could not well arrive at such a degree of wisdom and capacity without some singular adventures which I would be very desirous, I can assure you, to know from your own mouth. It will be no hard matter, madam, replied the mandarin, to gratify you in that; only I must premise to your majesty that I very much doubt whether you will credit what I shall have the honour to relate to you. I am not ignorant of the prejudice you have against the principles of our religion, and how you look upon as fables the very fundamental truths of it. But since your majesty is willing to know the principal events wherein I bore a part, it will be requisite to inform you that the soul is like a chameleon, which, according to the different bodies it passes through, takes different impressions, and is subject to all the passions of the body it inhabits. This is a point, madam, which you must have the goodness to admit (whatever you may have to allege against it) in order to hear my relation of some surprising histories, and such as will afterwards convince you of the truth of what I here advance. I have appeared in all parts of the world in very different forms; have consequently been of all religions and all sects; and, by a peculiar power, have preserved to this very day the remembrance of all the chief facts whereof I was an eye-witness or agent myself. That certainly must be very curious, replied Gulchinraz, with a smile; let me desire you to begin, then, for I promise to hear you with the utmost pleasure, and not to give you any interruption with the reflections I may make. What difficulties I have to propose I will reserve to the last, till you have finished your account and are come to the state of a mandarin, under the figure wherein I now behold you; but as the narration will in all appearance be of a long continuance, I will every evening set apart the time between our walking and supper, which I designed for the music and concert. The princess then signifying by her silence that she expected Fum-Hoam to speak, the grave mandarin began his story thus:

HISTORY OF MANDARIN FUM-HOAM

I CANNOT, madam, call to mind the first adventures of my life, without some horror; since the very moment I left the celestial sphere to come down upon the earth, I animated an unhappy infant who became afterwards a monster of cruelty. It was in Persia where I was born, under the name of Piurash. My father, who was but a poor shepherd, left me a very small estate; but I managed my intrigues so as to get into the confidence of Siamak, one of your Pischdadan kings, and obtained the first honours and dignities of the kingdom. The horrible luxury wherein I lived might have made me, one would think, look upon honours with some contempt; but the thirst of dominion was so predominant in my soul that I made a scruple of nothing to attain it. As I was Siamak's chief favourite, I had every moment free access to him; but being weary of living sneakingly under him, I cruelly murdered him, and easily seized upon his throne; after which I committed so many crimes that the world looked upon me as an abominable tyrant. There was no violence, no injustice that I stuck at; no new punishment that I did not invent to destroy those who pretended to oppose my will; but Heaven, who was weary, no doubt, to see me commit so many crimes, was willing to humble me with a cruel distemper. The extreme disorder wherein I had passed my youthful days occasioned a putrefaction in my bowels; insomuch, that I became, even while alive, the food of the vilest creatures without any hopes of getting rid of them. My body became, in short, one great ulcer; and, dying as I did, in long and terrible torments, I left behind me in Persia a fearful example of the Divine justice. But observe, madam, continued Fum-Hoam, a surprising metamorphosis for its singularity! My soul was no sooner departed out of the body of this cruel King of Persia, but it was immediately enclosed in that of a flea. Though this change was a great humiliation to me, yet for some time at least I had the satisfaction not to see myself deprived of human blood, which I was so greedy of before; and had several opportunities in this little body of exercising some singular strokes of my vengeance. When I was Piurash I had a seraglio filled with the most beautiful women in the East, and kept by slaves, who at the least turn of my eye trembled for fear. No sooner was I dead than one of my wives, whom I loved best, and who made sincere returns, as I thought, to my endearments, gave an uncontrolled loose to her passion; she fell distractedly in love with a young Persian who worked in my gardens, and who, to gain the easier admittance, counterfeited a fool; she introduced him into her chamber, and gave him the place I was accustomed to have.

You will hardly forbear laughing, madam, when I tell you how I swelled in my little body with rage, to hear my favourite sultana's railleries, the imprecations wherewith she loaded my memory, and the transports wherewith she received the caresses of her lover. I threw myself that instant with fury upon the beautifullest body in all Persia, bit her in a thousand places, and made her all over blood; till at last, being mad, and blinded with my growing rage, I threw myself designedly into my perfidious sultana's fingers, and there received my death.—Ah! ah! a very pleasant and jocular adventure! cried Gulchinraz, laughing; but what became of the soul of the illustrious Fum-Hoam afterwards?—You are very pleasant, madam, I perceive, replied the mandarin, the conclusion of this story I knew would cure your seriousness; but though you look upon it as a mere fiction it is nevertheless very true.

STORY OF THE HINDU MOUNTEBANK
AND HIS DOG

WHEN I left the body of that insect, continued Fum-Hoam, I passed into a little dog belonging to a mountebank, whose name was Kalim, and who was at that time at Arrakan. I had an instinct equal to the wit of men, was extremely beautiful, and surprisingly quick at learning anything, so that every one was for buying. me ; but the mountebank set me at so high a price that no one would come up to it. My pretty little tricks, however, were the whole talk of the town of Arrakan, and raised the curiosity of a certain very rich and jolly widow, who sent for my master ; but when he came into her house, so blinded was he with the sprightliness and vivacity of her eyes, that he changed his mind concerning me. Dariyah, for that was the widow's name, was at first delighted with my little size ; and after she had seen all my exercises was still more taken with me. What will you take for this little creature ? said she to Kalim.—Madam, replied he, I mean not to sell him, but to present him to you ; but it is upon a condition which I fear you will not accept of. I can no longer bear the sight of so much beauty without being sensibly affected with it. I love you, madam ; and though I here pass for a mountebank, I am of an illustrious birth and parentage ; answer, then, my love, with an equal return of yours, and suffer me to be happy in the enjoyment of you ; for that is the price I set upon my dog.

Dariyah was so surprised at this proposal that she fell into a violent passion. Be you who you will, said she, be gone out of my presence, or I will call my slaves to chastise you!—I would not advise you, madam, to do so, answered my master; I fear not your threats, and can soon defeat their malice. These words enraged the beautiful widow to such a degree that she called for her slaves and ordered them to treat him roughly; but my master had no sooner blown a little powder that he took out of a box among them, than, instead of falling upon him, they let fly at each other with so much fury that they fell down on the floor like so many dead men. Whereupon Kalim, addressing himself to Dariyah: You see, madam, said he, one part of my secrets; I will leave you in your present surprise. You will reflect upon the honourable passion I have for you; in four days time I will come with my dog again to your gate, and then I hope you will give me a more favourable reception than you have done to-day.

✳   ✳   ✳   ✳   ✳   ✳

The Mandarin Fum-Hoam was going on with his story, when word was brought the queen that supper was upon the table.—I am sorry for it, said she, for I sadly want to know how the fair widow received him.—Your majesty shall know that to-morrow, answered the mandarin; for I will not fail to be at your closet-door at the hour appointed.—I beg you will, added she, for you cannot do me a greater pleasure. And so she rose up to go to sup with the sultan her husband, and the King of Georgia, and Fum-Hoam retired to his own house.

CONTINUATION OF THE STORY OF THE HINDU MOUNTEBANK AND HIS DOG

THE Queen of China went next day into the walks, where she found the mandarin waiting for her ; she therefore brought him with her into her closet, and when every one had taken his proper place he re-assumed his discourse thus :

My master, as soon as he retired, left the widow in great consternation. His youth, good mien, and handsome address were frequently in her thoughts ; my little tricks and activities were perpetually before her ; and it was not without much impatience on her side that the fourth day came. We were introduced by her own orders into the bed-chamber ; and my master, having first put me into her arms, threw himself at her feet. My fair Dariyah, said he, forget, I beseech you, the insult I put upon you when I was last here. I was con-strained to do it to avoid the effects of your anger ; but, if to declare that I love you be an offence, I must own that I am a thousand times more culpable now than I was before. The heart, however, that I offer you, madam, is not unworthy of your acceptance. I am son to one of the King of Golconda's wazirs ; my father, who has no other child but me, was for marrying me against my inclination ; to avoid an engagement I had such an aversion to, I ran away (for his menaces made me leave Golconda) with a purse full of gold that I took from him. In two years time I travelled through the Indies and a great part of Persia. I joined myself in company with one of the ablest mountebanks in the East, got into his confidence, and was admitted to all his secrets; and we were returning together upon our way to Golconda (where I understood my father was dead), when I had the misfortune to lose him at Bantan by an accident occasioned by fire, which all his knowledge could not preserve him from.   He went to sup in the country at a great lord's house, where there chanced to be hard drinking.   The company sat great part of the night at table; and as the wine had heated their brains they fell all asleep in the dining-room.   The slaves followed the example of their master; one was so drunk that he set fire to a kind of office not far distant from them, so that they were all suffocated before any help could come. I was much concerned for the loss of my master, but took possession of all his drugs and of a certain book wherein all his secrets were contained.   I then came to Arrakan with a design to make no long stay; the little feats of my dog raised your curiosity; you sent for me to your house, and from that moment I have entirely lost my liberty.   Be then my wife, my beautiful Dariyah; delay no longer the happiness of one who loves you to excess, and go with me to Golconda, where you shall partake of the immense riches the wazir, my father, left me at his death.

My master spoke these words, continued Fum-Hoam, with such a passionate accent, that Dariyah suffered herself to be persuaded; she gave him her promise, and received his, and it was not long after that I saw them congratulating each other upon the happiness of their mutual enjoyment.   After they had adjusted measures to see one another frequently, Kalim retired, and left me with his new spouse, whom I loved beyond what anyone can imagine ; for never was there anything more amiable than she. Love danced incessantly in her eyes, which seemed more bright and shining than two stars ; an enchanting grace appeared in all her actions ; her smiles, her ordinary words, her least motions, her sighs, her complaints—nay, her very frowns and contempts, had a certain charm in them that went directly to the heart ; and therefore you may judge, madam, whether Kalim had not reason to think himself happy in the possession of so charming a wife. But as jealousy has always its eyes open, it was not long before a young Indian lord, who was greatly in love with my new mistress, took notice of the frequent visits that Kalim made her ; he spoke to her of it in a manner insolent enough ; and as she used him not very civilly for it, the young enraged lover spread reports everywhere exceedingly prejudicial to her reputation, which, coming soon to her ears, filled her with grief and disconsolation. She had her reasons for concealing her marriage ; she had scarce been two months a widow, and to declare it as yet would be discovering her infamy and giving the world a handle to reproach her with incontinence. Kalim proposed to her to go with him to Golconda, but he could not prevail. She was loath to give such a blow to her reputation, and therefore she entreated him to absent himself from Arrakan for a few days to let these injurious reports blow over, which cruel order he obeyed with great reluctance, pretending to her to go into Persia.

All this while Dariyah, overwhelmed with the bitterness of grief, was devising in her mind some expedient to reconcile the interest of her love and her reputation together. She was extremely pensive for the absence of Kalim; when, bethinking herself that I knew her mind perfectly, and very frequently made her slaves understand it, she redoubled her tears, and kissing me very tenderly: Ah! would to God, said she, that thou couldest this moment bring my husband thither, as thou makest my slaves come, upon any little sign! how much should I be obliged to thee!—Dariyah, madam, had scarcely ended these words when, jumping from her lap, I went hastily down the stairs, and, as good luck would have it, getting out of the sink-hole, I met Kalim in the street, disguised like an old woman; but so perfectly changed in his whole figure and make, that without my smelling, which was very exquisite, I could not have known him. I leaped into his arms, expressing a thousand little endearments; and the tender husband, making use of this pretence to get into the house, knocked at the door, and was carried in to Dariyah, as an honest poor woman in the neighbourhood, who had just brought again her dog, whom she had just found in the street. It was no hard matter for Dariyah to know Kalim in this disguise, especially when, as she was squeezing his hand, she saw some tears trickle down from his eyes. She ordered her slaves therefore to withdraw; and after a whole hour spent in his arms, without ever once opening her mouth, her heart was so full of joy and sorrow both, she gave it out in the family that she could not better recompense this good old woman for the service she had done her than in keeping her to have an eye over her slaves. So that Kalim continued with Dariyah, and enjoyed, with great ease and quiet, the pleasure of being beloved by

one of the finest women in Hind, when his good
fortune was all on a sudden ruined by a very odd sort of
accident.

Kalim and his dear wife were so intoxicated with
their happiness that they were perpetually together.
So sudden a transition from grief to joy occasioned a
great disorder in my mistress; she was seized with
a fever, and for four or five days that Kalim spent at
her bedside no one took care of me or remembered to
give me any water. I lay usually with a young slave,
who waited on Dariyah, and for whom I had a great
kindness; but she not understanding by the barking
and moan that I made what a violent thirst I had,
instead of giving me something to drink, fed me with
perfumed conserves, which I loved mightily; but they
only helped to inflame the violent heat that burned up
my entrails, and which proceeded at last to such excess
that I found myself forced by an unknown power to
bite the young girl's thigh. Whether it was her
modesty that made her conceal the wound, or that
she thought it not so great as it was, but she told
nobody of it, until the venom I had infused had entered
so deep that by the time Dariyah came to recover of her
fever her slave began to shew too manifest symptoms
of the effects of her madness. They found out the cause
of her malady by the dread I had of water, and were
more confirmed in the thing when they saw that, with
eyes sparkling with fury, I fell upon all the slaves in the
house, and pursued them without barking, but with open
mouth all over foam.

My mistress was greatly concerned to see me reduced
to this sad state, and was sensible of a double loss, in that

she was obliged likewise to have the girl smothered. For besides the love she had for me, I was a kind of sentinel at her chamber-door while she was shut in with her husband; my barking let her know when her slaves were coming up; nor was it possible for her to be surprised while I kept such strict watch for her security. Judge you, then, madam, what a violent shock and mortification it must be for her to prevail with herself to give orders for me to be taken and cast into the river. Her orders, however, were executed very punctually. They seized me, they tied a stone about my neck, and carried me to the river Martaban. Dariyah fell into tears at the remembrance of my pretty little actions, and Kalim endeavoured by the most tender caresses to assuage her grief; when her deceased husband's two brothers entered her apartment, at a time she was ill prepared for such a visit. The condition wherein they found her with Kalim, could no longer permit them to be deceived with his appearing in the habit of an old woman. They had reason to suspect that their sister had given herself up to lasciviousness; and being sufficiently convinced of the outrage she had done to their brother's memory, they fell upon her and Kalim, whom she held in her arms, and stabbed them in twenty places.

While this bloody and cruel scene was acting, I was struggling in the river; but having happily bit the string asunder, which was tied to the stone that made me sink, I rose above the water again, which was so very cold, that it extinguished the madness in me; so that I found myself cured of the raging heat that had devoured me, and, taking myself to my heels, ran as fast as I could back again to my Dariyah's house. But how was I surprised, when at my first entrance I saw nothing but blood and horror everywhere! The murderers of Kalim and my dear mistress were still in the house. I fell upon them, I bit them as high as I could reach; and, had my strength been equal to my rage, I should have quite devoured them. They were informed, however, that I was mad, and had therefore recourse to the common medicines to cure themselves; but whether our gods were determined to punish them for their brutal cruelty, or that some remains of madness were still lurking in me, it so happened that in a short time they died raving mad, after having almost devoured each other.—As for me, madam, being overwhelmed with despair, which I testified by such dismal howlings as drew tears from the eyes of every bystander, I threw myself upon the bodies of this unhappy couple, whose death I was the innocent cause of; (for had I been in my usual situation, I should have prevented their surprise). I licked their wounds, and refusing all kind of nourishment, died in a short time with grief at their feet, and was burned together with them on the same pile.

     *   *   *   *   *   *

Ah! lovely little dog, cried the Queen of Gannan, how sorely do I lament thy fate, and that of this unhappy couple! But wise Fum-Hoam, said she, you were without doubt, happier in the body you next inhabited? — Not very much, madam, answered the mandarin.

STORY OF MASSUMAH

WITHOUT ever yet going out of Hind, I entered into a young maid of Bisnaghar, and was born of parents, famous for the nobility of their ancestors, as well as the immensity of their riches. My name was Massumah, and my father, who had no more children than me, made it his whole care to find me out a deserving husband when I came to be seventeen years old. I was not in the least handsome; on the contrary, I was a little deformed; yet, for all that, one of the finest lords in all Bisnaghar, and as brave as ever were the Indian heroes of old, made his addresses to marry me. I had wit in abundance, and that made some amends for the defects of my person. We loved one another with a boundless flame which enjoyment did not extinguish. But we had scarce been married six months when there broke out a fierce war between the Kings of Bisnaghar and Narsing. Mansur (for that was my husband's name) went to the assistance of his prince; and, having the command of a principal part of the army, like a thunder-bolt of war, cut down everything that opposed his valour, and made victory entirely incline to our side; when, suffering himself to be carried away by too inconsiderate an ardour, he penetrated the enemy's army, and forced his way into the very midst of them. Everyone fled at the weight of his blows; but as he was not followed and supported by his own men, the enemy, being ashamed to see themselves so slaughtered by a single hero, rallied again, and surrounded him. It was to no purpose for them to shew deference to his bravery, or call to him to take quarter. Mansur answered their civility only with the strokes of his sabre; and, throwing himself like a lion among them, defended his life to the last gasp, till, pierced through and through with a thousand stabs, he died upon heaps of his slaughtered enemies, and made even those by whom he fell envy the fate of a death so heroic.

If my husband's death had happened at the beginning of the battle things had worn quite a different face; but fortune had already declared for the King of Bisnaghar, though it was at a dear rate enough, since he lost in my husband the support of his crown. After the victory our soldiers found the dead body with fury still painted in his eyes, and in this condition they brought him home. Ah, madam! my grief upon this occasion was so exquisite that I could neither utter the least complaint nor shed a single tear. My eyes were covered with a thick mourning veil, and I fell into a fit which continued so long that it was not without much difficulty I was at length recovered to a life which I detested. To rend my clothes, to scratch my face and breast, and tear my hair, were the least signs of my pungent sorrow; and still more to increase it, I had my husband's body embalmed with the most costly perfumes, laid him on a bed of state, and both day and night gave him incessant tokens of my sincere love, by watering his corpse with my tears. I had led this melancholy life for about eight days, when a certain good widow, whose room looked into my house, came running to my father's one morning, quite out of breath.—Sir, said she, your daughter has hitherto passed for a pattern of conjugal virtue; but come now and see her forfeit in one moment that character which we all thought she had justly acquired. She is actually now in the arms of a new lover, who is solacing her for the loss of the brave and illustrious Mansur.

My father, continued Fum-Hoam, was exceedingly startled at this news, so different from what my sentiments had all along appeared to be. At the woman's solicitation, he took his poniard, and coming along with her as far as my chamber door, was not a little surprised to find no other object of my love, than the body of my dear departed husband. It was that sweet mouth, which death had now deprived of all its lively colour, that I was kissing a thousand times, when this woman, without knowing the true motive of my tenderness, and trusting to an obscure view, ran to inform my father of the dishonour she imagined I was bringing upon my family. The old gentleman would, no doubt, have nearly destroyed her, had she not fled away and escaped his anger. He then related to me the occasion of his visit; and, taking pity on the sad condition I was in, thought the best way to remedy my grief would be to remove the object of it. For which reason, in pursuance of the king's order, he had a stately funeral pile erected before my house; and, notwithstanding my earnest entreaties to the contrary, was making preparation, according to the custom of the country, to reduce my husband's body to ashes. But seeing myself about to be deprived of the dear object of my love, whom death had so cruelly taken from me, I roared like a lion bereaved of its whelps; and as the fire was lighting, I went up to the terrace of my house, and throwing myself boldly through the

flames had the comfort to die embracing my dear
Mansur.

*   *   *   *   *   *

I had no sooner left the body of this virtuous Hindu,
than I passed successively into several others ; wherein
there happened nothing remarkable.   I was a bee, a
cricket, and a mouse.—Oh ! how many secret matters,
replied Gulchinraz, must you have seen under the last
mentioned form !—It would be an endless work, madam,
continued the mandarin, to pretend to recount to you
all the knavish tricks I have seen and heard under that
shape.   How many virgins have I seen, who had the
reputation of being such, give themselves up to sad
disorders !   How many widows married again in private,
or living in incontinence !   How many old men sunk
into children by the extravagance of their conduct !
How many rich men reduced to extreme misery by
their debaucheries !   How many beggars made insolent
by wealth !   What a number of hypocrites could I have
unmasked had I had then the use of speech !   How
many kadis have I seen selling justice !   And how
many bonzes, darwayshes, and kalandars, have I known
to be mere profligates under the outward shew of mortification and piety !   For, in short, madam, there was
neither chamber nor closet, court of justice nor council-
room, nor any other apartment so closely shut, that I
could not easily get into it ; and nothing, you know,
escapes the eye of him who sees all things, and has
no obstruction to hinder his sight.   But, after having
lived seven years in the skin of this little beast, and
gone through great part of Persia and the Indies, I
died at last, as most part of my species do, being
caught and strangled by a cat.

ADVENTURES OF THE IMAN ABZINDARUD

IN an instant I found myself at Ormuz, in the body of a certain young man, named Abzindarud, who, by profound reading of the Koran, came to be made an Iman. Notwithstanding this promotion, which should have made me more circumspect in my conduct, I was still a libertine, till the great Prophet thought fit to restore me to the right way by a punishment that has something very singular in it. There was a widow in the neighbourhood, very beautiful, and a little suspected of gallantry; she was choked with a bone, which she swallowed in eating too greedily; and, as her house depended upon my mosque, I was called to perform the abdest, and feeling an emotion in myself at the sight of so much beauty, I could not forbear crying out, though I was very indiscreet in so doing: Ah! great Prophet, how happy should I have thought myself to have tasted with this fair widow the pleasures which are reserved for true believers with the houri! No sooner, madam, had I said these words, which but ill became my character and function, than my hand, which was then upon her face, moved involuntarily, so that my finger, I know not how, slipped into her mouth, and her teeth closed upon it, and bit me so violently, that I could not forbear squalling grievously. My astonishment was as great as my pain; for, notwithstanding all my endeavours, I could not get away my hand. It was to no purpose to ask pardon of the Prophet for my insolence; my prayers were not heard; and therefore, to avoid scandal, I e'en took the resolution to cut off my finger, which I accordingly did, and returned home all bloody, pretending I had met with this unlucky accident, of which I was a long time ill, by some awkwardness of my own. So odd a punishment made me reflect deeply, and apply myself so diligently to the offices of my function, that I was soon looked upon as a man much beloved by the Prophet; and I was so entirely addicted to prayer, that whenever any person came into my mosque they always found me either reading the Koran or in some profound meditation.

So much virtue and piety raised the envy of the other Imans, and they set a young woman to tempt me to defile myself with her; but I bravely withstood the temptation, and sent away the impudent baggage with threats. But she, being exasperated at this manner of treating her, was resolved to be revenged of me. To this purpose she abandoned herself to one of these Imans; and no sooner did she find herself with child, but, carrying her impudence to the highest pitch, she had the hardiness to accuse me of having committed violence upon her, even in the mosque where I officiated. So gross a profanation as this enraged all the people against me: my brother Imans had no pity for me; on the contrary, they, by their credit, got me thrown into a dark and dismal dungeon, where I suffered most cruelly, until the time that this unhappy woman was in labour. The Kadi carried me that moment to her bed-side, taking the occasion to question her, when her pains were sharpest upon her; but she making the same declaration again, I should certainly have been executed had I not had recourse to the same Prophet who punished me so severely in the case of the widow. Mighty Mohammed!

said I, taking the child in my arms, which this slanderous woman had just brought into the world; thou who art the true father of believers, the source of light and truth, suffer not the impostor to triumph over my innocence; but untie the tongue of this infant, that he may himself declare who his true father is!

No sooner had I ended the prayer, which I spoke with much fervency, and accompanied with my tears, but —would you believe it, madam?—this new-born infant began to speak very distinctly. He named the Iman who was his father, declared me wholly innocent of the profanation whereof I was accused, and added that it was at the solicitation of the same Iman, who was then present, and of two other of his brethren, that his mother had undertook to ruin me, and to take away my reputation with my life. After so extraordinary a declaration, I was soon avenged of my enemies. The calumniatress and the three Imans, overcome by the force of truth, confessed their crime, and were carried out of the town and burned alive. I had my mosque restored to me again, and from that time was always looked upon at Ormuz with the greatest respect imaginable. In gratitude to the child who had declared my innocence to the world, I took care of his education, and provided him with a good nurse. In process of time he came to succeed in my employ; for before he was weaned from the breast he gave some signs of his sanctity, and on two memorable occasions shewed manifest proofs of the choice that Mohammed had made of him to be the support of his religion.

One day, as the nurse was holding him in her arms, she chanced to see a very handsome Persian nobleman, well dressed and well mounted, pass by. Would to God, cried she aloud, that my child may be like that fine lord! Whereupon the child left the breast, and looking steadfastly upon the nobleman, pronounced these words very distinctly: Good Lord! forbid that I may be ever like that man, whose conscience is a sink of iniquity! The nurse was strangely surprised at this answer, when a man who was whipped passed by the door. God forbid, said she again, that ever my child come to this fate! But the child, turning to her, expressed a different sentiment of the matter. You must learn, said he to her, never to judge by appearances. That fine nobleman, whom you saw pass by, is in reality guilty of the crime for which this man is punished. His innocence makes him easy under his sufferings, and in the midst of these outrages he is continually saying to himself: I am content; God is sufficient for me, and it is He who will keep an account of what I endure! So that this man, by his patience and resignation to the will of God, has attained to a very eminent degree of merit, whereunto I wish with all my heart that I may ever arrive.

As every good Mohammedan is obliged once in his life to go to Al-Madinah and Meccah, and I had not yet taken that pilgrimage, I obtained leave of the King of Ormuz, and left the care of my mosque and of this young child in the hands of my muezzin. After a vast deal of fatigue, I arrived at the tomb of the Holy Prophet. I returned him my thanks for his visible protection of me; and, when I had offered the usual sacrifice upon the Mountain of Arafat, I took the road which leads to Ormuz; but it was so late before I got thither, that the gates were shut, so that I was forced to stay all night in the suburbs; and being in some perplexity about my lodging, I asked a little shelter of a man whom I saw standing at the gate of an elegant house. The man very readily asked me to come in, and carried me into a fine hall where supper was served up, and a woman about forty years old, of a very courteous behaviour, sat at our table. We passed the evening very merrily. At last I was conducted into a chamber and left to myself. I shut my door, went to bed, and had been in a very sound sleep some hours, when on a sudden I was awakened by a frightful apparition which took hold of my arm.

My hair stood on end with fear, when, by the clear moonlight, I could see distinctly a man stark naked, stabbed in thirty places, and the blood gushing out from every part of him. Fear nothing, said he, wise Abzindarud; I am in no condition to do you any harm; on the contrary, I stand in need of your assistance to be revenged: only hear me with attention. I was not long since the master of this house, and was making preparations to go to Ispahan, when my wife, who supped with you last night, took the advantage of this opportunity to assassinate me by the help of my brother, who had criminal commerce with her. After they had both stabbed me in this very chamber, they threw me into a well in one of the little gardens belonging to the house, and afterwards filled it up. A crime of this nature ought not to go unpunished. Go, therefore, to the Kadi as soon as you are out of the house, inform him of what I tell you, that he may punish the authors of my death, and let my body have such a burial as every Mohammedan who has exactly followed the law of Mohammed deserves.

You may imagine, madam, how I passed the re-
mainder of the night after the apparition was gone.
As soon as it was peep of day I got out of the house as
fast as I could, without ever taking leave of my host;
and going to the Kadi's house I related to him all that
had happened to me. It was well he was acquainted
with the chief incidents of my life before, or otherwise he
would have hardly believed my account; but as it was,
he took instantly some of his asses with him to the
house, and ordering the well that was filled up to be
cleared, he had no sooner discovered the certain proofs
of the murder than the woman and the accomplice confessed the crime, and accordingly were executed for it.
The corpse was decently buried; and, as I assisted at
that doleful ceremony, I spared not my prayers for the
repose of his soul. Afterwards I returned to my own
house; and had scarce got to sleep the same night, when
the apparition appeared to me again, but in a quite different manner from what it did at first. I am pleased
with what you have done, said he to me; your charitable
zeal has procured me a burial; I thank you, and am
willing to gratify you for your trouble. Ask, therefore,
whatever you desire most, and I have a promise from the
great Prophet that it shall be granted.

After I had mused for some time, having no concern
with the world, I neither desired honours nor high places.
All that I desire, said I to the apparition, is to have
warning of the hour of my death eight days before it
comes, that like a good Mohammedan I may without
horror bear the sight of the Supreme Judge of both
our good and evil actions, when I shall be ready to go
and give an account thereof.—I agree to your request,

answered the apparition, and will come myself to give you information of it; do you continue always to follow the law of the great Prophet, to say the five prayers appointed in the Koran, to observe the ablution so much recommended by Mohammed, and you shall see the terrible day approach without fear. When I awoke I reported this second apparition to four or five of my friends; but they only laughed at me, and would give no credit to it. As for myself, being fully persuaded that it was not the effect of a heated imagination, I applied myself wholly to the practice of good actions, and to bringing up the child with care, whose education I had taken upon me.

Twenty years were now past, in all which time this young man went on in the way of perfection. I made him my muezzin, and had sufficient reason to be satisfied with his gratitude. One day, five or six of my friends came to see me, and I made them stay to dinner. That day we passed very agreeably; and a great storm happening a little before night, I entreated them to take a supper and a bed with me. We had almost done supper when I heard one knock at my gate. I ran with a light to see who it was that should want me at such an unseasonable hour, but how great was my surprise to find it was the man who had appeared to me twice before! Virtuous man, said he, I keep my word with you, and am come to inform you that within eight days you shall no longer be reckoned among the number of the living. As soon as I heard this terrible sentence I felt a great trembling all over me, and returned into the room so terrified that my friends were alarmed at it; but when I came to tell them the cause, though there were two in the company to whom about twenty years before I had related my adventures, they all treated it lightly, and observed that the fastings of Ramadan, and the extraordinary austerities I had imposed upon myself, had seized upon my brain. It was in vain to remind them of the dead person's history, his murder, and his apparitions; they persisted still in the same infidelity; but being myself persuaded of the truth of the prediction, I fell into a deep melancholy; not that I had any regret to part with life, but a dread and apprehension of being not sufficiently pure to appear before the Sovereign Creator of all things. I began then to repent of my wish, but having prepared very seriously for that passage, the nearer I approached to the appointed day the more I found my soul easy and undisturbed. My pupil was dissolved in tears; but seeing me much better than was usual with me, he endeavoured to persuade himself that the time of our separation was not yet so near.

The fatal day arrived at last, when these same friends of mine came all to my house; they found me busy in reading the Divine book, which the angel of the Lord dictated to the sovereign Prophet, and could not refrain from weeping. The day passed without any accident; the night came, I was still alive, and began myself to believe that the apparition had deceived me, when, having occasion to cross my court-yard, several balusters that made a kind of gallery on the top of the house tumbled down and fell upon my head. At the noise of this disaster my friends ran to me, and finding me all bloody and expiring, were too severely convinced of the prediction which the spectre had foretold.

*   *   *   *   *   *

These are incidents somewhat singular, said the Queen of China, and they please me the more because they seem not to agree so well with your system of transmigration; but I will not stand with you for so small a matter. Proceed, Sage Fum-Hoam, and recount what became of you next. The mandarin blushed a little at this gentle reproof, and then went on thus :

STORY OF THE BEAUTIFUL AL-RAYULF

I PASSED over the seas, madam, to Visapur, and came into the family of a rich Hindu merchant, whose daughter I animated. For eight years after I was born, my mother had no other child but myself, and my father, being desirous to revenge himself of fortune for refusing him a son, endeavoured to procure me all those perfections which not only distinguish a woman from the rest of her sex, but even make an accomplished man. As I possessed every disposition necessary to learn the most abstracted sciences, and was active, beautiful, and well shaped, I had all kinds of masters who were proper to improve both my mind and body: and succeeded so perfectly well in every exercise, that in a short time I was become the subject of all conversations in Visapur.

No sooner was I sixteen, and arrived at an age wherein the graces had lavished all their charms upon my person, than there was not a young Hindu of quality who did not use his best endeavours to obtain me for his spouse; but, by what cruel caprice I cannot tell, my father despised all their addresses, and was resolved to give me to a wazir, who was extremely old. Accordingly, I married him, though fitter to be my great grandfather than my husband, and thereby put an end to the hopes of all my suitors. The sciences, which I was mistress of to a great degree, had given me frequent occasions to read many matters of gallantry; but as my passions did not yet begin to work, the reading of them occasioned no emotion in me. But love, who was offended at my simplicity, raised a revolt in all my senses, and by continual reflections made me comprehend the reason of the tears of so many lovers for their mistresses, and that the height of happiness consisted in loving and being beloved again. Thus guided by nature, love, and conversation with my female friends, who knew the detestation I had for the old wazir, I was extremely smitten without ever knowing the object I desired to possess. My husband had a sister, who was a widow lady, and much about his age; she had an infinite deal of wit; and as she had for above twenty years a sort of academy at her house of the most learned persons in Visapur, she earnestly entreated her brother to make me one at their assembly. He consented, and no sooner was I introduced than I was loaded with commendations for some works I read to them; but the praises that touched me most came from a young Hindu lord, whose name was Da'ud. Our eyes met each other so frequently, and with such eager glances, that we were soon made sensible of all the emotions of a violent passion. Da'ud, under borrowed names, charmed the ears of all the academics with his fine verses and his tender and passionate songs; and he could easily perceive that those which I composed grew by degrees tenderer and tenderer. Hearing me frequently speak mysteriously, and what he himself knew only how to expound, he took courage at last to write to me, and to declare the love he felt for me in his letter. I received a vast pleasure in reading it, and it was not long unanswered; after which we wrote to each other very regularly. We had continued this epistolary commerce to my great satisfaction something more than a month, when, by the negligence of our porter, the note I had written to Da'ud fell unluckily into the hands of my old husband; and he, supposing me guilty in the most essential point, produced it to my father. Ah! madam, continued Fum-Hoam, what cruelty and hard heartedness did I meet with in these two old men! Their first design was to stab me in a thousand places; but being both desirous to preserve their reputation, which they thought I had mortally wounded, they devised an expedient of a very singular nature. Directly over the place where I was accustomed to dress my head there stood a marble bust, representing one of our ancient kings; it was placed upon a cornice and fastened by an iron pin, which went through the wall into a room which was never used. They so ordered this pin that by pulling out the key which went through the hole of it, the bust might fall upon me; and then watching me through a hole they had made in the wall, they observed when I went to dress my head, and let the bust fall so suddenly that it crushed me to pieces before ever I saw it coming, and thus punished me for a crime which I never committed.

* * * * * *

4

I greatly pity that unhappy Hindu, said Gulchinraz, and think fathers very blameable who dishonour them-selves by unsuitable matches. — That is very true, madam, continued Fum-Hoam ; it was the source of my misfortune, to which the sciences, wherein my father had me instructed, contributed not a little ; and I am, from my own experience, fully satisfied that the care to govern her family should be the only employ of a virtuous wife ; and that it is next to a miracle if pride or some other more dangerous passion make not a woman neglect her duty when she once comes to apply herself to the study of learning, and affects to surpass the rest of her sex.

HISTORY OF JIZDAD

WHEN I left the body of this unhappy victim to avarice and interest, I found myself in an instant trans-ported into a village not far from Iolkos, which nature had enriched with all its gifts. The air was wholesome and pure, the water as clear as crystal, which, falling from the top of Mount Petras, divided itself into a thousand rivulets, exceedingly cool, and watered the plains, which were very beautiful. The fields were stored with cattle of all kinds, and the earth enclosed in its bosom mines of gold and silver, which the covetous-ness of mankind had not as yet dug up. A rich shepherd of this village, who dwelt in the most pleasant part of it, where he had built him a very commodious house, was my father. He called me Jizdad, and Fortune, who was lavish of her favours, made me appear in those parts under the form of one of the greatest beauties that had ever been seen in Greece.

As I was one time, in imitation of my companions, who spent whole days by the clear fountains or in the dark forest in pursuit of the fallow-deer, scouring through our woods, and had out-ran my greyhound, a very frightful figure of a shepherd met me. My fear gave wings to my feet, and I ran as fast as I could, but the monster of a man pursuing me very nimbly, I found it would be but vain to trust my fate to my heels, and therefore turned about, and let fly a dart at him; but, as I had no sure hand, I missed my aim, and the brute came up to me that moment, with an attempt, no doubt, to revenge my contempt of him at the expense of my honour, when a lovely graceful youth ran to my cries, and cut his head asunder with one stroke of his sabre. I was so exceedingly terrified when my deliverer came up to me that I had scarce strength to thank him, much less had I power to resist his desires; and though he did not attack me with such brutality as the insolent fellow he had just then killed, yet he was no less daring in his enterprise, and attained the same end, though in a different way. I had no sooner recovered my spirits than I was struck with the most pungent sorrow, and loaded him with a thousand reproaches for the horrid deed he had done. My tears and repeated cries gave him no time to excuse the extravagancies of his passion; he was apprehensive they would bring company to the place, and therefore mounted his horse, and rode away as quick as lightning. It was to no purpose to tear my hair or

disfigure my face; my despair was no relief to my sorrow
which every day increased more and more, when I came
to perceive that I carried in my womb the certain marks
of my misfortune.

It was the custom at Iolkos to have every year a
feast, in order to engage the young shepherdesses there-
abouts to avoid the surprises of love; and the feast began
usually with purification, which was done by bathing in
a little river that rose out of the mountain. All the pre-
tences that I could make would not excuse me from being
at this feast; I was obliged to do as the rest of my companions did, and so we all went to the river-side, where
we undressed ourselves under a tent set up for that purpose. I had a veil which hung over my body, but not
thinking that sufficient to conceal my weakness, and
imagining to hide it better, I plunged myself hastily into
the water up to my neck; but as soon, madam, as I came
to feel the coldness of it, the miserable fruit of my
betrayer's indiscretion so leapt within me, that I swooned
away in my companions' arms; and as I had in my looks
all the symptons of a dying person, they concluded to
carry me home to my mother. Nobody had hitherto
perceived my fault; the simplicity of these girls made
them not suspect the condition I was in; but the moment
my mother cast her eyes upon me: Wretched creature,
said she, crying out very imprudently, would to God
thou hadst died the moment thou wast born !—Ah !
see you not here the occasion of her faintings ? With
this my companions opened their eyes, and were but too
much convinced of my fault; then, stealing out one by
one, they went and reported the news of my misfortune
everywhere. My death was decreed by the laws of

Iolkos. A disgrace of this kind cannot be washed out but by one's blood, especially when he who is the author of it does not appear to marry the person he has dishonoured. So that as soon as I came to myself I could read my sentence in the looks of every spectator about me.

The uneasiness of the state I was in, the shame that would redound upon my family, and the fear of punishment, all together made me miscarry ; and hereupon I was soon conveyed to the place of execution, where, as a victim to the brutal passions of men, I was to suffer certain death ; and, what was a great addition to my father's grief, he, by the custom established at Iolkos, was obliged to cut short the course of that unhappy life which himself had given me under the aspect of malevolent stars. I invoked Heaven with all earnestness ; I besought the gods to make known my innocence and the involuntariness of my crime ; I called to witness the trees under which I unhappily chanced to be conversant with that rash man ; but the gods seemed deaf to my prayers, and I was reaching out my neck to the knife, which my father held in his trembling hand, when Prince Kuluf, son to the late King of Iolkos, and who himself about a month before had ascended the throne, stayed my father's hand. Hold, shepherd, said he ; suspend thy resentment and obey no longer a law that is too rigorous, and which 'I abolish this moment. This beautiful young woman is not culpable ; and Heaven, who will not suffer the innocent to be oppressed, sent me hither to save her life. As I was myself the person that robbed her of her honour under those very trees, it is but just that I should repair my fault by making her my wife. Consider her, therefore, henceforward, as your queen, and do justice to the virtues of the beautiful Jizdad.

You may imagine, madam, what effects these words of the king had upon the minds of all the shepherds and shepherdesses. In a moment the forest rung with a thousand shouts of joy, and the names of Kuluf and Jizdad were repeated without intermission. The king called his guards, who stood at some distance from the place designed for my punishment, and, embracing me before them all, took me, together with my father and mother, into his chariot, and carried us to his palace, where I was married to him with all the solemnities due to his rank. But I must own to you, madam, that the splendour of the throne to which I was advanced, did not affect me near so much as did my justification. I was not at all elated to see myself raised above my companions. I always remembered the meanness of my birth, and taking great delight in succouring the distressed, I let not a day pass without doing some remarkable kindness to my people. This made my husband love me very tenderly, and my subjects in a manner adore me; insomuch that it was not without abundance of tears that at seven years' end I died, and left no posterity behind me.

STORY OF HUSCHANK AND GULBAZI

As soon as I had quitted the body of Jizdad, I entered into that of a young child, whom a dyer in the suburbs of Shirah, while he was washing his stuffs in the River of Baudamir, found in an ebony trunk which the current of the water threw up just by him. The man, as soon as he had broken open the lock, was surprised to find a boy dressed in rich linen, and adorned with jewels, which made him believe that he must needs be born of some illustrious parents. I held out my little hands as if I implored his succour, and begged my life, and he was so sensibly touched with my situation that he carried me home, and gave me to his wife, who divided her milk between a daughter she had then at her breast and me. When I was grown up to a youth's estate, I found I had no inclination to my reputed father's trade, and therefore employed all my time in hunting, and at night, when I returned from my sport, I used always to bring home more game than would feed the whole family. My foster-sister's name was Gulbazi, and the dyer called me Huschank. Though I had a very great respect for Gulbazi, as supposing her to be my sister, yet I perceived so much beauty in her that I could not look upon her without some strange emotions. One night, as I was presenting her with a young stag, I fell at her feet, and embraced her very tenderly. Huschank, said she to me, Heaven is my witness, with what purity I love you, and how much I am concerned for your life. You cost me many a tear every day ; nor can I see you encounter wild beasts without horror, for I have this daily dread upon my spirits that at one time or other you will be brought home bathed in your own blood. In the name of all tenderness, my dear brother, leave off this violent exercise and let us have a little more of your company at home !—Ah ! my charming Gulbazi, cried I, do not persuade me to follow a mean

employment, and to which I have an utter aversion !
I will never be a dyer ; my bow and arrows will maintain me ; and I had a thousand times left my father's
house ere this, and gone into the queen's army, but that
there is some secret charm in this place which detains
me.   You are my sister, most adorable Gulbazi, and I
cannot without offence pass the bounds of the most strict
friendship and affection ; but what would I give that the
passion I feel for you were legitimate !   Yes, I swear to
you by Mohammed, that were I in possession of the
whole universe, I would set the crown thereof upon your
head, even though your condition were more humble
than it is !—Alas ! my dear brother, answered Gulbazi,
with a flood of tears, how exactly do your sentiments
correspond with my own !   Ten thousand times have
I wished that we had not been joined together by the
bands of consanguinity ; and, notwithstanding all these
invincible obstacles, I still find my love increasing for
you every moment ; I blame myself often for the caresses
I give you ; they alarm my shame and modesty ; and I
dread more than death the least shadow of a crime.—
Why then do you detain me here ? said I to her, with
more than ordinary transport.   Why should we thus
constantly expose our feeble virtue to temptations ?
Adieu, Gulbazi ! I must avoid for ever your dangerous
charms, and this is the last kiss you will receive from
your dear Huschank !

This resolution, madam, continued Fum-Hoam, how
many tears soever it might cost us, I had the courage
to execute.   Next morning at break of day I went and
offered my service to one of the Queen of Persia's
wazirs ; and being unwilling to own myself a dyer's

son, I told him I knew not my father's name ; but
that, if I might judge by the nobleness of my spirit
I flattered myself I could do such renowned actions as
would make the queen herself not ashamed to own me
for her son.—This little vivacity of mine made him
smile ; he gave me, however, an immediate employ,
and, being willing to know whether my courage was
equal to my pretensions, recommended me to his father-
in-law, the prime wazir, who ordered me to serve him in
the capacity of aide-de-camp. Their general was then just
going to fight a great battle. I charged always at his
elbow and under the eye of my protector. I saved both
their lives that day, and performed such prodigious acts
of courage that the enemy looked upon me as the tutelar
god of Persia, and durst not abide my blows. Thus all
the campaign through I carried victory along with me,
and the wazir, astonished at my courage, did me the .
honour to declare publicly that the success of that day
and the following ones was wholly owing to me. The
enemy, in short, were entirely defeated ; we made them
tributary to the queen, and I was sent to Ispahan to lay
at her feet the marks of their submission and obedience.

Dugmi (for that was the queen's name) had been
left a widow by Kudaddan, King of Persia (by whom
she had only two daughters), much about six months,
when I came before her. The wazirs had often pressed
her to give them a sovereign. I was very handsome,
and my name was become so famous, that she took
great notice of me. If my parentage was obscure, my
great exploits had so advanced it that I was looked
upon as one descended from those first heroes, who, as
they tell us, governed Persia in the most obscure ages

of antiquity; and the more I endeavoured to conceal my origin the more was the mystery supposed to be merely an artifice to prove the affection of Dugmi's heart. In short, the princess herself was so blinded with the notions of my birth, that from that very moment I thought I could discern that I was not indifferent to her.

The Queen of Persia was something more than five-and-thirty, but I never saw so fine a woman in my life. She was so exceedingly well made, that one could not behold her without admiration; her hair, which was blacker than ebony, was finely contrasted by the fairest and most lively complexion; a delicate proportion and exact regularity appeared in every feature of her face; and the whole was a collection of charms sufficient to captivate the most indifferent heart, and above the power of eloquence to describe. The fire of her eyes was sufficient to raise a flame in the most serene breast; her mouth, which she only opened to load me with praise, displayed a set of the finest and most regular teeth in the world; her hand, which she gave me to kiss, seemed to be made only for sceptres and crowns; and a noble boldness and air of majesty raised and supported all these perfections. The truth is, I was so astonished at the sight of them, that, forgetting in that instant my dear Gulbazi, I entirely lost the use of my reason. What became of me, madam, I cannot tell; but as soon as I recovered myself out of the deliquium, I perceived I was in the arms of one of the queen's old slaves, who gave me to understand that my mistress had tied on my arm her own picture set with diamonds of extra-ordinary value; and after some inconceivable transports

of joy I retired to the prime wazir's house, as he had
ordered me. In five days' time he himself came to
town, and as I was relating to him in what manner
the queen received me, he was so surprised with the
magnificence of her present, that embracing me very
tenderly : — My lord Huschank, said he, Fortune,
I see, begins to look upon you with a favourable eye. I
will make her acknowledge your merit; and before a
month be over your head, doubt not but to place you
upon the throne of Persia.—What! me, my lord! said I,
surprised; by what means can you think of effecting it?
—By marrying you to Queen Dugmi, replied he. Such
a hero as you alone deserves to be our sovereign, and
since the choice depends solely upon her, I will die if I
bring it not to pass!

The wazir, not doubtful of my gratitude, and thinking that this advancement would be a means to bind me
eternally to him, did his utmost endeavours to keep his
word. He went to wait on the queen, and having
extolled my services to her he perceived, by her blushing upon every occasion of mentioning my name, the
strong impression I made on her heart. He took the
advantage of this favourable situation, and persuading
her to believe that a person of my exalted valour could
not but be sprung from some illustrious family, he conjured her, in the name of all Persia, to make me her
husband; and putting the other wazirs and soldiers, who
were witnesses of my glorious actions, upon the same
request, he reduced her to this at last, that she only
required some time to consider before she resolved upon
a matter of such importance; and so, without seeming to
gratify the strong inclination she had conceived for me,

she consented in a few days afterwards to place me on the Persian throne.

I own to you, madam, that I was not a little intoxicated with love and ambition. Dugmi was the most charming princess in the world. She seemed not to be above twenty, and I thought myself the happiest man living to see with what goodness she received my love. One night, as I was embracing her knees in profound respect, I thought she seemed a little uneasy in her mind. What troubles my queen? said I to her, trembling; does she repent of the promise she has given to her wazirs?—No, Huschank, said she to me, my sentiments must always be subservient to the interest of my duty; and the desire of all Persia is a sovereign law to me.—A sovereign law, madam! cried I, with some emotion. Can you believe that I will ever be indebted to your subjects, and not to your own inclination, for the inestimable happiness of possessing you? Ah! too adorable Dugmi, how sovereign soever the laws of state may be, a real affection makes them submit to those of love. He will owe all to the object of his passion, and looks upon politics as an obstacle that generally crosses the happiness of true lovers. As I was saying these words I marked the queen's countenance, and saw a visible alteration in it. Her troubled looks, which seemed to search for mine, were afraid at the same time to meet them and had she not recalled her usual dignity, her beautiful eyes, which seemed then more languishing than ever, had perhaps given me some intimations of the most private sentiments of her heart. Huschank, said she to me, your passion is violent, nor am I calm and composed enough to answer you upon that head. Let me get a little rest, I beseech you, which your company and the sense of your merit have bereaved me of since the time I first beheld you. I was throwing myself again at her feet; but she lifted me up, and giving me her hand to kiss, obliged me to retire. However, I gave her a look at parting that discovered the disorder of my soul. At length, madam, the evening preceding our marriage arrived, and as I lay me down to take a little rest a fearful dream disturbed all the pleasure of my sleep. My dear Gulbazi, I thought, appeared to me all in tears. What are you going to do, Huschank? said she to me. Have you so soon forgotten all the tenderness I had for you? Rash young man, the splendour of a throne dazzles you! But tremble to set your foot thereon, for in so doing you will commit a most hideous crime unless I am partaker with you. I waked on a sudden in a most terrible fright. What signifies this extravagant dream? said I to myself; it is not worth minding. I cannot marry Gulbazi without offering a violence to nature. But how much soever I resolved against it, I could not get over my terror. It grew more and more upon me, until they came to dress me in all my splendid attire, and the greatest lords of Persia conducted me into the mosque belonging to the palace, where I was married to the charming Dugmi.

How much reason soever the queen and I had to be satisfied with each other, it is certain we were both in very great disorder, notwithstanding all we could do to suppress it. I perceived it first in my consort, but imputed it only to her regret at having married a person she knew nothing of, and scrupled not to mention the great uneasiness that my suspicions gave me. No, no, my dear Huschank, said she to me, your suspicions are injurious to my love. I can now own to you without a blush to what degree it is I love you; but a dream which I had last night gives me some pain. The King Bahaman, my father, appeared to me; he forbade me to marry you, and foretold innumerable mischiefs to befall me if I did not obey him. As I have no great reason to be so well pleased with my father, as to respect his memory, I have made no scruple, even contrary to his express orders, to give you my hand. This is all the matter that troubles me.—Ah! my dear queen, said I to her again, much such another dream has had a like effect upon me, but I have regarded it no more than you. Our heated imaginations occasion these phantoms, but our love will soon break through the impediment they would put to our mutual satisfaction. In short, we passed the rest of the day with ease and tranquility enough. The night came; my spouse was undressed, and her slaves put her to bed. And I too, after I had taken my leave of the wazirs, whom I loaded with presents (especially the two to whom I was indebted for my throne) went to lie by her side. There was nothing now, one would have thought, to oppose my desires, but only Dugmi's bashfulness, which I conjured her to banish for ever, when happening to espy, by the help of the wax-lights in the room, as the bosom of my shirt was open, the perfect mark of a tulip on my stomach—Oh, Heavens! said she, shrieking violently, this is the interpretation of my dream! and then, pushing me from her with all her might, she threw herself out of bed, and ran to a closet where an old slave lay, who had brought her up, and hastily shut the door.

You may imagine, madam, continued the mandarin, in what surprise and astonishment I was left. I put on my gown and ran to the door, but they refused me admittance; so that after much entreaty I broke it open, and found the queen fallen into a swoon in the old slave's arms, whose name was Sunghir. What is the reason, said I to her, of all this uneasiness? Why does the queen, who has had all along hitherto so much kindness for me, fly from me with horror? Unfold this secret, I conjure you. Sunghir made no reply, but opening my gown, and shewing me the tulip—Ah! said she, the queen has sufficient reason; that fatal mark has reduced her to this condition. Dugmi that moment opened her eyes, and turning them languishingly upon me—Ah! dear Huschank, said she, praised be the great Prophet, that I did not defile my bed with incest; you are my son!—Your son, madam! replied I, with the utmost astonishment, that is impossible; and since I must inform you of my birth, which I was willing to conceal because of its meanness, I am the son of a dyer in the suburbs of Shiraz, surnamed Topal, because he is a cripple. I could not bring myself to like so mechanic a life; my courage gained me some glory in your armies, and my queen had the goodness to requite me with her hand and her heart for some gallant actions of mine which had the good fortune to please her.—Huschank, replied the queen, with a languishing voice, Heaven grant that what you tell me be true, and that Topal may be able to rid my mind of the secret horror of this marriage, which nature inspired but my love surmounted! Let us, then, live like brother and sister till this mystery be unriddled, and to-morrow set forward for Shiraz.

I could not but comply with the queen's request. The next day we departed, and arrived at the palace of Shiraz, where we sent to find out Topal. But how great was the poor man's surprise when he was brought into a closet, where only were Dugmi, her slave, and myself, and told by what means I became King of Persia! He fell prostrate at our feet; but the queen, raising him up—Topal, said she, it but ill becomes you to use such a posture to me; rather praise Heaven for having blessed you with a son whose shining valour has merited a throne, and live in future with us in such plenty and honours as are reserved for the father of the illustrious Huschank.—Ah, madam! replied Topal trembling, Huschank is not my son.—Who then is my father? said I, turning as pale as death.—I cannot tell, my good lord, answered the old man. It is now about nineteen years since I found you in an ebony trunk, which floated on the River Baudamir, and stuck in the stuffs which I was then washing. The richness of the linen and the jewels wherewith you were adorned made me believe that you were of an illustrious family, and that some malignant star had destined you to lose your life before you could know the use of it. I took you out of the trunk; my wife brought you up, together with my daughter Gulbazi, and you left me, sir, the moment I came to understand the aversion you had to my profession, and was about to inform you of the mystery of your birth. I was so surprised at this dis-course of Topal that I never observed the queen, as she fell back upon her sofa all drowned in tears. I fell instantly at her feet. Let me but know at least, said I, to what adventure I owe my life, and why I came to be thrown into the River Baudamir.—Ah! my son, cried Dugmi, how can I tell you a thing that I cannot think on without horror, or in what terms shall I do it? But as this horrid secret is known to none but faithful Sunghir and myself, and you have all the interest that can be to conceal it, I shall run no hazard in relating it to you, how unwilling soever I am to do it.

.

HISTORY OF DUGMI, QUEEN OF PERSIA

BAHAMAN, my father, King of Persia, resided for some part of the year at Shiraz. He had no other children but me, and would to God I had died the moment I was born! The sultana, my mother, died when I was scarce twelve years old; and to my misfortune, I was but too beautiful. My father, who was generally well beloved by his subjects, laid the death of my mother sore to heart. His wazirs in vain represented to him the unreasonableness of his immoderate grief; he regarded them not, but shut himself up in his seraglio, and would see nobody for above three months. I shared in his sorrow, as much as my age would permit; and he, won by my endearments which I did not then understand the consequence of, could not look upon me without conceiving a criminal passion. I had not discretion enough at that age to distinguish his sentiments; I acted from nature only, and the tenderness he perceived I had for him served only to kindle that

5

horrible fire that burnt in his veins when I drew near;
however, my fourteenth year of age, which improved my
reason, made me more reserved towards him. This
grieved him exceedingly, and made him complain to me;
but I knew not how to answer his complaints, and only
endeavoured to avoid them as much as I could; when,
all on a sudden, I found myself seized with an illness
unknown to me before. I lost my appetite, I had
continual vomitings, and felt strange emotions within
me. This made me very uneasy; and the ignorance of
our physicians had nearly proved fatal to me, when my
father fell dangerously ill, and all the care that could be
taken of him was not enough to drive the angel of death
from his bed, whose approach he dreaded exceedingly;
however, when he found he had not many moments to
live, and was going to give an account of his deeds
before the awful tribunal of God, he ordered everybody,
except Sunghir and myself, to leave the room; and
calling to me :—Come hither, said he, my daughter,
receive my last farewell, and grant me your pardon for
the fault which the execrable passion I had for you
made me commit. You were much too wise and too
virtuous willingly to comply with it; but I took the
advantage of a deep sleep, which every night I cast you
and Sunghir into, and by that means gave myself up to
the most detestable crime of abusing your innocence.
This, my dear Dugmi, is the cause of your illness.—
You may imagine, sir, continued the Queen of Persia,
my condition at the hearing of this. Rage and despair
made me thunder out a thousand imprecations against
Bahaman. He heard them with humiliation. I have
deserved all this and more, said he; but still let it be

concealed; all Persia is hitherto ignorant of my crime and your shame. I give you this in charge, Sunghir, added he, speaking to the woman, that you take Dugmi hence; her just fury may perhaps discover a secret that ought to be buried in everlasting oblivion. I am now going to leave some orders about the affairs of my kingdom. Sunghir pulled me out of Bahaman's chamber; he immediately made the wazirs come in, and having proclaimed me Queen of Persia made an order that whomsoever I should choose, him should they acknowledge for their king. As my father had always governed his subjects with great lenity, and was not a little beloved by them, his orders were punctually executed; for no sooner was he dead than they forced me from one of the lower apartments of the palace, where I was giving myself up to despair, and placed me upon the throne. To the same apartment I retired again, under pretence of lamenting the loss of a monarch whom I then detested, and whose memory I still detest, where I continued six months without ever appearing in public, but always bewailing the infamy my cruel fate had brought upon me. When my hour was come, I was delivered of a child, who came into the world with the plain mark of a tulip upon his breast. It was Sunghir who received the fruit of my father's detestable love, which I could not myself look upon without horror. My bowels recoiled at the sight of it; and, in the first transport of my fury I ordered Sunghir to throw it in the River Baudamir, which runs at the foot of the palace. She went out immediately, and returned in a quarter of an hour, assuring me that she had executed my orders. Ah, sir! how exceedingly powerful is nature! my blood chilled at the shocking

5—2

recital ; I repented of my cruelty, and bewailed the unhappy infant with tears of blood.   After I had spent a
considerable time in sorrow, and was now perfectly
recovered, I appeared in public again ; and, notwithstanding the melancholy which hung always about me,
my people thought me so fine a woman, that they were
perpetually urging me to give them a monarch, whose
posterity might govern Persia.   In vain I married, about
three years after the death of Bahaman, the Prince
Kudaddan, who joined Circassia to my kingdoms.
That monarch had only daughters by me, and I sincerely
lamented his death, which happened some eight months
ago, by a fall from his horse ; for he was both a gallant
and a virtuous prince.   He loved me with extreme
tenderness, and it was not without extreme reluctance
that I came so soon into your arms.   I was forced to
love you by the voice of nature ; that same nature
opposed the inclination I had to admit you to my bed.
Bahaman's ghost cautioned me to decline our marriage ;
I rejected his counsel, as the effect of his mad jealousy ;
but, thanks be to Heaven ! the mark upon your bosom
has delivered me from the commission of a second crime
no less horrible than the first.   The linen, the jewels,
and the ebony trunk, wherein Sunghir assured me afterwards that she exposed you upon the Baudamir, the
plain and natural declaration of Topal, and my heart,
which is a more certain proof than all, assure me that
you are my son.   Receive, then, my dear Huschank,
these embraces, pure and separate from all criminal
passion ; and as there is no necessity for the people to
know secrets of such importance as this, choose you
out a wife in all Persia, and marry her in private.   I

will adopt your children, and make them pass for mine. This, my dear Huschank, will now be the summit of my joy and felicity.

CONTINUATION AND CONCLUSION OF THE STORY OF HUSCHANK AND GULBAZI

AH, madam! said I, very readily, the woman is already found; it shall be the lovely Gulbazi, daughter to Topal. We have now loved one another these six years with all imaginable purity; I esteemed her as my sister, and fearing lest our passion should become criminal left the good man's house, whom I imagined my father. Grief and despair made me engage in your army. I sought for death, and had doubtless found it, had not Heaven, which favoured me so visibly, suffered me to destroy your enemies like a thunderbolt without receiving the least wound myself. Let me entreat you to consent, therefore, madam, that I may have this adorable creature, who, next to yourself, may justly be called the model of all perfections.—I consent with all my heart, answered Dugmi; order Topal to go for Gulbazi, for I have an impatient desire to see and embrace her. I executed, madam, continued Fum-Hoam, the Queen of Persia's orders. Gulbazi appeared in an hour's time, with all the modesty peculiar to her age, and was received by the queen with every endear-ment imaginable. That princess made me notice a thousand beauties in her which I had not perceived before ; and telling her she had discovered that I was the late king's nephew, and had on that account some scruple to live with me as husband and wife, desired that we might instantly marry, and expected no other acknowledgment but that we and Topal should keep the secret inviolable.

It is not to be expressed, madam, with what satisfaction Gulbazi and I received the queen's orders, which we immediately executed. In short, I was married to this lovely young creature ; and the queen took to herself five sons I had by Gulbazi, and they consequently passed for her own children. In the midst of all this happiness and apparent reason for contentment, Dugmi would every now and then give herself up to melancholy ; and I have sometimes seen, as she looked at me, the tears drop involuntarily from her eyes. I used every effort, by inventing always some new pleasure or other, to dissipate the sad ideas which the remembrance of the king, her father, brought to her mind ; but all would not do. She sunk into a sad dejection of soul that preyed upon her continually. At length she fell sick, and the whole art of physic could not save her life. She died in mine and Gulbazi's arms, having desired me, in presence of all the wazirs, to marry that charming woman, who had passed for her favourite.

I was extremely troubled for the death of my mother ; according to her orders, however, I raised Gulbazi to the throne, and had afterwards three daughters by her. At length, when we had lived together in perfect union to a good old age, honoured and respected both by our children and subjects, we quitted the cares which attend a crown. We left the sovereignty to our eldest son, and, having settled a considerable portion upon the other four and their sisters, reserved to ourselves only Circassia, whither we retired ; and had the consolation to see all our children live in peace and unity ; till, by the will of the great Prophet, Gulbazi and I, both in one day, quitted a life which would have been burdensome to the survivor.

This history, I confess, said the Queen of Gannan, has given me a great deal of pleasure, and the circumstances of it are very affecting ; but what became of you afterwards ?

HISTORY OF THE BEAUTIFUL HENGU

I WENT, continued the mandarin, into the body of a young woman of Kananor, whose name was Hengu. My father, who died before I was born, sold fiquaa ; and my mother, who continued the business after his decease, brought me up with as much care as her circumstances would permit. I lived always retired in a little neat apartment, with an old slave named Gabra, where I spent my days in such works as are proper for our sex ; and enjoyed this secret tranquility, without any passion to disturb me, when an unlucky accident happened in our house which disconcerted all my felicity.

Some Hindu gentlemen happened one day to quarrel in our shop ; and though we did all we could to prevent any mischief, yet one of the company received a stab with a poniard, and was dangerously wounded. We sent immediately for a surgeon to dress him; but the gentleman falling into a swoon, it was not thought advisable to carry him to his own house, and therefore my mother lent him a bed. The wound was deep; but not being mortal the young Hindu was soon out of danger. He returned my mother many thanks for the care she had taken of him; and before he left the house took the opportunity, when there were many people in the shop and my mother very busy, to come into my chamber, leaning upon his slave's arm, without my being apprised of the visit. I was surprised, indeed, at the sight of him; but my beauty made such an impression upon his spirits that he had like to have died away.—My dear friend, said he to his slave, you have not deceived me; this certainly is the most charming creature upon earth, and how happy should I think myself if she could love me with the same ardour with which I adore her.

I confess, madam, I was in the utmost confusion, for never did I see a handsomer man in my life than Kotza-Rashid (that was the gentleman's name), and I found my vanity so well pleased with his praises and respectful carriage that I was perfectly enchanted. After some time, however, I said to him.—Sir, I know too well the distance between you and me ever to think of becoming your wife, and I have too much virtue to be your mistress; I beg you, therefore, to cease your railleries, which are no handsome return for the care we have taken of your life.—Ah! madam, replied Kotza-Rashid, I speak seriously; I never saw any thing so perfect as you; and I call all our gods to witness, and to punish me with the most cruel death, if I place not my whole happiness in

the love of my adorable Hengu!—Gabra, who had all
this while spoken nothing, believing that she saw
sincerity painted in the eyes of my lover, said,—Sir, my
young mistress is not to be deluded by words; for,
though she is inferior to you in point of birth, her beauty,
if she were once known to our sultan, might place her
upon the throne of Kananor.—Ah! I know that but too
well, cried Kotza-Rashid; nor do I pretend to her heart
but by the most honourable means.—What shall I say,
madam, continued Fum-Hoam, Gabra was won by the
presents of my lover; he feigned a relapse, to gain an
opportunity of seeing me more conveniently; and for a
whole month he spent in my company all the time that
my mother was in her shop; he was always tender and
submissive; and I in my turn loved him with an equal
passion. In short, after we had in the presence of Gabra
entered into engagements which I thought solemn and
sincere, I gave myself up to my love without reserve.
My mother knew nothing of our intrigue; she would
never have consented to this private marriage, and therefore Gabra advised me not to mention a word of it to her.
It was high time, however, for the secret to be out; my
husband had left his lodging for some time, not thinking
it decent to stay any longer, and I was on the point of
becoming a parent. What to do upon this conjuncture
I did not well know; but my going away, which was
proposed, seemed to me the best expedient. One very
dark night, therefore, I left our house, accompanied by
Gabra. My husband waited for us at the outward gate,
and carried us to a stately palace which he had about a
league from Kananor, and it was there I first began to
enjoy his dear company with freedom; but that pleasure

was soon interrupted by a piece of news which touched
me very sensibly. My mother was so affected by my
running away that she fell dangerously sick upon it ; she
was seized with a very violent fever and died in a few
days, uttering curses and imprecations upon me which
too soon had their effect. I fell into a sad dejection of
mind upon my mother's death, which I was sensible I
had occasioned, and would a thousand times have stabbed
myself had it not been for the care that Gabra and
Kotza-Rashid took of me. Their assiduity dried up my
tears ; and for two years, which I passed in such delights
as tender and mutual lovers taste, I thought no more of
the matter.

Kotza-Rashid was one of the most charming and
entertaining men living ; he was perpetually at my knees,
and protesting to me that his love should last as long as
his life ; when on a sudden I thought I perceived some
coldness in him, and endeavouring to find out the cause
of it to no purpose, gave myself up entirely to grief, and
never after had a moment's rest. My sleep when I laid
me down at any time was most strangely disturbed. I
thought I saw ten thousand extravagant phantoms that
are not in nature, and every one more fantastical than
another ; and my frightful dreams always ended in my
mother's threatening me that I should soon be punished
for my want of tenderness to her.

Kotza-Rashid, who now began to neglect me much,
and for fifteen days together could stay in Kananor without any consideration of my affliction, seemed one day a
little sensible of my misfortune ; and after a few slight
endearments proposed that we should go and take the
air some distance from his castle. As I had no other

will than his, I made ready to obey him ; and after I
had dressed myself a little, to repair the injury which
grief and want of rest had done to my beauty, Gabra
and I went into a palanquin, and Kotza-Rashid rode on
horseback. In this manner we went about two good
leagues till we came to a little country house that
belonged to him. It was the most pleasant situation
that ever I saw. An old Hindu who had the care of it
opened us the gate ; the gardens were exceedingly neat,
and a fountain of clear delicious water seemed to invite
us to sit down by the side of its basin, where we were
served with the most excellent fruit. I observed a very
great uneasiness in Kotza-Rashid's looks; he ate nothing,
and turned his eyes from me. What is the matter with
my dear spouse? said I to him, tenderly; wherein have I
had the misfortune to displease you ? A flood of tears
that ran down my cheeks with these words completed
the confusion of my soul. I died away in Gabra's arms,
and when I came to myself was in the greatest consternation imaginable to see that Kotza-Rashid was gone,
and to find a green velvet purse that was very heavy
lying at my feet.

Gabra presently took up the purse and opened it ;
it was full of gold, and there was in it a letter directed
to me. But imagine, madam, what a condition I was
in when I came to read in it words much to this
purpose:

" Some particular reasons oblige me to marry. In
eight days I am to have the Governor of Kananor's
daughter, and to-morrow must bring her to my palace :
so that you, Hengu, must yield her up the place that
belongs to her. To make you some amends for the loss

of my heart, I leave you absolute mistress of this house and of all that belongs to it; I make you a present of them, together with five thousand rupees of gold. Endeavour to live easy with Gabra, and be silent in this affair if you would not displease

"KOTZA-RASHID."

I shall not pretend, madam, said the mandarin, to relate to you the rage I was in after I had recovered from the first surprise that my reading this letter had occasioned. None but a person who has been provoked to the last degree can be sensible of my condition. My resentment, indeed, was so keen that I wondered with myself why I did not instantly expire; and my heart, left naked to the assault of jealousy and fury, meditated the blackest designs. Unhappy Hengu! said I to myself, since it is a violence done to thy sex to deny thee the use of arms and the pleasure of washing off thy affront with blood, find out another way to avenge thyself on the ungrateful villain who forsakes thee; let him and thy hated rival both die by the subtlest poison.—But how can I execute, continued I, this ridiculous project? Are not all avenues shut against me, and how can I think to succeed therein? No; rather die than survive thy husband's infidelity! And with these words, I seized on my poinard, and was going to rid myself of all my torments, when Gabra wrested it from me, and promised that, without running any risk, she would undertake both to destroy my rival and recover my dear Kotza-Rashid's heart; but that to succeed therein great dissimulation would be necessary. This promise stopped the source of my tears and I prepared myself to hear with attention, when the old Hindu who had the care of the place came, he and his daughters together, and fell down at my feet. Madam, said he to me, I come to do homage to my new mistress; here is a writing wherein Kotza-Rashid invests you with all the goods he has in this place. We were his slaves, we are now become yours; and we hope to find in you as much goodness as we did in Kotza-Rashid, who was one of the best masters in the world. I received the good man's homage and his daughters' with courtesy; and finding that I wanted rest retired into an apartment, very plain but charmingly neat, which had a prospect into the delicious fields that belonged to the house.

Here I found all my clothes and ornaments, which my perfidious husband had caused privately to be brought there; and the sight of them renewed my sorrows. Is it then for ever, my dear spouse, said I, that I have lost you? You have basely deceived me; and abusing my simplicity and your oaths, you have abandoned me to put yourself in the arms of another. Oh! I never will survive this hard fate.—As sure as you are alive, said Gabra to me again, depend on me, my dear Hengu, and you shall soon be revenged. This fresh promise of Gabra appeased my sorrow a little; she told me her design, and I listened to her with impatience. Kotza-Rashid loves you too well, said she, to abandon you for ever. It will not be long before he comes hither again, and will inform himself from your slaves in what manner you live; pretend, therefore, to be very easy; shew as much as you can such a freedom of spirit as argues an unconcern for him, and depend upon it my contrivance will not want for success.

I followed Gabra's advice very exactly. Before the old man and his daughter I put a restraint upon myself

—nay, I affected a good deal of gaiety, and spoke often against the engagement of our affections and as the foible of our sex. All which, being carried to Kotza-Rashid, he began to imagine that he might now come and see me without any fear of reproaches. In short, one day, when I least of all expected him, and as I was walking in the garden, I saw him come up to me. I am very well pleased with you, Hengu, said he to me ; you have taken the right method ; passion and resentment would have banished you for ever from my heart. Live quiet and peaceable in this place, and permit me some-times to come and interrupt your solitude. I answered him suitably to his desires, and according to the instructions which Gabra had given me ; and as our conversation could scarce end without some occasion or other to speak of his wife, I asked him whether she had beauty enough to give her the hope of fixing his heart for ever ; whereupon he drew me such a picture of her as almost killed me with vexation. I could indeed hardly contain myself ; but I knew how to enter into his sentiments so dexterously that he did not perceive my disorder, and continued his detail of every single perfection, both of body and mind ; he extolled her above all the beauties that had ever been in life. I stopped him. For though I yielded to her, I said, in all things else, yet as for hair, I knew no woman who had the vanity to think she had finer than I. He laughed at me for this ; the dispute grew hot ; and, since I was not allowed to come to his house, I desired him to bring me a lock of the fine hair, of which he so greatly boasted, that we might compare it with mine. He promised me he would ; and after he had spent the rest of the day with me he returned home. Gabra was hugely pleased with the use I made of her instructions; and, as soon as she heard what promise my faithless husband had made me, out she runs in all haste to look for poisonous herbs, stones, and roots unknown to any but herself; and by powerful charms, wherein she was versed from her childhood, prepares for the death and destruction of my rival.

The moment which I desired with so much impatience came at last. Kotza-Rashid, about fifteen days after his first visit, came to pay me another. See here, said he, the first thing he spoke to me, whether I am prepossessed in favour of my wife; look on this lock of hair, and be convinced that its blackness and lustre far exceed your own. I went near the window, as if to see it with a better light; and, pretending to look at it very earnestly, stole a little of it, which I slid into my bosom, and returned him the rest, after I had allowed, in compliance, and the better to blind him, that mine was not comparable to my rival's; hereupon he laughed very heartily, and seemed pleased with my sincerity. He was all the day in a charming humour, and did not leave me till very late.

No sooner had I parted from Kotza-Rashid, but, being full of resentment, I made ready to take vengeance on my rival with all the punctuality necessary in such horrid rites. The night had spread its thick shade over the earth, when Gabra and I, with our hair loose, and our bodies half naked, stood in the open field, and called the most mischievous jinnis to our aid. At our horrible incantations we saw the stars instantly lose their light, or, by fearful streaks of fire, shew the change of their situation. The moon crept into a thick cloud, and left us in such darkness that the lighted torches we held in our hands could hardly dissipate it. It seemed sometimes bloody and sometimes glaring with fire and flames ; and round about we distinctly saw fall a shower of burn- ing sparks instead of wholesome and refreshing dews. I began to tremble excessively at the sight of so many prodigies, when Gabra, beating the air three times with her powerful wand, and pronouncing the most barbarous words with horrible contortions, shook the hair which I had taken from Kotza-Rashid upon the flaming torch, and conjured the infernal deities, that, as that hair burned and consumed, the person whose it was might be consumed and destroyed.

I began to please myself with the full vengeance I was to have, and fancied I already saw my rival on fire, when on a sudden I found myself seized with a violent heat which burned my entrails. My blood curdled, my heart shrivelled up, my limbs consumed away, and, to Gabra's great astonishment, I fell to the ground and groaned hideously. Ah ! perfidious Kotza-Rashid ! cried I, with a dying tone, you knew too well what I intended to do with your wife's hair ; you have certainly brought me my own which I once gave you, when I had the happiness to please you ; and in seeking my rival's destruction I have met my own. I had scarcely time to pronounce these words, when my soul, disappointed of its revenge, went out of my miserable body, with cries sufficiently dreadful to terrify the stoutest heart ; and Gabra, who would not live after me, stabbed herself immediately with a dagger.

·   ⁂   ⁂   ⁂   ⁂   ⁂   ⁂

But let us waive, madam, continued Fum-Hoam, all reflections upon a death so melancholy, and which I deserved so well. When I had left the body of this unhappy young woman, I was for a long while, without interruption, in different conditions of life, wherein there was nothing remarkable. For what pleasure would it be to your Majesty to hear a recital of the dangers I underwent in the form of a serpent ; the sad and uneasy life I led when I was an owl and a bat; the amorous complaints I made under the figure of a tender nightingale; or the malicious tricks I studied when I was an ape ?—Your tricks, when an ape, replied the Queen, interrupting him, I have a great desire to know; and you will do me no small pleasure if you will relate them. —Since your Majesty desires it, said the Mandarin, I will not be wanting to your satisfaction.

ADVENTURES OF THE APE MORUG

I was born in a forest of Hind, and some time after was taken with bird-lime, which I was fool enough to rub my eyes with ; being willing to imitate a huntsman, whom I saw washing himself in a basin of water. I was sold to a young Chinese who called me Morug ; and who, making me fast very severely when I would not obey his commands, brought me to be so nimble and active, that I passed for a prodigy. He bought me a little horse, which I managed with as much dexterity as the best riding-master ; and while he was in his gallop, I used to skip and jump upon him so nimbly

6

that I surprised everybody. In short, through all the cities of Hind where we passed, I was looked upon with admiration; and my master, who had made a considerable profit of me there, was resolved to return to Kambalu, where I got him as much money as in Hind. The children brought me great store of all kinds of fruit; and, because I played with them without hurting them, they were very fond of me, and caressed me much. Every day I brought home my purse, which was tied about my waist, full of silver, which I was sure either to win or pilfer from this young fry, who had no better sport than to divert themselves with me.

It so fell out that a certain good woman of Kambalu, whose house joined to the back part of that where my master lodged, chanced to die; and, as I happened to see the people carrying her out of her apartment, from the top of the house where I was sitting, it came into my head to try if I could imitate the moans I heard her make. I slipped nimbly into the chamber, put on the dead woman's shift and head clothes, and covering myself in the bed waited till the people's return from the burial to play a farce which nearly cost me my life. As soon as the woman's relations were come into the chamber, and were going to begin their lamentations again, I stretched my head out of the bed, and made most hideous grimaces. The good people were so terrified at this, that, taking me for the devil, they scoured out of the room, and each person was only solicitous to save himself. Presently, the whole house was in an uproar, and the community of bonzes was sent to in all haste to acquaint them with the strangeness of this adventure. The eldest of the priests assembled his brethren; and, everyone arming himself with a torch, they came two and two into the dead person's chamber. All this while I lay snug in the bed; and seeing this jolly train as they came in, could perceive that fear was painted in their looks, which gave me the more courage. No sooner had a dozen of them entered the room, than I sprang out of the bed, and jumping upon the shoulders of their chief bit his nose and ears to that degree that I made him cry out bitterly; insomuch that his comrades tumbled one over another, and left him to my fury. I then shut the door, and beat him at my ease; and, after I had torn his gown to tatters, and thrown the old woman's clothes in his face, I whipt out at the window, recovered the top of the house, and so got safe into my master's lodging.

The poor bonze, after his first fright was over, knew, no doubt, who it was he had to deal with; but being very feeble he took my blows patiently; and yet as a man of quick invention, who could make an advantage of everything, no sooner did he see me out of the chamber than he opened the door and called to the other bonzes, and reproached them with their cowardice. He told them he had been encountering one of the most powerful devils he ever knew, who, after an obstinate defence (of which he had several marks to shew), was compelled to yield him the victory. After this he caused the window where I got in to be walled up, and so returned home loaded with presents; and everybody afterwards looked upon him as a holy man. But he was not yet satisfied; I might still appear upon the top of the house, and thus discover the pious fraud; and therefore, getting intelligence where my master lived, he came as soon as it was

light to pay him a visit, and, telling him the whole
adventure, desired of him, in all kindness, to change his
lodging. There is not, indeed, any material difference
between a kind of quack (which my master was) and
such a bonze as this; so that they soon agreed, and we
went to live at a distant part of the town, which prevented the truth of this comical adventure from ever
being known at Kambalu.

To be short, the wonders I performed were the
whole talk of the town; my fame was carried even into
the sultan's seraglio; and Alishank, his favourite sultana,
whom he had just advanced to the throne, having a desire
to see me, that monarch, who could deny her nothing,
ordered my master to make me go through all my
exercises before her. She was so taken with my activity
and address that she could not forbear expressing her
desire to have me herself; so that my master Yvam (for
that was his name) was obliged to present me to her,
and be content with a very considerable gratification
from the King of China.

I was so accustomed to live with Yvam that I
would not obey the sultana. I grew melancholy; and
the sultan, to please Alishank, sent for my master, and
committed him to the care of one of his chief eunuchs,
whom he commanded to attend my master into the
seraglio, as often as the sultana desired to see him, and
to leave him upon no account whatever. I no sooner
got sight of my master again than I revived my former
gaiety. He was very young and handsome, so that
Alishank could not look upon him without conceiving
desires injurious to the sultan's honour. Her eyes were
soon the interpreters of her heart. Yvam understood her

meaning, and the eunuch, who was to be present at their interviews, being gained by the strength of money, the two lovers were left at their liberty. One day, when the sultan was gone a-hunting, and was not to return again for four days, I chanced to be by as the sultana was caressing my master, and heard him ask her who her parents were, and how long she had been in the seraglio. I have only been here a year, said she ; but this year, how long has it been ! I hate the sultan as much as I love you, my dear Yvam ; and the more I see you, the more I find my hate increases ; but since you are desirous to know who I am, I will relate to you some of the principal events of my life, and how it was that I came to this honour which I so little esteem, and which other sultanas seek with so much eagerness.

ADVENTURES OF THE SULTANA ALISHANK

My mother, whose name was Dogandar, was the only daughter of a rich jeweller of Ceylon, but a very severe man. There was in the neighbourhood a young Hindu named Ganim, who, having seen her frequently at the window, grew passionately in love with her ; and he being a very beautiful man himself, it was not long before he was beloved again. My mother, however, knowing he was not rich enough to gain her father's consent to marry her, resolved to run away with him, and retire into some island in the Indian Sea. After they had taken proper measures for the execution of this design, my mother took with her all the gold and precious stones she could get, and embarked with her lover in a vessel that was bound for Timor. They were cast by the violence of a storm upon the coast of Sumatra ; and my mother, who was then big with me, and almost dead with the tossing of the vessel, no sooner had set her foot on shore than, unwilling to venture her life at sea again, she proposed to Ganim to stay in that island ; and the better to conceal herself from her father's pursuit, she let the vessel she had hired proceed on its voyage to Timor, and retiring to a good widow's house, who lived at Achim, gave her to understand that she and Ganim were two comedians who had been shipwrecked on that coast and saved in the ship's boat. The woman believed what she said ; and as my mother spent a good deal of money, which made the poor woman a little more easy in life, she was very diligent in attending upon her.

After some months' stay at Achim, my mother was delivered of me ; and nature had expended her store in my production, for I was her masterpiece of beauty. My parents' chief concern was the care of my education. They had been seven years in this city, and, perceiving they had not brought wealth enough with them to live at the rate they had hitherto done, after they had parted with most of their jewels, were thinking of returning to Ceylon, when one night the good woman with whom they lived came home full of joy. I have good news to tell you, said she ; there is a company of comedians just now arrived, who may very probably belong to you, because they have been shipwrecked in several places before their landing in the Island of Sumatra, and have these eight or ten years been travelling all over Hind. Dogandar and Ganim could not forbear smiling at the woman's notion. That may very well be, answered my mother, but I will see them act before I make myself known to them, and if I find they belong to our company I will make their joy the more by the surprise of coming upon them when they least of all expect me. The old woman was satisfied with these reasons. She undertook to secure us places, and we went the first time they acted, which was some few days after this discourse.

The company was made up of very good actors, and Dogandar, seeing her substance grow less and less every day, fell suddenly into a very odd resolution. My dear husband, said she to Ganim, an expedient has just now come into my head that will secure us against want and misery; let us turn comedians. My father that moment cried out with joy, embracing my mother very tenderly, That thought, my dear, I have long entertained, but durst not propose it to you.—But why so nice? said she. Nobody knows us here, and as we have all along lived in obscurity, who can tell but that our condition is truly the same with what we are now going to embrace? nor will our old landlady fail to make the world believe that this has formerly been the profession of our life. But do you think you have a talent for it?—I own, answered Ganim, that this has always been my reigning passion; and that, if I had been permitted to follow my own inclination, and my love for you had not detained me in my youthful days, I should, doubtless, have joined myself to the first company that passed through Ceylon.—I never carried my desires so far, continued Dogandar;

but I have frequently wished that young women of my condition had been permitted to tread the stage. I am willing to believe I could distinguish myself as well by an easy and natural manner of acting as by the practice of the most austere virtue, for virtue is by no means inconsistent with that course of life ; and if those who have hitherto embraced it had but endeavoured to be unblameable in their morals, they would not have rendered disgraceful a profession which on other accounts deserves not to be condemned, since its only tendency is to correct the vices of mankind by setting before their eyes a true and natural picture of the faults and extravagancies they daily commit.—You reason justly, my dear Dogandar, replied Ganim ; let us turn comedians.

This resolution, continued the Sultana Alishank, was most punctually followed. Next day my father and mother went and offered themselves to the company, and having each chosen the part wherein they thought they should best succeed, they spoke with so much eloquence and observed such propriety of action that the whole audience returned home charmed with the play and with their two new actors. My mother was somewhat more than three-and-twenty ; but never was there a creature more beautiful. All the young noblemen of Achim, thinking to have as favourable access to her as to the generality of actresses, were incessantly visiting her. She received them with great civility, but soon gave them their answer by informing them that her talents were wholly confined to the theatre. This, however, they could hardly credit ; and therefore, to tempt her further, were continually sending her the richest presents ; but she refused them all, and at length established her reputation so well at Achim that everybody looked upon her with admiration.

The company having remained three years in this city resolved to go through all the rest of the Island of Sumatra. My father and mother, who by this time had got a considerable deal of money, began to doubt with themselves whether they should go along with them or not ; but overcome with the earnest entreaties of the rest, and accustomed to a kind of adoration that exceedingly gratified their vanity, they resolved not to leave them. They accordingly established themselves in several places, one after another, with very great success ; and, coming to fix for some time at Palimban, my mother resolved to give me a short part to perform. I was then about thirteen, and very well shaped for my age. My mother's instructions did not a little help me ; and I received such applause at my first appearing on the stage that they feared it would have turned my brain. As I grew in age I increased in beauty, and applied myself so diligently to my new profession that in a very short time I became as great an actress as my mother. Thus everything was gay about us ; we lived at ease, were esteemed by everybody, and had abundant reason to be content with our little fortune, when our happiness was all quashed at once by a very cruel accident.

In a new tragedy, called *Innocence Oppressed*, Ganim acted the part of a man persecuted by a favourite of the King of Hind, who was in love with his wife. My mother, who acted the wife, was so far from yielding, on account of the favourite's persecution, that she treated him with the utmost disdain. Ganim is falsely accused of crimes that merit death ; and in one of the last scenes his enemy brings him a cup of poison and a poniard. My father, before he chooses which of the deaths he will die, outbraves his rival in a speech full of constancy and boldness, recommends to his wife to avenge him if possible, and, having taken a tender farewell of her, strikes the poniard into the middle of his breast. Just as he is going to expire, his innocence is found out, and the King of Hind, enraged against his favourite, comes to inform my mother, the widow, that she has got her revenge, for that he himself has just then cut off the head of her persecutor.

This play got the company a vast deal of money, and my mother acted her part therein so very naturally that she always drew tears from the audience; but that which was but a fiction, was, very unluckily for her, turned into a reality. The actor, who represented the favourite, was in good earnest in love with my mother; and, being well convinced of her virtue, he thought with himself that, as long as Ganim was alive, he could have no hope of possessing her; he, therefore, to get rid of a man whom he reckoned the only obstacle to his happiness, invented one of the blackest plots that ever was contrived, for, sharpening to a point the dagger wherewith my father was to stab himself when he came to the conclusion of his part, he struck it with such force that it plunged into his body quite up to the hilt. What a surprise was he in to see his blood gush out upon my mother's face, who was then embracing him! But soon knowing the villainy of the other actor's soul, he seized him by the throat, and gave him several blows with the same weapon which laid him flat upon the stage; and that moment himself expiring, had only time to put the poniard into my mother's hand, signifying thereby plainly enough the part which he meant her to perform. Her rage made her almost distracted; she ran to the assassin that moment, and taking advantage of his fall and wounds, threw herself upon him and stabbed him in a thousand places, thus revenging my father's death, who had just expired in my arms. Never was there a scene in reality bloodier than this; and it would certainly have been still more so had not I seized the dagger as my mother was turning it to her breast, and immediately wrested it out of her hand. She then threw herself upon my father's body, heaving such sighs as would have softened the most obdurate heart; nor was there, indeed, any of the spectators who did not shed tears in abundance at so sad and affecting a spectacle.

What more shall I say, my dear Yvam? continued the sultana. Ever after that fatal day my mother detested her profession; and having spent a considerable time in bewailing her loss of Ganim, she resolved to return again to Ceylon; and if her father would not pardon her elopement, there to put an end to her life. Accordingly, we went on board the first vessel which set sail for that island, and had a very favourable wind, when we discovered two pirate ships making full at us. As everyone chooses to lose his life rather than his liberty, we made ready to engage them with great courage. The fight was bloody; but, notwithstanding all the resistance we could make, which indeed was more than credible, the pirates in a short time became our masters, and massacred everyone who opposed their fury. It was not enough for me to be deprived of my liberty. Mine was the hard fate to lose my mother likewise, in the heat of the action, for being wounded in the breast with an arrow she died in my arms, who was unable to give her any relief. What became of me in that moment, my dear Yvam, I cannot tell; I fell into a swoon, and when I came to myself found I was in the pirates' vessel, and that they had thrown my mother's body into the sea. This redoubled my sighs and tears; many reproachful things I said against these barbarians, but they understood me not, and made the best of their way for the coast of Egypt.

As beauty has a power to overcome the most savage and cruel nations, these pirates beheld me with admiration; the majesty that appeared in my whole person, and the innumerable graces which adorned me, made such an impression on their hearts, that they could not turn their eyes from looking upon me, insomuch that they even forgot sometimes to take care of the vessel. Though the grief I was in had made a considerable alteration in me, yet I could see nothing in all their actions but surprise, and was several times for taking advantage of the astonishment they were in to throw myself into the sea; but they, perceiving my design, carried me down into a cabin, where there could be no danger of my doing myself any mischief. They then came down one by one to take a view of me; and as if they aimed at the possession of my person, and everyone thought he had a right to pretend to it, they first began to dispute the matter over seriously; but a quarrel arising, they fell to abusing each other. From words they proceeded to blows, and in a short time there was to be seen on our deck one of the most bloody fights that can possibly be imagined. The pirates

of the other ship, surprised at this cruel division, were
coming on board us to make peace ; but instead of
ending the quarrel they fomented it, and disputing the
honour of my conquest they fell upon each other with
such rage and fury that in less than three hours'
time they were almost all dead of their wounds. So
that I was left alone in one vessel, whilst the other,
which was almost empty, was bearing away before
the wind.

Since the death of my mother I had been very
indifferent to everything I saw, and better pleased to
be left to the discretion of the sea and all its monsters
than to these pirates, and had waited my death with
a deal of unconcern, when I found myself very inclinable
to fall asleep. I laid me down, therefore, regardless what
fate might determine for me, and fell into a dream which
had something uncommon in it. I fancied I was upon
the deck of the little vessel I was in, and saw a magnificent chariot rising out of the sea, all shining with mother-
of-pearl, and drawn by four sea monsters much like our
horses. In the middle of the chariot there sat a man
half naked, of a venerable aspect. A large beard fell
down to his stomach, and in his right hand he held a
spear, which was everywhere beset with precious stones.
He was surrounded by a great number of men and women,
of a very beautiful form as low as their waist, but whose
bodies terminated in the tail of a fish ; and though in
the water, they danced very sprightly and passionately
to the sound of some instruments whose harmony was
delightful. I was wonderfully pleased with my dream,
and could not forbear admiring this extraordinary sight,
when the man lifted up his eyes to heaven, and reading

there, doubtless, the misfortunes which threatened my life, shed some tears, and looked upon me with extreme pity. How do I bewail thee, unhappy Alishank! said he; but thou canst not avoid thy destiny. And at these words, striking the sea with his spear, he made a wide gulf, where himself and his whole retinue were buried in a moment. The winds then began to blow terribly; the sea, which before was calm, grew boisterous; mountains of water carried the vessel as high as heaven, and in an instant threw it down into those abysses which in all probability were to be my grave. The thunder, with its most hideous roaring, and the violent tossings of the ship awoke me at that instant, and I soon perceived that the end of my dream was too certainly coming to pass.

During this terrible storm, which lasted two days and two nights, and all the while drove my vessel into open sea, the water came in on every side and threw me at last upon a rock, where that love of life, with which nature never fails to inspire us when in danger, made me forget my insensibility and seize on a plank of the ship, which was now broken into a thousand pieces; and suffering myself to drive where fortune should please to direct me, I was at length cast on shore at the foot of a mountain inhabited by savages. Some of their women happened luckily to be on the coast when I came on shore; they made me throw up the water I had swallowed, and perceiving some signs of life, carried me into one of their cottages, where they took great care to chafe and warm me. My eyes, though covered with the shadow of death, still resembled the brightness of half-rough or ill-polished diamonds, which have not so good a lustre as others;

and my lips, which before outvied the coral, were then of a violet colour; but notwithstanding this cloud disfigured my beauty, these barbarians were so taken with it that they spared no pains to preserve my life. When I had recovered the use of my senses, how great was my sorrow to find myself in the arms of such frightful figures of women as scarce could be called human! Their language more resembled the howling of wild beasts than anything else; and as I could not under-stand what they said, I answered them only in sighs which discovered my affliction. Indeed the evils I had suffered had almost deprived me of the use of speech.

For the first eight days, wherein these women as well as their husbands used all kind offices to recover me from the cruel fatigue I had undergone, I could perceive that my honour was safe among them, and was the more convinced of it by the several sorts of adoration which they paid to me as a divinity. My sorrow at length began to wear off, cheerfulness made me appear a thousand times more beautiful, my charms recovered their former lustre; and arming myself with constancy against the assaults of fortune, I was resolved to bear with courage whatever calamities I had still to undergo. I therefore began to accustom myself to this extraordinary kind of life, and in fewer than four months understood enough of these islanders' language to com-prehend their meaning. I came then to be informed that their custom was in light little barks to scour along the seas, and to sell all the slaves they could find, and that their first intention was to have used me in the same manner; but upon the sight of so many charms and graces in my face, they looked upon me as their tutelar goddess, and were so far from selling me that they would treat me as their queen while I continued among them, and would expose themselves to any danger for the preservation of my life and honour.

I was not a little pleased to know the kind intentions of these savages. I desired them to persist in their favourable impressions of me, and promised to requite them with all the gratitude in my power. From that moment I endeavoured to civilize them as much as I could, and to teach them my language. I instructed them in our Hindu customs, and shewed them how to dress their provisions according to our fashion ; all which made these good people look upon me with admiration. When I found myself in the humour I would sometimes act by myself whole comedies before them, with which they were highly delighted. By these means I not only amused myself, but was continually increasing their affection for me. In this manner I lived with them for a year, until on a certain day, which they kept as a festival, their enemies made a descent upon the island and took me away from them. I seem yet to behold the distraction of those poor savages: they raised the most terrible outcries, pursued their enemies with inconceivable fury, and sacrificed to their rage everything which opposed their valour. But all their efforts were in vain. I was put into a bark, and carried to an island not far distant from thence. But as soon as I was well got on shore, my little fleet of islanders came after me and landed. Never was there a battle fought with so much intrepidity as this. They made a terrible slaughter among my ravishers; and after they had set their habitations on fire, they carried me triumphantly to a bark, which they placed in the middle of their fleet, and rending the air with acclamations of joy made the best of their way to their own island. I cannot, my dear Yvam, continued the sultana, represent to you the great satisfaction it gave me to see the tender assiduities of these poor savages; and I was returning them my thanks in the most affectionate terms, when a terrible storm arose, which dispersed all our fleet, and drove the vessel I was in to sea, notwithstanding I had ten or twelve savages on board, who used all their skill and dexterity to make the land.

The more the storm increased the further we were driven from the island; and it lasted so long, and blew so hard that in fewer than four days we were near five hundred leagues from home. At length we were thrown upon a rock not far distant from land, and there went ashore; but we were all so weak with hunger and fatigue, we could hardly support ourselves. My islanders found some turtles, and ate them raw; but I was, for my own part, so afflicted with this fresh misfortune that my thoughts ran upon nothing but dying. The poor savages were greatly concerned to see me in such dejection; they did all they could to comfort me, with the hopes of recovering their island again; and one of them brought me a large piece of honeycomb, which he had found in a cleft of a rock, and entreated me to eat it. This nourishment recovered the strength I had lost; and being resolved to advance with them into the country, we drew our bark ashore, covered it among the weeds, and traversed several parts of the country without being able to discover whether it was inhabited. We came at last to a high point of ground, from whence we could

7

discern some huts; and then, returning the way we had
come, we ran our bark out to sea again, and coasted
along the shore, till we came over against them; but
just as we were going to land we were surprised by three
brigantines that lay hid behind a rock, and were then
putting out to sea.   My savages at first were for preparing to defend themselves, but I begged them not to
venture their lives in such an unequal fight, which they
complied with; and so we went undismayed on board
one of the brigantines.   But how great was my grief to
see these poor creatures immediately loaded with chains!
My cries were sufficient to make the most inhuman heart
relent: but I had got among a parcel of barbarians, who
were more cruel than wild beasts.   I understood nothing
of their language; they disregarded my tears, and, as my
islanders could not help shewing by their furious looks
some resentment of their breach of faith, the perfidious
villains massacred them before my eyes, giving me to
understand they would treat me in the same manner,
unless I dried up my tears.   I would gladly have thrown
myself into the sea; but to prevent this they chained
me down, and after a month's sailing, wherein they
threatened my honour unless I would consent to receive
nourishment, they sold me to a slave merchant, who
brought me over into China.   I must own to you, my
dear Yvam, continued the sultana, that of all my misfortunes nothing ever touched me so feelingly as the loss
of my islanders.   I fell into a great dejection of spirit,
which alarmed the merchant; and as my melancholy
made great alteration in my beauty he thought the only
way to cure it was to let me know he designed me for
the King of China's seraglio; that honour, however, did

not flatter my vanity, and I came to Kambalu just as a victim is brought to the altar.

It is the custom, as you cannot but know, on a certain day appointed for that purpose, to have all the young women who are to be presented to that monarch appear in a large outer room of the palace ; but that there may be no art in the case, they are all dressed alike at the expense of the prime wazir. The Sultan of China, who you know is very old and much more homely, had several times gone along the room disguised like a woman to take a near view and examination of us ; after which, putting on his robes, all beset with the most refulgent precious stones, he seated himself upon his throne, and making us pass in review before him, gave a sign to the wazir, when any one had the honour to please him, to put us within the rails of his throne. We were above a hundred and fifty in all, but the sultan only took three for himself, whereof I had the misfortune to be one. As to the others, he bought about sixty of them, which he presented among his chief officers, and the rest he ordered to be sent away.

The extreme melancholy which appeared in my looks gave the sultan much uneasiness. Dear Alishank, said he to me, squeezing me very gently, the division of such a heart as mine, I perceive, does not please you, and the other two sultanas I have chosen alarm you. Well, then, to shew you how much I love you, I will give them away to my prime wazir.—Ah ! sir, said I, throwing myself at his feet, this sacrifice is such a proof of your love as I shall always endeavour to merit by a strict performance of the duty I owe to so powerful a monarch, whom I will continue to respect as long as I live.—It is not respect, says the sultan to me, taking me up in his arms, but it is love that I require of you. You do not answer me, adorable light of my life! Are not you mistress of your own heart? Ah! I would die with grief sooner than put any force upon your inclinations!—I must confess I was sensibly touched with such tender and submissive language. I have no affection for anyone, said I, and I wish still to continue in the same indifference. —Ah! my dear Alishank, replied the amorous monarch, that assurance has restored my life.—What shall I say, Yvam? continued the sultana; after a great many respectful denials I at last consented to gratify the king's ardent desires. As soon as he had received this agreeable intelligence, I was put into the hands of seven old slaves of the seraglio, who are appointed to attend on his favourites. They first conducted me to a bath, and afterwards to the King of China's apartment, who waited for me with the greatest impatience, and as soon as I entered the chamber he ran to me, and, dismissing the slaves, helped to undress me himself, and entreated me to come to bed. I felt a chilling horror thrill through my whole frame, and the night habiliments, wherein the sultan lay, made him seem still more ugly in my eyes; I was, however, obliged to obey, and he the next day proclaimed me Queen of China. So much goodness, one would imagine, must have endeared him to me; but still I cannot endure his embraces, though I am not in a condition to refuse them. I find, however, that my aversion to him every day increases, and am very sensible it proceeds in a great measure from the love which I have for my dear Yvam. Why is he not the Sultan of China? or why may not I live with him out of the seraglio, and be eased of all this grandeur which is but a burden to me ?

    *   *   *   *   *   *

    This, madam, continued Fum - Hoam, is what I heard the beautiful Alishank relate, when I was in the form of an ape. I shall now proceed to inform your Majesty of the sultana's further adventures.

CONTINUATION OF THE ADVENTURES OF THE APE MORUG, AND OF THE SULTANA ALISHANK

    Love ever makes happy lovers blind, of which Alishank and Yvam were but too sad an instance. That beautiful person forgot all her melancholy in the arms of my master ; but she forgot at the same time the laws of honour and her duty. Adored, as she was, by one of the most powerful monarchs upon earth, she could want nothing that tended to her satisfaction ; but she made an ill use of it. The immense riches she had at her disposal, the excessive honours perpetually paid her, and the tender love of her husband, could not all make her enter into herself ; she had nothing in her thoughts but her dear Yvam, and how to devote those nights to him which she did not pass with the sultan.

    My master's chamber was at the entrance of the seraglio ; and to come at it, there were two large galleries where a number of women and very wakeful eunuchs lay ; but the madness of Alishank's passion had such dominion over her, that she prevailed with the eunuch, who was to guard her lover, to put an infusion of prepared laudanum into a sort of sherbet which they used to give the women and eunuchs every night, and taking advantage of their sleep, she went to Yvam. This passed on for some time; but, as ill luck would have it, hitting her foot one night against a parcel of arms which stood against the chief eunuch's door, her fall made such a noise that it awoke him. He jumped out of bed, and seizing Alishank who was wrapped in a great cloak, held a dagger to her throat, and so carried her into his own apartment; but was in the highest surprise, when, by the light of his lamp, he perceived it was the Queen of China. Gabao, said she, my going out of the seraglio at this time of night may give you room to suspect some irregularity in my conduct, which is no way blameable; for curiosity was my only fault. I request it may be a secret, however, and you may depend upon it, you shall have no cause to repent this piece of service. Gabao had time enough to recover his surprise; and, seeing the queen in a disguise so inconsistent with her honour, and wherein she discovered so many charms, he could not forbear conceiving desires, which (how inconsistent soever they were) entirely dissipated the terror she was in. The eunuch's rash and indiscreet discourse, some actions in him a little too free, and to which she herself perhaps gave occasion, made her instantly take the expedient to get from him. Having repulsed him with the greatest disdain, she seemed violently enraged at his insolence, and treated him, in short, with such a haughty air that he durst no longer hold her in his profane arms; and she, taking the opportunity of this mark of respect to disentangle herself, slipped away nimbly, and recovered her chamber before he perceived she was gone.

It is scarcely to be conceived how exceedingly uneasy this accident made Alishank, and how it raised her indignation to think of having been exposed to the insolent embraces of this eunuch, which she was resolved to revenge by one of the boldest strokes imaginable. The Sultan of China never failed to dine with her, and Gabao used always to be present. As the conversation naturally turned upon the blind obedience his subjects paid him, she told the king she would be well pleased to try the experiment with one of his eunuchs, upon a slight occasion; but that she desired the eunuch, whoever he was, should be entirely at her disposal.—You may easily satisfy yourself on that point, my dear queen, answered the good king; choose you any, even from Gabao to the lowest slave I have; I make you a present of him, and from this moment you have an absolute power over his life and death.—Since your Majesty has so much goodness, replied Alishank, with an air full of joy, Gabao himself is the person I make choice of; and the matter of obedience I require of him is this, that from the present moment he begins to be voluntarily mute; insomuch, that on any account whatever, even though your august Majesty should ask him a question or order him to speak, he presume not to answer, either by word of mouth or by any sign whatever until I give him permission; and that if he obey not this order with the most exact submission, he may assure himself I will have him thrown into the canal in the garden, with a stone about his neck.

An order of so singular a nature made the sultan laugh heartily; he confirmed to the queen the present he had made her of the chief of his eunuchs, and began to divert himself by asking him a thousand questions about the duties of his office, but could not draw from him so much as a single answer. At every question the king asked, the queen cast a furious look upon Gabao, who was sorely vexed at her resolution, but for his heart he knew not what to do. If he opened his mouth to explain to the sultan the last night's adventure, his death was sure ; if he held his tongue and said nothing of it, he saw he must fall into the power of an inexorable mistress, who wanted but an opportunity to destroy one who was witness of the irregularity of her conduct, and could inform her husband of it ; he made choice, however, of the latter resolution, in hopes of mollifying the sultana's heart by his submission ; but in this he was mistaken.

As soon as Alishank retired from the sultan's presence, she found all her hatred against Gabao awaken in her breast; while he lay prostrate upon the ground, not daring to lift up his eyes towards her, with his blood chilled in his veins through fear. Rise up, said she, and follow me. He readily obeyed her, and was two days together exposed to all the questions of the sultana's slaves, without speaking a word. On the third day Alishank went into the garden, and stayed there till almost night, seemingly very easy, and delighted with everything, when, on a sudden, she desired to bathe herself in the canal. The water was low ; and as soon as a tent was erected by the side of the canal for the purpose, she called Gabao in. Come, undress me, said she. The poor man trembled exceedingly, not knowing where this ceremony would end. He, however, obeyed her commands, till at length, transported at the sight of so many charms as the

sultana maliciously disclosed, he forgot the severe order
he had received, and in a kind of ecstacy, which he
could not restrain, cried out, Good God! how beautiful
she is.—Seize him, said Alishank, immediately; tie a
stone about his neck, and cast him into the canal.—
The people were not very ready to execute her orders,
believing her only in jest; when, putting herself into a
violent passion, I will be obeyed! said she. At which
words the eunuchs fell upon Gabao, tied his hands
behind his back, and a stone about his neck; but still
supposing the affair would end in some slight punishment, when she commanded them peremptorily to throw
the poor man into the canal. Though her orders were
executed with some reluctance, yet Gabao was nevertheless drowned in a few moments and the queen saw
him die with a satisfaction so great, that it rendered
her an object of detestation even to her slaves.

As soon as Gabao was dead, Alishank sent the
sultan word of the disobedience and punishment of his
slave. He was much surprised and concerned at it,
but shewed no signs of displeasure to his wife; on the
contrary, he had the goodness to approve of the chastise-
ment she had inflicted on the chief of his eunuchs.
But though the king seemed satisfied with this cruel
action of the queen, yet other people were not so; for
Gabao was well beloved in the seraglio, and used his
power with much lenity; so that the great severity of
his successor served to render his memory still more
regretted. They endeavoured, therefore, to find out the
reason of the queen's taking this vengeance, as she was
always before reckoned a sweet-tempered lady; and a certain female slave, who was some relation to Gabao, having

observed how remarkably sound herself and companions slept every night, began to think with herself that it must of necessity be the effect of some drug or other being mixed with the sherbet. For several days, therefore, she abstained from drinking any, and by that means soon became acquainted with the queen's treason ; and following her as far as Yvam's door, without making the least noise, was presently assured of Alishank's infidelity. Accordingly, she acquainted the sultan with the discovery she had made, who could at first scarcely believe a thing so incredible ; but being at length convinced of his dishonour by his own eyes, he ordered Yvam to be burnt alive, and Alishank's head to be cut off.

While they were throwing Alishank's body into the flames which consumed my poor master, I made my escape over the walls of the seraglio, got into the woods, and there continued for seven or eight months, in the deepest regret for my late delicious life, until I met with a company of comedians, and leaping on the waggon that carried their baggage I was very well received by them. The truth is, I drew a great number of people to them by my nimble and active tricks; nay, sometimes I acted a dumb part, and made such grimaces as they taught me, a little before the play began ; and it was one of these unlucky parts which cost me my life. One day, as I was in a soldier's dress, to act a sort of bully, and standing at the play-house door, a company of Hindus began to quarrel with each other, and in a moment's time twelve or fifteen sabres were drawn. I could not endure to be an idle spectator in this scene, but longed to be in the midst of them ; taking, therefore, my sabre in my hand, I laid about me as others did. It was not in my power greatly to hurt those I encountered, because my sabre was of wood; however, one of these brutes, being violently enraged at a blow I had given him on the face, made no distinction whether I was a man or an ape, but with a single back-stroke of his sabre took off my head. My death occasioned much grief among all the comedians, for I brought them in a great deal of money.

※　　※　　※　　※　　※　　※

Ah! what a pity was that! cried the Queen of Gannan; deuce take that hot-headed fellow for his pains! The adventures, however, of the ape, and the Sultana Alishank, have been very entertaining; nor should I grudge to hear a further account of the unlucky pranks of that animal. — They were innumerable, madam, answered the mandarin Fum-Hoam; but such frivolous stories would only weary your Majesty's patience; for which reason, I have omitted a thousand little tricks, such as I, since the time I was an ape, have imitated, and which have nothing remarkable in them; with your permission, then, I will pass on to some new adventures. —With all my heart, answered Gulchinraz; I take great pleasure in hearing you relate them.

STORY OF MAGMU, MIDWIFE OF ASTRAKHAN

As soon as I left the body of the ape, Morug, I found myself in a moment transported into Tartary, and animated the body of a midwife's daughter at Astrakhan, who had not many scruples about her own conduct, and knew how to enjoy the first years of my youth, much to her own humour and advantage; for which purpose she instructed me perfectly in the art of pleasing. They called me Magmu; and though I was naturally handsome enough, yet I had such art in setting off my beauty, that when I undertook to make a conquest it was impossible to escape me. Not a word proceeded out of my mouth that was not studied, neither did I open nor shut my lips but with design. To know perfectly well how to counterfeit a violent passion, to sigh *apropos*, to make an attractive gesture, to trifle agreeably, and to collect the various graces of dumb eloquence into one single smile, were all arts in which I excelled. In short, I had such ambition to surpass all other young women of my age that I was whole hours before the glass, to examine what clothes gave the greatest lustre to my beauty, what coloured stuffs best became me, which was the most graceful way of tying up my hair, and how a curl might hang loose upon my neck to the greatest advantage; how to open, shut, or move my lips with an air, to shew my teeth without affectation, to appear with a full or side face, as best suited the occasion, and to adjust my veil with a good grace; in short, madam, it seemed as if some invisible being gave life to my gestures and actions, and all the constituent parts appeared to have received a peculiar polish from the hand of that able master; and I changed myself into so many different forms that I sometimes looked upon myself with admiration; and if I may so say, even adored my own hand, which knew so well how to infuse the soul of every beauty into a body of itself sufficiently defective. These were the snares I

spread with so much address, and wherein I caught and
retained my admirers. You would be almost astonished,
madam, for instance, to see a lover I had just smiled on
tenderly, go out of his senses, and seem as much enchanted as if he had got into some great magician's
circle. I changed one into a lion by my disdain ;
another into a dog by his ready obedience to my least
motion ; another into a hare by his timidity and dread
of displeasing me, or the fear of being roughly handled
by his rivals ; and almost all, into such unclean beasts
as only take pleasure in mire and dirt,

If the love of a beautiful, virtuous, young lady
elevates the hearts of her adorers, making heroes of
them, and striking, as it were, the sparks of bravery
and generosity out of them ; the passion which men
entertain for a coquette, such as I was, being widely
distant from the path of honour, not only destroys the
seeds of virtue but carries prevailing vices to the
greatest height. My house was the general rendezvous
of all the vicious youths in Astrakhan. Gaming and
assemblies every night, under the protection of a Kadi,
furnished them with all sorts of diversions ; and I was
the only subject of the discourses, the amorous looks
and wanton thoughts of all those who frequented it.
This monstrous course of life continued as long as I was
young ; but when my hair began to turn white, and
wrinkles appeared on my face, all my lovers, one after
another, quickly disappeared ; and with them fled the
plenty that used to reign in my house. I now found by
experience that at a certain age one may have new
passions but want new adorers. Far from having preserved in my youth a stock sufficient to maintain me

in ease when advanced in years, I had been always too
profuse, and must have lived in the utmost poverty, if I
had not in my latter years applied myself to the profession of midwifery, which my mother had taught me
in my youth.

It would fill several volumes to describe all the
adventures wherein I had a part, and how many young
women, widows, and unknown persons, applied themselves to me; but I shall pass by these incidents, and
relate to you only that which put an end to my life.
One very dark night, while I was fast asleep in my
bed, two men came and knocked loudly at my door,
and calling me by my name ordered me in the name
of the Governor of Astrakhan, to come quickly to help
one of his wives, who was then in labour. As my
profession obliged me to go out at all hours of the
night, I came down in great haste to go along with
the men; no sooner had they turned the corner of
our street than they threatened to stab me if I attempted
to cry out, and, covering my eyes with a handkerchief,
they made me walk in this manner a full hour, and at
length brought me into a neat apartment, where they
unbound my eyes, and put me into the hands of a young
man about twenty, whose face was covered with a double
veil.

I seemed to be in no small concern, when the man
assured me I had nothing to apprehend. Be not afraid,
said he ; only make ready to deliver a woman in the
chamber to which I shall conduct you. This room had
but one lamp in it, which gave a very faint light, and by
its glimmering infused a secret horror, which was still
more augmented by the complaints and bitter cries which

came from beneath a canopy of green cloth. I drew near towards it, and there saw a young person whose eyes, though drowned in tears, seemed full of vivacity ; and the moment. I told her who I was she redoubled her tears, and embracing me very tenderly, conjured me to prevail with her inhuman brother to save at least the miserable fruit of her frailty. With these words her affliction was so great that she fainted away ; and some few moments after, by the help of a very strong pain, I assisted her to bring into the world a most beautiful boy. But no sooner was the little infant born than the young woman's barbarous brother, looking steadfastly upon him, found all his rage return into his heart, and taking the child in one hand and presenting the mother a poinard with the other, ordered her to plunge it instantly into the little innocent's breast.—I yet, madam, tremble with horror at the recital of so much cruelty ! The unhappy woman, not able to bear this horrid proposition, died away a second time ; when the inhuman monster, putting the poinard into her hand, directed it to the infant's throat, and so took away his life ; then taking the dead body of a young man, about twenty years old, all bloody, out of a chest, he set it directly over against his sister. As soon as this sad victim of enraged fury had recovered her spirits, and seen in what condition the dead body and her son were, she screamed out. Barbarous villain ! said she, finish thy crime upon me ; for after thou hast deprived me of what is most dear to me in the world, without considering it is thy master's blood thou hast spilt, can'st thou be so cruel as to let me live ? Ah ! I will deprive thee of that pleasure ! and since thou hast made me against my will the murderer of my son, I know how to revenge the crime upon myself; not doubting but that Heaven will punish thee for thy inhumanity! And with these words she plunged the poinard into her heart, and vomited up her indignant soul in streams of blood. I shrieked violently at this last catastrophe; but the cruel villain, not willing to have any witness of his horrid crimes, struck off my head with one blow of his sabre.

     *   *   *   *   *   *

How do I pity the fate of this unhappy person! said the Queen of China; what baseness is there in the whole conduct of this barbarous brother! and how concerned am I, that you cannot relate me the particulars of her misfortune, whose body it was that was set before her, and the true motive of this monster's fury!—Above thirty years after this adventure, replied the mandarin, I was informed of the whole transaction, and will relate to you the particulars in its proper time; but to follow, madam, the order of things, you must know, that after I ceased to animate the midwife, I went into the Mogul's country, and entered into the body of the Sultan of Agra's only son.

ADVENTURES OF MOGIRADDIN, KING OF AGRA, AND OF RUZ-BAHARI, PRINCESS OF PEGU

My father, Moaggim, Sultan of Agra, had no other child than me; he called me Mogiraddin, and when I was eighteen years of age I had the misfortune to lose him. I succeeded him, however, on the throne, and after a

short time spent in mourning and the care of my kingdom, had some thoughts of choosing me a wife. I had
heard vast commendations of the exceeding great beauty
of Ruz-Bahari, the only daughter of the Sultan of Pegu,
who at fifteen had eclipsed all the princesses of the
East; but being resolved to judge for myself, I left the
administration of my kingdom to three of my wazirs,
and after passing over the Mogul's country and the
Gulf of Bengal, I arrived in the city of Pegu accompanied only by three persons, amongst whom my
governor was one.   The princess frequently appeared
in public, and when at any time she lifted up her veil
everyone was enchanted with the charms which overspread her face; she played at the mall the day I arrived
in the city, and I must own to you, madam, that from
the first moment I beheld her my liberty was lost; nay,
I became in a manner distracted, and when I came into
the good woman's house, which my governor had hired
for me, I threw myself upon a sofa, and passed the rest
of the day and all the succeeding night in very great
disorder.   When I had duly considered the matter, I
perceived this manner of life could never advance my
interest with the princess; and therefore determined to
resume my usual temper, and ate that day with a good
appetite.

The old woman with whom I lodged was of a very
gay temper, and I took much pleasure in talking with her.
One day, as our discourse turned upon Ruz-Bahari, I
was given to understand, to my great concern, that the
princess was as whimsical as beautiful, and that the king,
her father, severely repented an oath he had made, to
let her dispose of herself in marriage, because more than

8

twenty princes had paid their addresses to her, every
one seeming handsomer than the rest; and yet, upon
some slight reason or other, she had refused them all.
The least trifle served for a pretence, and was with
her a material blemish. One was too gay, another too
melancholy; one had a jealous look, another was in love
with himself; such a prince had too small eyes, such a
one too large ones; this man had either too flat or too
high a nose, and the next either too much or too little
wit; in short, madam, whether it was merely her caprice,
a peculiar aversion to marriage, or a natural love of
liberty, so it was that she had never yet met with a man
who entirely hit her taste. As soon as I heard what disposition she was of, I was resolved to take a method
quite different from that which had been pursued by all
those princes who had failed in their endeavours to gain
her affection. They had uniformly treated her with the
most servile adoration, and were of course despised; for
my part I proposed to affect the utmost indifference for
the whole sex, but more especially for the princess. I
went, therefore, to make my compliments to the King of
Pegu, and gave him to understand that I was the Sultan
of Agra. He pressed me to lodge in a palace adjoining
to his own, which was separated only by a parterre of
very choice flowers. I saw him several times successively,
without making the least mention of Ruz-Bahari; and
being surprised at my little curiosity in not appearing
desirous to see the princess, he rallied me on the occasion
with a considerable deal of wit. Sir, said I, I am not
come hither, as other princes do, to admire the charming
Ruz-Bahari; it was merely the pleasure of travelling
which occasioned me to leave my kingdom. Thanks to

our great Prophet! the most celebrated beauties I have seen could never make any impression on my heart. Besides, I understand the princess has refused the addresses of the most accomplished princes of the East, finding some fault or other with every one of them; since therefore I, who pretend to no beauty, and by hunting and travelling have been far from improving my complexion, even though I were not indifferent to the sex, cannot compare with the meanest of those whom she has rejected. I must even make the insensibility with which I am blessed, my preservation against the like disgrace.— We shall soon see whether you are able to keep your word, said the King of Pegu to me, smiling; to-morrow I invite you to dine with Ruz-Bahari, and am extremely apprehensive you will not find your resolution capable of resisting my daughter's charms.

The less eagerness I discovered to see the princess, the more the king pressed me to accept of his invitation; and, though I had in reality the most eager desire to behold her, yet I raised many difficulties; nor did I at last consent till it seemed necessary, consistent with good manners, not longer to refuse. On the day following, however, I failed not to be at court by dinner-time. I chose to be dressed very plain, and, though I was enraptured with the princess's charms, I was yet so far master of my actions as not to discover the least admiration of her. Ruz-Bahari, who had been informed of my discourse the night before, spared nothing to improve her natural beauty. She had added every ornament that could increase the lustre of her charms, and was so concerned to see the little notice I took of her (not so much as saying one polite thing to flatter her vanity), that she

8—2

was ready to die with vexation. It was a great pleasure to me to see the effect of my precaution; and as I had a strict watch over myself, I preserved such gaiety and freedom of spirit through the whole entertainment that the princess was not able to sit it out, but presently withdrew, pretending a slight indisposition. I, too, rose from the table, apparently as unconcerned as when I came in, but in reality the most in love of any man living.—This conduct I pursued for a whole month; that is, I all along affected the most perfect insensibility, and by this means brought the princess so effectually to change her manners, that she gave me to understand, notwithstanding all my indifference to her, I was the only prince who had ever yet occasioned her a sigh. It was with much apparent reluctance I was brought to comply, but at length I consented to marry her with her father's permission, which she readily obtained.

Great preparations were made for celebrating the nuptials with all the magnificence befitting our con-dition, and the day drew near; when, one evening, as I was mentioning to the princess the great obligations I found myself under to her for preferring me before the finest princes of the East—I cannot well tell, sir, said she, by what fatality this came to pass. I had vowed never to be in love, and slighted the offers of all the monarchs upon earth; their passion was only a fatigue to me, but your insensibility gave me an uneasiness which I did all in my power to dissipate, not having any intention of engaging myself to you; but in the present situation of our affairs I shall not blush to own that, had you continued your indifference much longer, I should have fallen into despair.—Ah, beautiful princess! said I,

I never was a moment without loving you; your first looks reached my heart, and I only affected an insensibility to your whole sex in order to inflame you. I redoubled my indifference in proportion as I saw your love increase, and by this innocent artifice have arrived at the height of my felicity, since in two days I shall possess the adorable Ruz-Bahari.

This declaration, which was a little too ingenuous, made the princess blush. She was secretly chagrined at having been so imposed on, and fell into a sudden gloom which it was not in my power to dissipate the whole day. On the morrow I found her somewhat easier, and flattered myself she had forgiven the artifice I had made use of; but I soon discovered my mistake, and how dangerous a thing it is to be too sincere with women. We were sitting at dinner with the King of Pegu, and I was going to eat the wing of a pheasant, when a bee chanced to sting me on the cheek, which gave me such exquisite pain for a moment that the wing fell out of my hand upon the princess's robe. She instantly took occasion to quarrel with me, seemed highly offended at the accident, pretended I did it on purpose to affront her, and without regarding my excuses rose hastily from the table, and declared to her father she would never be my wife.

You may imagine, madam, my surprise, and the King of Pegu's anger. It was in vain for him to make use of his authority; she regarded it not, and gave him to understand that she would stab herself to the heart rather than give me her hand. After I had in vain endeavoured for five or six days, by every possible method of submission, to appease her anger, I fell into the utmost despair, and was for making some attempts upon my life, and punishing one folly by another, when my governor staying my arm—Sir, said he, I will revenge you of this capricious princess, and in a short time make her repent severely the treating you with so much cruelty. Let me have but this one night to consult a jinni, who never fails me, and I will engage for the success of this matter.

Everything which flattered my passion abated my grief. I hearkened, therefore, to my governor, but had not much rest that night. In the morning he explained to me the reason of Ruz-Bahari's unaccountable resentment. The motive, said he to me, which occasions the princess to treat her lovers in so haughty a manner is this: she keeps in her possession a little piece of gold, which a skilful fairy once gave to her mother, and while that continues in her custody all the efforts of her lovers will be in vain; nor indeed can anyone become her husband without incurring the greatest misfortunes, unless she presents him with this piece of gold, or he gets it from her by some stratagem. It is constantly tied to her girdle with a gold chain, and she does not put it off the whole night long. The jinni who has promised me his protection has engaged to procure it me in a short time, but the better to deceive the princess it will be proper to take leave of the king and quit the city; in the meanwhile, depend upon me for the execution of the project. I followed my governor's advice implicitly; and shall now, madam, relate to you the method which the jinni pursued to revenge me.

Ruz-Bahari was accustomed every evening to walk in the gardens belonging to the palace, and sitting one afternoon by the side of a basin, ruminating a little by herself, she saw when she came to rise, a lizard running upon her. Having an extreme aversion to this sort of reptiles, she screamed out terribly, and tearing her robe in pieces did her utmost to get rid of it, but all to no purpose. It got between her golden girdle and her stays, and there twisted itself in such a manner that the princess could think of no other expedient to get quit of the creature but loosening her girdle and throwing it with the piece of gold, into the basin near which she was sitting. When the princess was somewhat recovered from her fright, she looked in the water for her piece of gold; but it was to no purpose, for the gold and the lizard had both disappeared. Never was any person more grieved with an accident than the princess with this. She had the basin emptied to the very last drop, and the pipes, which carried the water either in or out of it broken into pieces; but all their searches proved ineffectual, and her concern for the loss of the piece of gold became so violent that she retired to her apartment, and would receive no consolation.

My governor did not deceive me. The jinni who had taken the shape of a lizard brought him the piece of gold, which he put into my hands. I then washed my face with a certain water he gave me, which entirely changed my features, and presenting myself, as he advised me, to the king, who wanted a groom, in order to serve him in that capacity, was received into the stables. For eight or nine days and nights I performed the offices of my new vocation, during all which time the princess continued weeping, without once closing her eyes. The King of Pegu was greatly afflicted at his daughter's situation. He proclaimed by sound of trumpet that he would give a hundred thousand pieces of gold to anyone who would bring the piece that was lost. The next day I presented myself before the king, as I was instructed, and shewed both him and the princess the chain which belonged to the piece, and promised in ten days to procure the piece itself, provided I might for so many nights be permitted to lie in the glass-closet at the end of one of the galleries of the palace, which was the only recompense I would desire. I was looked upon as a vain, silly fellow, but my proposal was nevertheless accepted, and the princess was so charmed with the hope of again recovering the piece that her joy nearly proved as fatal as her grief had threatened. The night came. I was conducted into the glass-closet, where they fastened me in ; nor could I well tell what I had to do there, when the jinni appeared to me in the shape of a young child. I have just now, said he to me, cast the princess and all her slaves into a deep sleep ; promise me that you will marry her and I will conduct you into her apartment. —I swear to you, said I, by the gutter of gold, and by the black stone, which are at Meccah, that I will not only make her my spouse, but will likewise promise never to have any other wife as long as I live.—This is suffi-cient, said the jinni. As for the last article of your oath, that I will excuse you. He then pushed back one of the glasses, which was a kind of private door into Ruz-Bahari's apartment, where he made me first go into the bath which had been prepared for the princess, and then led me to her bed. As soon as it was day the jinni awoke me, and carried me back to the closet, whence in about an hour the king's people came and let me out. For nine nights together I went on at this rate, at the expiration of which time the jinni transported me and my three officers into the city of Agra, without suffering me to perform my promise; but, on the contrary, desired me to preserve the piece of gold. I was not a little surprised to find myself in my own palace at a time when I least of all expected it, and could not forbear upbraiding the jinni. Be not uneasy about your mistress, said he, she has not yet been sufficiently punished for her caprice; you shall see her again at a convenient time.

While I waited with impatience the result of these promises, Ruz-Bahari was plunged in the deepest sorrow and despair to find the groom was gone without returning her the piece of gold; but how greatly was her anguish increased, when at the end of two months she found herself with child, without being able to account in what manner it could possibly happen! As she was in the glass-closet one day, musing and considering with herself, she accidently pushed slightly against one of the sashes, which immediately flew open, and discovered the communication between that place and her apartment. How great was her confusion upon the sight of this! Heavens! cried she to herself; has a sorry groom been able to obtain what I have denied to the Sultan of Agra? Ah, Mogiraddin! you are sufficiently revenged on my capricious humour, did you but know my present shame and dishonour! At these words the princess melted into tears; and being for some time buried in thought, she at length resolved to leave the palace. For this purpose she took with her a purse full of gold; and putting on the habit of a slave went out at one of the garden gates, and walked the whole day without taking any refreshment. About the close of the evening she arrived at the entrance of a village, near a fountain, at which an old woman was washing her linen, and desired to have a lodging in her house that night; and to encourage her the more, presented her with a piece of gold. The good old woman conducted her to her cottage, treated her with the utmost tenderness and assiduity, and having given her a good homely supper, obliged her to make use of her own bed, while she herself slept on the straw.

Ruz-Bahari was so fatigued with her journey that she grew exceedingly drowsy, and when she went to bed immediately fell asleep, and waked not till the next morning, when she was disturbed very early with the singing of birds. But how great was her surprise when she opened her eyelids to find that, instead of being in the old woman's house, she was lying on a bed of green turf, in a very agreeable country, and clothed in a peasant's habit, but without her purse. What this extraordinary change meant she was at a loss to imagine, and the more she considered, the more her surprise and grief increased. But how mortifying was her condition when she understood from a young man, a tailor, who was passing that way, that she was in the Mogul's country, and just at the gates of Agra! This news, though it seemed incredible, made her ready to die with grief; she could not comprehend how it was possible to pass over such a vast tract of land in a single night, and was so deeply affected with the thought that she died away in the young man's arms, whose name was Sabur. But notwithstanding all

her melancholy, she was still exceeding beautiful, so that
the affliction she was in raised compassion in the tailor's
heart. Charming stranger! said he to her, as soon as
she had come to herself, your spirits seem to be cruelly
agitated; come to my house, which is at the entrance of
the suburbs of Agra, where you shall be treated with
kindness, and my mother and I will endeavour by every
assistance in our power to dispel the black cloud of
melancholy which sits upon your countenance.

Ruz-Bahari found herself in a condition too deplorable to refuse the tailor's offer. She followed him to a
little plain house, but extremely neat, where his mother
received her with all possible civility. If the sorrowful
princess had not been with child, she might have thought
herself happy in this quiet retreat; but this was a misfortune she knew not how to conceal, and Sabur having
proposed to marry her, she listened to his offer, more to
save her honour than from any inclination for him, and
accordingly became his wife in eight days. From that
time she began to appear a little more gay, especially in
her husband's company; but when she was alone, and
began to consider with herself that, after refusing to marry
the Sultan of Agra, she had suffered the embraces of a
filthy groom, and was now thrown into the arms of a poor
tailor, she felt herself most severely humbled, and became
very disconsolate. She had, however, all the reason in
the world to be content, had she not been born a princess,
for her husband was a young man of the foremost rank
in his profession, and had a very good reputation in Agra.
He constantly shewed an excessive love for her; let her
want for nothing she could desire; and, except the time
he went to work at his master's, would not be a moment

out of her company. This behaviour, so uncommon in a person of his condition, gained upon the princess's heart to such a degree that she soon lost the remembrance of her former quality, and came in time to love her husband with the greatest degree of tenderness.

It was a little more than six months since Ruz-Bahari, who now called herself Lama, had been married to the tailor; she lived very retired, and seemed to be with child much from that time. When talking with her husband one night, he reproached her with her want of curiosity in not having ever expressed the least desire to see the Sultan of Agra.—Ruz-Bahari blushed at the reproof. What avails it, said she, to see this monarch? An honest wife should have no eyes but for her husband. —I agree with you, replied the tailor; but as you were not born for Mogiraddin, you may safely see him without exciting my jealousy. To-day he goes a hunting, and will pass by your window; and I am desirous you should observe how well he sits a horse.—I will not do it, replied she; for I hate the sultan, though I do not know for why.—You hate him! answered the tailor, why what has he ever done to you?—Nothing! said the princess, rather briskly; but I have dreamed he was the cause of all my misfortunes, and I am one, you must know, who has great faith in dreams.—A good reason indeed, said he. Well, Lama, my absolute will and pleasure is that you stand at the window when he passes by; or rather, I beg you to give me this small token of your obedience; I shall myself be one of the retinue, and will notice whether you obey my orders. Ruz-Bahari at first only answered her husband with tears, which he affected not to perceive. You shall be

obeyed, said she; and, since you require it, I will see
the king pass by.

The tailor went out, and about an hour after, the
Princess of Pegu, hearing a great noise in the street,
went to the window just as I was passing by the door.
Surprised to see so beautiful a female in such a place,
I looked very earnestly at her and enquired who she was,
which threw her into the utmost confusion. She retired
from the window, full of vexation, and I proceeded on my
way. As soon as the first violence of her passion was
over, she could not forbear shedding a torrent of tears.
O Heavens! cried she to herself, had it not been for my
unpardonable caprice I had now been the wife of that
powerful monarch. Good God! what a difference! O
Mogiraddin, Mogiraddin! I am justly punished for my
contempt of thee! These words made her tears flow
afresh, and she continued weeping and lamenting till her
husband came from hunting. Well, Lama, said he to
her, did you see the sultan?—You would have it so,
replied she, and I was obliged to obey your orders.—Did
you not think he was richly dressed? continued he.—Yes,
surely, answered she.—Ah! but this is nothing, said he
again; he is shortly to be married, and I intend to take
you to court. There are splendid preparations making
for that joyful day, and my master and I are to fit on his
his wedding clothes, while my master's wife and you dress
the princess he has chosen, and who is to be here in a
few days; the robes are now actually making for her.—
Though the princess trembled at this proposition and
made many objections, there was no help for it; she
found herself constrained to obey. Nay, the tailor did
more; he had the robes of the intended queen brought

several times to his house, and assuring his wife she was much of the same size with herself, put them always upon her to see if anything wanted amendment. How grieved soever Ruz-Bahari might be to see herself dressed in such magnificent robes, and so very unsuitable to her station, she could nevertheless scarce refrain from laughter when she saw how they shaped the queen's clothes upon her. This princess, if she be like what I am at present, is of a pretty jolly size, said she to her husband.—She is very lusty, said Sabur to her again; the king loves to have them so.

At length the evening preceding the day whereon the sultan's marriage was to be celebrated arrived, and Sabur forgot not at break of day to awaken his wife, whom, notwithstanding all her reluctance, he carried with him to court. He was received by an officer of his acquaintance, who conducted them into the apartments, and was every moment extolling the happiness of the princess who was to be married to the sultan, assuring them he was one of the best princes in the world. All this was as so many daggers to the breast of Ruz-Bahari, nor could she bear to see such magnificence without many a bitter sigh. She was now in the chamber where the new queen was to sleep, when some messengers brought word the king was approaching, and within a few paces of the door. The poor princess, not being able to hear this without the most violent emotion, fell upon a sofa. O Heavens! said she, speaking to her husband, what an imprudent thing it was of you to bring a woman in my condition to such a place as this! I find I shall this moment bring into the world the child with which I am pregnant; yesterday I had a fall, but did not think it would have produced so grievous a consequence. The tailor seemed to be in great confusion. Ah ! my dear friend, said he to the officer who attended, what will become of us ?—Why, said the man, you must e'en put a good face on it ; set your wife upon this cushion, and I will go out of the chamber the way which I know the king comes, and will so hamper the lock that it cannot be opened. I will then tell his Majesty the apartment is not yet set in order, and afterwards run as fast as possible for my wife, to help to convey yours home, or give her all necessary assistance ; and I hope we shall extricate ourselves from this difficulty without the sultan's perceiving it. Everything was done as the officer promised. —I went not into the apartment, continued Fum-Hoam ; the woman who was to assist Ruz-Bahari came in a few minutes after, and, without having time to be removed, she was delivered in the royal chamber of a most beautiful boy. The tailor was in transports of joy, hardly to be expressed. Faith, my dear Lama, said he, since you are delivered in the queen's apartment, the damage will not be much increased if we put you in her bed too.—The man is surely distracted, answered Ruz-Bahari, to think of such an absurdity.—Say what you will, answered the tailor, the bed is made, and in it you shall lie !—The princess, notwithstanding all she could say to the contrary, was accordingly carried to the queen's bed; and though she had a strange perturbation and disorder upon her spirits for an hour or two, yet it was not long before she fell into a sound sleep, which held her till pretty late the next morning.

Ruz-Bahari no sooner saw the light than she immediately opened her curtains, and was strangely surprised to find twelve female slaves standing round her bed in the most profound silence, frequently bowing their bodies very low, in token that they attended her commands. I fancy, said she presently, the women are mad, or perhaps my senses are not yet recovered from the vapours of sleep.—You are not asleep, madam, said the eldest of these women; the Sultan of Agra, your husband, and to whom you gave a successor yesterday, waits till your apartment be open that he may be permitted to wait on you. Shall I inform him you may now be seen ? — Ruz-Bahari was so confounded at a request apparently so extravagant that she made no reply : her silence was therefore interpreted favourably. The old woman ran to the door and I made my entrance, all shining with precious stones, and sat down on a sofa by the Princess of Pegu's bedside. My queen ! said I, embracing her, it is high time now to put an end to your astonishment, and to restore you to your true husband ; since the groom of Pegu, the tailor in the suburbs of Agra, and the Sultan Mogiraddin are one and the same person ; though a certain jinni, who is my protector, had so disguised them that it was impossible for you to discern the imposture. I have a thousand times entreated him to put a period to your pain, and have represented to him, but in vain, that your punishment was too great for the uneasiness you gave me the evening before our intended marriage.—Pride and stateliness of temper, said he to me, do well enough become a princess ; but then it should be a noble pride, directed by wisdom and not by caprice ; nor shall the queen, your spouse, be restored to you till self-conviction has made her fully sensible of the faults she committed in rejecting the homage of so

many princes, and refusing to marry you on so trifling
an occasion. All that I can do for you is to convey her
into your arms without her knowing herself to be there;
and I enjoin you to compel her to come to your palace at
the time when she shall be ready to be delivered.—I was
obliged to obey the sovereign orders of the jinni, who in
one night transported you to the gates of Agra. I
assumed, therefore, by virtue of a certain water, with
which I rub my face when I have occasion, the figure
of that young tailor whom you married. But now Ruz-
Bahari is to take her own name and quit that of Lama,
as I have relinquished that of Sabur to be henceforth
the Sultan Mogiraddin only. You know the rest, your
punishment is now at an end, and I conjure you, my fair
queen, to forget that I was the instrument of it!

Ruz-Bahari was so amazed at the account I gave
her, continued the mandarin, that she could not return
my caresses, but looked on me with eyes bathed in tears,
which joy and sorrow equally occasioned; and as soon
as she had recovered her speech—My dear lord, said she,
what afflictions have I suffered since your departure
from Pegu! what shame have I felt, to think myself
dishonoured by a groom! what cruel necessity was I
under to marry a tailor, to secure my honour, and to
rescue me from the miseries of want! and what uneasiness did not yourself occasion me, whilst you were
under that shape, by obliging me to see you pass before
my window, to try on the queen's clothes, and to come
to this palace, where I had so terrible an apprehension
of meeting you! Ah, sir! I could not pardon you the
many uneasy hours you have cost me, and which the
jinni has enabled me to sustain, but that you assure me

9

it was not in your power to make them expire when you pleased !—Forget all your trouble, thou dearest essence of my life ! said I, interrupting her ; and think of nothing but the happiness which we are in future to enjoy with undisturbed tranquility.—Ruz-Bahari, madam, continued Fum-Hoam, received my excuses with great tenderness ; we lived together in perfect union for almost twenty years ; till, as I was one day hunting, I was drowned in attempting to ford a river, into which my horse threw me.

                ✳   ✳   ✳   ✳   ✳   ✳

The history you have told me, said Gulchinraz, is full of marvellous incidents ; and I do not a little pity the fate of the unhappy Princess of Pegu, till the moment in which Mogiraddin assured her that he himself was the tailor.   To speak freely, I think your jinni was a little too severe, and should not have punished the poor lady's caprice with quite so much rigour.   But after you had lost your life in the water, what became of you then ?

ADVENTURES OF THE PHYSICIAN BANU-RAZID

I ENTERED into the body of a young man, who was born at Astrakhan, the son of an Arabian physician, then in the king's service.   My father performed such wonderful cures that they almost esteemed him as a divinity ; and as I had a great fancy for the profession, he took care to instruct me in it.   When I came to be about fifteen years of age,—Banu-Razid, said he to me very often, there is no acquiring a thorough knowledge of the sciences without the watchfulness of a crow, the greediness of a swine, the patience of a dog, and the fawnings of a cat. If you know these precepts perfectly, you will, one day or other, become a great man; but if you do not, you will be always grovelling and mean, nor ever distinguish yourself in any kind of life whatever.

Enamoured with these maxims, I applied myself entirely to my studies, and in fewer than ten years made so great proficiency, that after my father's death I was appointed one of the King of Astrakhan's physicians. I was hardly eight-and-twenty years old when I acquitted myself in that employ with infinite success, and had got so far into the sultan's good opinion that I became his favourite. That monarch, indeed, so greatly esteemed me, that he could not live without my company, and therefore allowed me the peculiar privilege of going into the inner apartments of the seraglio at any hour of the day. The chief reason why he permitted me to enter a place which was prohibited to every man besides, was his knowledge of my strong aversion to the sex, and how I detested the horrid effects of love. I had, indeed, read so much of the disasters that usually attend this strange passion, that I guarded myself against it, and had taken a firm resolution never to let my heart be surprised. When the sultan used to rally me upon my insensibility that way,—Sir, said I to him, I do not hate women, but I fear them. They may disturb the quiet of my life, and it is for this reason I look upon them with such indifference. God grant that I may persevere in the design I have taken of preserving my liberty! This,

madam, in a great measure, is the subject of the conversation I often had with the sultan ; and one day, as we
were talking together much to the same purpose, word
was brought him that his prime wazir, Hussan ibn San,
had fallen into a kind of madness, which several times
had seized him very violently ; and, having a tender
esteem for the wazir, he ordered me to hasten to his
assistance. The information which was brought the sultan
was but too true ; I found Hussan ibn San so very
delirious, that I was obliged to have him tied down.
His madness increased every moment, and it was seven
or eight hours, after I had let him blood in the foot,
before he began to recover his senses. Banu-Razid,
said he to me, you see me just going to appear before
the tribunal of Almighty God ; I feel already the cold and
freezing wind of death, which blows continually at the
side of my bed, and all the art of physic is not able to
save my life.—Sir, said I, your distemper is not so
incurable as you imagine ; only endeavour to overcome
this melancholy humour, which gets the better of you.
Is there anyone in all Astrakhan who has more reason
to be happy than you ?—Ah, my dear friend ! said he,
squeezing my hand ; how deceitful are appearances !
There is, it is true, no person who ought, in all human
appearance, to be better satisfied with his fortune than
myself. I have more riches than a man need desire ;
my seraglio is full of the fairest Circassian women ; and
my daughter, the only one I have, is a beauty not inferior
to any of the houri. This is the bright outside of my
family ; but a worm, which has been gnawing me above
these thirty years, brings perpetually to my remembrance
a chain of crimes that make me even abhor myself.

Since that fatal day I have never once tasted true repose, but have been constantly tormented with the cruel motions of the Suiderez. I see before my eyes the frightful ghosts of a sister and her son, whom I have most barbarously murdered. Their blood, and the blood of one of our sultans, rise up every moment against me. I tremble when I think that within a few hours they will be upbraiding me with my inhumanity before the tribunal of God. Ah, my dear Banu-Razid! what answer shall I make to the Sovereign Judge of all our actions? Can I think (how great soever my contrition may be for my having committed the horrid crimes which yet lie heavy upon me) He will not listen to the just complaints of these unhappy victims of my fury? But these things are so many enigmas to you, which it is necessary that I should explain.

HISTORY OF THE WAZIR HUSSAN IBN SAN

My father, as you cannot but remember, my dear Banu-Razid, said the wazir, was the favourite of Fakr al-Din, father to the Sultan Muza-Kazim, our present king; but perhaps you do not know that Fakr al-Din had two sons, Muza-Kazim the younger, and Alaku the elder, of whom we have not heard anything for more than thirty years past. The former loved me extremely; he raised me to the post which I have enjoyed ever since he came to the throne, and still continues his affection. The latter, jealous of the friend-ship his brother had for me, beheld with pain the little respect I paid him, notwithstanding he was the elder.

We are not masters either of our sympathies or anti-
pathies ; and whatever efforts I made to conquer this
aversion I could never gain so much upon myself as to
make my court to Alaku.   What likewise increased my
hatred to the prince was his falling in love with a young
widow, by which he became my rival, and was treated
more favourably than myself.

I carried my resentment a little too high, continued
the wazir, not considering the distance which was
between a prince and me ; and Alaku having complained to Fakr al-Din, I had orders to remove threescore
leagues from Astrakhan, and not to appear at court for
six months.   This punishment filled me with rage ; I
was incapable of hearkening either to reason or to the
remonstrances of my father ; I would not so much as
make the least excuse to the prince, who required only
my submission ;   and my father took my imprudent
conduct so much to heart that he fell sick, and with
a lingering fever at length gave up his soul to the
angel of death.

The Prince Muza-Kazim in this sad conjuncture
obtained leave of the sultan and his brother for my
return to Astrakhan.   I took possession of all my
father's effects ;   and as he had left me a sister of
exquisite beauty, I ardently wished that Muza-Kazim
might fall in love with her and make her his wife.   To
bring this about I feigned myself sick ;   he had the
goodness to visit me ;   and as I was informed of his
intention I ordered the amiable Pahrizad (for that was
my sister's name) to be at my bedside and without her
veil when the prince should come into my chamber.   I.
did not expect, my dear friend, that Alaku would accom-

pany his brother. The prince, to convince me he had forgotten my insolent behaviour, was desirous to give me this mark of his goodness. What aversion soever I had for him, I must do justice to truth by acknowledging he was a person of uncommon merit. He was not very tall, but the best-shaped person in Astrakhan; and his face was so regularly beautiful it was difficult to look upon him without admiring him. I was astonished at this visit; and if I had been but forewarned of the honour he intended me, should have taken particular care not to let him see Pahrizad; but the fault was committed, and I was under the necessity of putting a face upon it, though at the bottom of my soul I was exceedingly chagrined. My sister's beauty had an effect the direct contrary of my intentions. Muza-Kazim beheld her with indifference, and Alaku with such transport as pierced me to the heart. My grief, too, was the more sensible, as I thought I could perceive in Pahrizad's eyes that the prince's passion caused in her as much vanity as pleasure. I knew, however, how to disguise myself, and feigned not to see what had passed between these two lovers.

Accordingly, I redoubled my diligence in taking strict care of my sister, and entrusted the inspection of her conduct to an old slave, whom I thought incorruptible; but what will not gold and presents bring about! Alaku, under the pretence of passing whole weeks in hunting, kept himself concealed in my sister's apartment; he had promised to marry her at his accession to the throne, and Pahrizad, sensible of the sincerity of so amiable a prince, could not refuse satisfying his impatient desires. What shall I say, my dear

Banu-Razid ? I was absolutely ignorant of this secret conversation ; but that black fury with which I was perpetually agitated, and which every moment excited my resentment against Alaku, gave rise to a dream which was the occasion of all my misfortunes. I thought that in travelling through a forest I heard a terrible cry, and fancied it was the sound of my sister's voice. I ran to her, and found her in the paws of a ravenous lion, and Prince Alaku, sabre in hand, hastening to her assistance. This dream so disturbed me that I awoke in great agitation, and went to Pahrizad's apartment without knowing why. But, oh, what a surprise was I in when I saw her fast asleep in the prince's arms ! I could not govern the violent emotions of my soul ; but filled with rage stabbed the prince in a thousand places with my poinard. I rewarded my slave in the same manner, and then awaking my sister, shewed her the dreadful effects of my vengeance. She fell into frightful shrieks at this spectacle, and as I was afraid she would awake my slaves, I crammed a handkerchief into her mouth ; and having locked her up in one great chest, and Alaku and the old woman in another, I ordered them to be conveyed in the night-time by four slaves to a little house of mine at the gates of Astrakhan, without their knowing what they carried. I directed them afterwards to return to the city, and opening Pahrizad's chest, I was about to send her to keep her lover company, when, throwing herself at my feet : Barbarian, said she to me, before thou takest away my life, suffer me at least to bring into the world the wretched infant I bear in my womb ; he may be, perhaps, one day thy master, unless the effects of thy cruelty obstruct his passage. Let me, therefore, have the comfort of leaving after my decease an heir to my misfortunes. I need not recommend to you the concealing his birth ; if thou hast pity enough to let him live, thy own interest will make thee grant me this.—I could not help being overcome by her tears ; her delivery was hastened by the violence of her grief ; and, as I found she stood in need of some assistance, I ordered two slaves, who always lived in that house, instantly to fetch a midwife, without letting her know whither she was coming. My orders were obeyed ; the midwife came in an hour's time, and my sister, with her help, was delivered of a fine boy, being seven months gone, or somewhat more.

My first intention was to have placed the child with the midwife, and to have given her a purse of gold, which might be sufficient for his education, but unfortunately, casting my eyes upon him, I saw some features so much resembling those of Alaku, that I found all my hate, which was not quite extinguished, revive afresh, and would have prevailed on his mother to have stabbed him. So great was her horror at this proposal that she swooned away, upon which, O unparalleled barbarity ! I put the poniard myself into her hand, and directed it to the throat of her little son. When she came to herself she no sooner perceived the involuntary crime I had made her commit than she instantly took away her own life with the same weapon. The midwife, thus astonished, would have shrieked out, but I made her head fly from her shoulders with my sabre, and by the assistance of my two slaves buried all their bodies in the garden belonging to this house. Afterwards, that there should be no witness of so many crimes, I killed my two slaves, and interred them near the others.

The next morning I returned to Astrakhan, and caused it to be rumoured abroad that my sister had been stolen away. The absence of Prince Alaku occasioned it to be concluded that it was he who had dishonoured me. I complained to the sultan; he was dreadfully enraged, and became the more incensed when Muza-Kazim assured him that his brother was passionately in love with Pahrizad. Several years had elapsed without hearing any news of these unfortunate lovers, who were believed to be wandering about the world; and Fakr al-Din having paid the common tribute to nature, Muza-Kazim ascended the throne, to which I had paved the way for him by the murder of his brother. This prince, who had always given me extraordinary testimonies of his goodness, made me immediately his prime wazir. I have been possessed of this place, my dear friend, above twenty years; but I am far from being happy in it. I am incessantly tormented with remorse for my crimes, and have endeavoured, by all kinds of good works, to appease the anger of our great Prophet. I have founded two caravansaries, hospitals for the pilgrims of Meccah. I have built three mosques, where forty poor people are daily fed; I have caused prayers to be said in my behalf by the Imans of the kingdom; but nothing can drive away this black melancholy which devours me; all my vows are rejected! At last, thus sorely burdened with so many horrors with which the secret part of my life is blackened, I begged it as a favour of the Prophet that he would take me out of the world. This is the only prayer he seems to have given any attention to; he has sent me a most violent fever, madness precedes the fits, and I am sensible I have but a few moments to live. You will find in this casket of sandal wood—which I desire you will put into the sultan's hands—all my jewels, with my will. I have added to it a particular account of my horrid crimes. I ask him a thousand pardons ; he will curse my memory. Ah ! I too much deserve it. I regard myself as a monster not fit to see the light ; but, however, oblige me thus far, my dear Banu-Razid, not to carry the casket to Muza-Kazim till after I am dead.

I left the wazir, continued the mandarin, after having taken charge of the casket ; but scarce had I set my foot out of the chamber when, falling into new fits of madness, he was attacked with such violent convulsions that in spite of my assistance he was suffocated in a few moments.

CONTINUATION OF THE ADVENTURES OF THE PHYSICIAN BANU-RAZID

NEVER was surprise equal to that of the sultan upon reading the wazir's memorial which I presented him. He wept exceedingly, and bewailed the unfortunate Alaku ; and having summoned his privy council to communicate to them the news I had brought him, it was consulted whether that memorial should be made public, and possession taken of all the effects the wazir had bequeathed to Muza-Kazim, for the care of an only daughter he had left behind him, whose name was Simache. As I was charged with this commission, I caused all the rich furniture of the wazir to be brought into the seraglio, and conducted his daughter thither. She was scarce sixteen ; but, madam, what charms were in her face, and how did her tears affect me! I then attributed that to compassion which I soon found was the effect of a more violent affection, not imagining this beautiful young creature had made so strong an impression on my heart. Afterwards I presented her to the sultan Muza-Kazim ; and I did not well understand my true sentiments till I perceived with what surprise he looked at her, and heard him exclaim that he had never beheld anything in nature so perfect as Simache. I then discovered my unhappiness, and felt in my heart such struggles of jealousy as made me detest the sultan. In vain did I resist, and use all endeavours to subdue the growing passion, which I perceived would be fatal to me. Love triumphed ; and in spite of all my resolutions I yielded ; nor could I see Simache enter the seraglio without thinking I should become the victim of my grief.

Muza-Kazim was very handsome, but of an impetuous temper ; he did not delay a moment to make known to Simache all the violence of his passion. Ambition, and, perhaps, love, dried her tears in a few days, and I soon found that she was going to give herself up to the sultan's pleasure. I received this information with extraordinary transports of rage, and exhausted myself in reproaches the most extravagant and outrageous against Muza-Kazim, as if he had stolen away my mistress. I treated Simache as if she had engaged herself to me, and had afterwards proved perfidious and ungrateful. In short, madam, I so lost my reason, that they were obliged to keep me confined. Muza-Kazim, surprised at so extraordinary a distemper,

caused me to be brought before him that he might
be himself a witness of the condition I was in. Simache
was with him when I entered his closet ; her presence
recalled to my distracted mind a thousand extravagant
ideas ; I cast myself at her feet. I declared my passion,
and very probably did it in terms so singular and
pathetic that they reached the very soul of the fair
Simache. She comprehended in a moment the violence
of my passion, and discovered that it was herself who
had reduced me to that deplorable condition, and com-
paring it, no doubt, with that of the sultan, who shewed
to her nothing but an absolute power, to which she was
on the point of submitting, gave herself up to such a profound melancholy as astonished Muza-Kazim. What
endeavours soever he made use of to console her, he
could never effect it. This beautiful creature was in a
little time in the same condition as myself; she talked
of nothing but the tender Banu-Razid, and, in a word,
become equally distracted.

This extraordinary situation, which the sultan could
not but notice, mortified him exceedingly. He was tenderly fond of the beautiful Simache; but he was, at the
same time, exceedingly nice and delicate in affairs of
love ; and her condition would not permit him to make
her a favourite sultana, though he had been less delicate
than he was. For several days he caused all the ordinary remedies to be applied, and perceived that the whole
art of physic was ineffectual to restore her ; he therefore
determined to apply a remedy which his physicians
would never have prescribed, and which, indeed, was
wholly of his own invention. Accordingly, he sent for
a kadi, and ordered us both to be brought into his pre-

sence. Banu-Razid, said he to me, I am resolved to make a great conquest of myself. I adore the charming Simache, but as I am persuaded that you were born for each other, I give her to you. Live happily together ! Upon this the kadi made the contract, and we signed it without well knowing what we did. The sultan then made us go home to my house, where we were served with a most magnificent entertainment, at which he did me the honour to be present, till the whole company retired, and left me in full possession of the adorable Simache.

Our spirits, madam, were too much disordered for me to explain by what means they returned to their former situation, to which, it is highly probable, the felicity I experienced with my fair bride did not a little contribute. This only I know that in proportion as my reason returned, my charming spouse likewise recovered, and that the sultan found himself infinitely pleased in having furnished so simple and natural a remedy as that which so effectually restored us. These great benefits, however, did not suffice the great heart of Muza-Kazim ; he restored her all her father's estate, and made me prime wazir. I lived with my wife in perfect union, and had a great number of children ; and it was not before I was extremely old that I left a much decayed body, and passed into a new world unknown to all mankind before.

    ❊   ❊   ❊   ❊   ❊   ❊

I own to you, said Gulchinraz, that I think the conclusion of your history is very pleasant, particularly your cure, and has very well made amends for the relation of the unfortunate Pahrizad, whose catastrophe was so tragical. All the physic in the world put together could

never have formed a remedy like Muza-Kazim's, and I
believe one may cure in the beginning all kinds of folly
and madness by remedies proportioned to the causes
which produced them.   But continue, I beseech you,
your adventures, and tell me what you were in that
obscure part of the world you mentioned.

ADVENTURES OF KOLAO, THE WILD MAN

I ANIMATED a young savage, named Kolao, who lived
in the island Misamichis, so called from a certain river,
to which some of my ancestors gave that name; but I
cannot tell you, madam, in what part of the world it is
situated.   I have scarce an idea of the religion we pro-
fessed; I only know we adored the sun at his rising, and
that every morning, turning our faces to the east, we
saluted him three times, crying as loud as we were able,
Ho! Ho! Ho! after which, making profound reverences,
we prayed him to preserve our wives and children, to
give us strength to conquer all our enemies, and to grant
us fishing and hunting in abundance.

You may easily imagine, madam, continued Fum-
Hoam, how the first years of a life so plain and simple
passed away.   I was taught to use the bow, and when I
had attained eighteen years I chose me a wife.   I loved
her tenderly, and had by her six girls and a boy.   My
daughters were no sooner of age than they married; and
my son, whose bravery was respected throughout the
whole island, was also going to be married when a

violent distemper carried him off in four days. This loss went so near my heart that, having committed several extravagancies, I was going to plunge an arrow into my breast, when one of my companions arrested my arm. Why will you die, said he to me, Kolao, since there is still a remedy for your misfortunes ? Only hear me with attention. I have often heard my father say that one of the most considerable ancients of our nation was one day so dangerously ill that he lost the use of all his senses, and fell into such violent convulsions that for a long time he was imagined to be dead. He came, however, to himself again, and being asked by the people who were in the hut with him where he had been all the while he lay so senseless, he told them he had just come from the Country of Souls ; that by an extraordinary favour, never indulged to any person but himself, the sovereign of the kingdom, whose name was Pat-Kut-Parut, had permitted him to return to his own island to bring back an account of a country which till then had never been discovered ; that the country, moreover, was not above a hundred leagues distant from them ; that the ready way to it lay by the north side of the island ; and that, after wading and swimming through a lake of about forty leagues' breadth, which was full of seaweed, one might arrive at the kingdom of Pat-Kut-Parut ; and that by carrying a proper present to the monarch, he might have leave not only to converse with the souls of his old friends but even to bring away such as he pleased, provided their bodies were not yet corrupted.

This, said my comrade, is the account which our ancient related to those who were about him in the hut, and he would have been more particular in it, and told them the conversation he had had with the souls of his friends, had not our most cruel enemy, Death, closed his eyes that very moment. The tyrant was, doubtless, jealous of Pat-Kut-Parut's favour to him, and feared that at one time or other he would undertake to rescue some of his relations, and therefore snatched him from among us so suddenly. Your son is but just dead. Do you think you have courage enough to undertake so difficult a journey as that to the Country of Souls? I will bear you company, and we will either bring back your son's soul or die in the attempt.

I accepted this proposition very gladly; we were joined by three more of our comrades, and having made a great feast for all our friends, we took our bows and arrows, bracelets of coral, and some tobacco, to make a present of to Pat-Kut-Parut, and began our journey by break of day. We took our route by the north side of the island, and came in a few days to the lake which our ancient had mentioned, where we cut ourselves poles to sound the ford, and so went into the water, and waded at a great rate but with vast difficulty. When night came we struck our poles into the bottom of the water, and tied some cotton-filleting to the tops of them, in the nature of hammocks, and there slept till sunrise. After two days' travel in this manner, we at length got over the lake, landed in the country we so much wished for, and at our arrival were very agreeably surprised with an infinite number of spirits of bows, arrows, and clubs, which flew about before our eyes like so many little clouds; and by a certain unknown language gave us to understand that they had formerly been in the service of our fathers and companions. But not long after, we

10

were almost terrified to death ; for as we drew near a hut much like these in our island, except that it was prodigiously lofty, we perceived a man, or rather a giant, armed with a bow and a terrible club, who, looking upon us with eyes sparkling with rage, spoke to us in these words : Whoever you are, prepare yourselves to die for daring to pass this river, and come into the sacred realms of the dead ! I am Pat-Kut-Parut, the keeper, and master, and governor of all the souls !

The giant had already brandished his club to destroy us, when, throwing myself at his feet, I conjured him both with tears and words to excuse the rashness of an enterprise which justly merited his wrath.   Empty your whole quiver of arrows upon us, said I, or crush us with one blow of your mighty club ; our breasts and our heads are bare to you, and you are the sovereign arbiter of our life or death ; but if you have any sense of compassion in you, pardon our boldness on the account of an unhappy father who has only offended you out of too great tenderness for an only son he has lately lost ; and vouchsafe to accept of the presents we bring you from the country of the living, and receive us among the number of your friends. —These humble and submissive words touched the heart of Pat-Kut-Parut ; he seemed sensible of my grief, received my presents, bade me take courage, and to complete his favour and my consolation, assured me that before my departure he would give me my son's soul again.   In the mean time, he was pleased to regale me and my companions with an excellent liquor he had in his hut, and we drank it with the greater pleasure, because in a moment it restored us to the full possession of that strength we had lost in so laborious a journey.

While we were thus rejoicing and refreshing ourselves with him, the soul of my son came. I knew the
voice, and was ready to die with joy; but while I was
requesting the giant to give it me to carry back to his
body, it grew in an instant as big as an apple. He then
took it into his hands, and thrusting it into a little leather
bag, which he tied with a packthread, he hung it about
my neck and gave us audience of leave, with a strict
injunction as soon as we arrived in our island to lay my
son's body along in quite a new hut, and to open the
little bag at his mouth and so let in his soul; but to take
particular care that the bag was not opened till then, lest
it should slip out and return to his kingdom again, which
it did not leave, as he told us, without some reluctancy.

After I had received the bag, with all the transports
of excessive joy, we were, by the order of Pat-Kut-
Parut, shewn the dark and dismal place where the souls
of the wicked are confined. It was covered over with
nothing but branches of dried box, irregularly placed;
whereas the huts of the virtuous were beautifully adorned
with an infinite number of evergreens both within and
without, through which the sun continually came to visit
them and to refresh the branches of box and cedar
whereon they repose themselves. Around their huts we
saw the spirits of the bows, arrows, and clubs, wherewith
they diverted themselves in the same manner as when
they were in the land of the living. After we had considered these things with admiration, we drank each of us
two cups more of the same liquor he had given us before,
and so set forward on our journey. We entered the lake,
fixed our poles, slung our hammocks, and slept very
soundly; but whether it was the pleasure of the great

10—2

Pat-Kut-Parut to have it so, or some natural effect of the liquor we drank, so it was, that when we awoke we all found ourselves in our own island and within a hundred yards of my hut.

It is no difficult matter to conceive the joy of our comrades to see us get back, and to hear the strange accounts we gave of our journey and return. They could not believe that I had really got my son's soul in the bag which hung about my neck, and were very impatient to see it enter into his body again, in order to convince them of the truth of what we related. For this purpose we immediately built a new hut, and carried my son's corpse into it, which his mother and three other women had kept fresh by driving away the flies with large feather-flaps; and I was preparing to execute the orders Pat-Kut-Parut had given me, when an unexpected accident plunged me into the most cruel grief.

While I was employed in making the new hut, I left my wife the bag wherein my son's soul was enclosed. She had been present at the relation of the history of our journey, but the prohibition not to open the bag raised her curiosity; and though I had given her a strict and repeated charge not to meddle with it, yet she would be untying the packthread; when out flew the soul of my son to the country from whence we had brought it with so much difficulty, and I found the bag empty. It is impossible to express, continued the mandarin, the rage aud fury I was in. In the first transport of my passion I gave my wife such a terrible blow on the head with my club that I scattered her brains in the air; then taking my knife, the point and blade of which were of flint, out of a kind of sheath, I plunged it into my own heart, and fell down dead on my son's body, leaving my comrades in great tribulation at so sad a catastrophe, which had deprived them of the pleasure of knowing with more certainty the news from the kingdom of souls, and the state and condition of those of their own kindred.

✻   ✻   ✻   ✻   ✻   ✻

In good truth, these poor unhappy creatures, said the Queen of China, had a great loss, for that young man would doubtless have told them many a pleasant story. But when you left that body, what afterwards became of you?—I passed into a slave, replied the mandarin, named Ilul, who was sold to the daughter of the great Mogul's first physician, who dwelt at Agra.   In this condition there were no particular events that personally concerned me, my life was simple and uniform; but those wherein my young mistress had a part, and such as I heard while I was in her service, may possibly amuse your majesty for some moments.—You will do me, then, replied Gulchinraz, a singular pleasure in relating them.—If so, madam, continued the mandarin, I will endeavour to satisfy your curiosity.

ADVENTURES OF DARDOK; TOLD BY HER SLAVE ILUL

My young mistress's name was Dardok; the fine and sprightly air of her face pleased infinitely, and at fifteen she so far excelled all the young ladies of her age, both in the graces of her person and vivacity of her wit, that she became the admiration of all who beheld her.

Takfur, first physician to Prince Filu, Sultan of Hind, had made several voyages to Agra, and had contracted a firm friendship with my mistress's father ; and persuading himself that he could not but be happy with a person of so much fine sense and beauty, he desired her in marriage, claimed her for his wife, and carried he to Masulipatam, where the sultan his master had his usual residence.   Thus, tenderly beloved by his new wife, and highly respected by the sultan, who shewed him every mark of royal favour and confidence, he wanted nothing to complete his happiness, when a certain fakir named Barzalu, who, through all degrees of fortune had raised himself to be prime wazir, grew jealous of the kindness the sultan had for him.   The fakir in every step he had taken for his advancement to that high station had always distinguished himself by some new artifice, and therefore you may well imagine, madam, that it could not be long before he would contrive some plan for the removal of my master (for I went with Dardok to Hind).   But to let your majesty into the wazir's character it will be necessary to trace him from his first original.

Barzalu was born in the territories of Kabul, of a very mean extraction, and brought up as a cook ; but being weary of an employ so unsuitable to his genius, he quitted it and turned fakir.   After he had the whole day long wandered about the streets of Kabul, he used toretire at night to a little hut he had made himself in the suburbs, not far from a mosque.   As Barzalu one day came into the place where Prince Masdowan resided, who was then upon his travels in the Mogul's country, the prince had compassion on his poverty, and threw him some pieces of gold, ordering his slaves to keep him to dinner. The fakir, who had always a good appetite, went into the kitchen, where he found enough to satisfy his hunger, and then, bethinking himself of his former trade, began to assist the prince's officers in dressing the dinner.

Masdowan, who loved good eating, and soon perceived that the ragouts, and especially an excellent dish of partridge with coleworts, were not after the manner of his own cook's dressing, had him called up, and understanding that the fakir had dressed part of his dinner, he proposed to take him into his service. Barzalu, who was already weary of the profession of a fakir, accepted the prince's offer, and as he wanted no wit he soon insinuated himself into his good graces, was made privy to his pleasures, and sometimes even admitted to sit at his table. Sir, said he one day, I do not confine my talents to the kitchen only ; I am capable of something greater. This, if you please, is "A Treatise of Politics," written by me, which I would beg your highness to read, and then favour me with your opinion of it. The prince had the complaisance to read the fakir's manuscript. He found all his maxims very excellent, but oftentimes dangerous ; and making every day further trials of his capacity, as soon as he arrived at Masulipatam he introduced him to the Sultan of Hind, whose near relation he was, and recommended him as a man of very great merit. The sultan was mightily pleased with him, found he possessed a superior genius, raised him by degrees to be prime wazir, and at length blindly committed to him the administration of the whole kingdom.

The more humble and abject Barzalu was before he

was raised to this post, the more fierce and arrogant he became when he beheld himself sole favourite to the Sultan of Hind. He soon forgot his birth and first benefactor, who to be revenged failed not on every occasion to remind him of the story of the coleworts and partridges. These reproaches mortified the insolent wazir not a little; but he dissembled his resentment, and carried it so very submissively that to see him in the prince's house one would have really thought him still in his former condition of a fakir. Masdowan himself was deceived by him, and forgetting the maxims which Barzalu had laid down, was imprudent enough to trust himself without reserve in the power of this perfidious villain. They frequently joined together in their debauches, and one day, after an entertainment which had lasted ten or twelve hours, Masdowan was seized with a violent fit of the colic, which, being treated by the physicians as if it had been an indigestion, carried him off in two hours, notwithstanding all their endeavours to relieve him. Barzalu appeared in public extremely afflicted for the death of this prince, but from this time became more powerful with his sultan than ever, and got such an entire possession of that monarch that without his assistance and introduction there was no approaching the sultan.

In this disposition of affairs, you may easily conceive, madam, continued Fum-Hoam, with what eye he looked upon the late favours conferred on Takfur. He was, indeed, resolved by all manner of means to ruin him, and was restrained only by the passion he had conceived for Dardok, whom he had often seen making her court to the sultana. He knew not well,

at first, how to begin a declaration of his love. He
was satisfied she was virtuous, and very much dreaded
her wit, lest she should turn his professions into ridicule.
He had therefore several private conversations with
her, affected to impart to her what passed in the diwan,
and frequently consulted her about matters of state. He
perceived that she listened to him with pleasure on these
occasions, but that alone·did not answer his intended
purpose. At length, therefore, he gave her to understand that being absolute master of the sultan's will
he had nothing more to desire in the world but the
possession of her heart ; that he was in a condition to
expect the favours of the most beautiful women in
Masulipatam, but was insensible to all their endearments, and that no person in all Hind could have the
honour of captivating him except herself. My mistress,
who always put on her grave airs to Barzalu, could not
avoid laughing aloud at the conclusion of this discourse,
and this piece of levity highly affronted that vain minister.
You are not, then, in the humour, beautiful Dardok, said
he, to receive the proposals of one who means to adore
you, even in the high station wherein you see me.—No,
truly, sir, said she with louder laughter than before ; no
one but my husband has a right to my heart, it is all
his own ; and I know no person, how high soever his
condition may be, who shall attempt my virtue with
impunity. I will that moment be revenged of him !—
And what will you do to him ? replied the wazir, with
some warmth.—Not only receive him very scornfully,
answered the other, with great seriousness, but immediately publish his infamy throughout all Masulipatam,
and even demand justice of the sultan himself for the

insult; and that virtuous monarch is too much an enemy to seduction and adultery to suffer the author of such an outrageous attempt to go unpunished.

The blood flushed in Barzalu's face at these words; he bit his lips almost through to prevent his spleen from rising, and that grand politician, defeated by the brisk air and lofty repulse of my young mistress, pretending it was time to be at the diwan, burst from her presence, mad with rage at a conversation from which he had expected such very different success. For some months, however, he dissembled the concern this affront gave him; but the sultan happening to be one day a little disordered with some physic which Takfur had prescribed him, this vile minister had the baseness to insinuate that his enemies might have corrupted the physician, and that a post whereon his master's life depended ought not to be entrusted to a stranger (for Takfur, madam, was born in the Mogul's country), and then proceeded in his discourse with so much malignity that Filu, who put a blind confidence in him, ordered his physician to depart out of Masulipatam in four-and-twenty hours, and entirely to quit his dominions within a month.

The blow of a thunder-bolt would have less surprised Takfur than so positive an order; he was with Dardok when a wazir of his acquaintance came to inform him of his disgrace, and he was at first overwhelmed with grief. What have I done, cried he, to be treated with so much · rigour? It was but yesterday the sultan gave me a thousand tokens of his goodness, and under the shadow of his favour I have lived honoured and respected in Masulipatam. Peace and plenty reigned in my house; but now he withdraws his munificent hand from underneath me, and leaves me like a slender reed, which the least blast of wind can easily blow to the ground.

Dardok, who was present at these complaints, as soon as the sultan's messenger was gone, embraced her husband very tenderly.   Light of my life ! said she to him, why do you afflict yourself for so slight a matter ? Know ye not the favour of princes is as inconstant as the sea, and that courtiers have the same power over them that boisterous winds have upon that perfidious element ? nor are the best built vessels secure from storms.   Believe me, my dear Takfur, instead of being concerned at your disgrace, you ought rather to praise and magnify the great Prophet, who hath inspired your secret enemy to be content with our banishment ; for I well know the hand from whence the empoisoned arrow is lanced that now pierces your heart.   The base Barzalu takes this method to revenge himself for the fruitless attempt he made upon your honour.   But it will not be long before this outrage will draw upon him the indignation of the Sultan of Hind.   That monarch will in time open his eyes, and punish the miserable fakir, who is the cause of our present woe.   Takfur listened to the consolation of Dardok, and their minds were restored to their former tranquillity.   Let us then be gone, soul of my life ! said he ; you are to me instead of everything, and we have wealth enough in Agra to compensate for the loss of these honours and preferments, of which we are unjustly deprived.   The sultan will one day be made sensible of my innocence, and perhaps be concerned for having treated me with so much severity.

After they had thus ended their complaints, Takfur and Dardok went into their palanquin, attended by their

slaves, whereof I was one. We had some difficulty in
passing over the high mountains which lie between
Masulipatam and Golconda, but we afterwards came
into a beautiful vale in the kingdom of Orixa, where
we beheld above a thousand tents, placed in lines like
so many streets. One might easily perceive a vast
bustle in this little camp, and joy was painted upon the
countenance of every common soldier. As we came to
a large pavilion of blue velvet fringed with gold, which
was surrounded by fifty guards clothed in blue satin
embroidered with gold, we alighted out of our palanquin
to take a nearer view of this gay sight, when the person
who seemed to have the command of the guards came
up to us, and desired Dardok and her husband to come
into a most elegant tent ; where, having presented them
with all sorts of refreshments, he addressed himself to
my mistress in terms to this effect :

HISTORY OF KORKUD AND HIS FOUR SONS

You seem astonished, madam, at the magnificence
you behold in this country, and therefore you are to
know that the beautiful Muwarrakh, Princess of Orixa,
and only daughter to the Sultan Mohadin, is lately
married to one of my sons, whose name is Amru ; and it
is to celebrate that illustrious day, designed as a splendid
festival, that these soldiers and people are assembled
together. As for myself, my name is Korkud ; and by
the grace of the Holy Prophet fortune at length is grown
weary of persecuting me, and has lately declared in my

favour, since I have the honour of entering into an
alliance with the sultan, my master. Before this happy
day there was not an inhabitant in the whole kingdom
so unfortunate as myself. If I had shares in several
ships they all perished at sea; if I ventured to game, I
was sure to lose my money; if I bought any merchandise,
the goods decayed upon my hands for want of sale, and
I was obliged to throw them away; if I fell in love, my
rivals, though inferior in merit, were either preferred
before me, or I was jilted by my mistresses; in short, it
was enough for me to undertake anything to make it un-
successful. Under what unlucky planet was I born,
said I to myself, thus to be always exposed to the cruel
shafts of fortune? or is it written upon the table of light
that I shall never succeed in any project I undertake?

Quite dejected with these melancholy reflections, I fell
asleep on the sofa and had a very remarkable dream. I
thought there appeared to me a little old man dressed
wholly in white. Korkud, said he to me, I have a mind
to put an end to your misery; take this basket; go
to the Mountain of Gerahem; stay one night in Eve's
Cave, and there you will find a remedy for all your
misfortunes. I awoke full of this dream, and was
astonished to find that there was in reality a basket of
a moderate size close by my side. I obeyed the little
old man in white, embarked on the Indian Ocean, and
having passed the Straits of Bab al-Mandeb, entered the
Red Sea, and arrived at Meccah. I thence went to the
Cave of Gerahem, where I obtained permission to lie all
night; but as I was going to fall asleep the little old
man appeared a second time. You complain of your
misery, said he to me, but behold, Korkud, where the

wife of the Sultan Adam dwelt, after she had disobeyed
God; is not your house more pleasant and more commodious than this cave of hers? and yet you are not
contented.   It is the nature of man to be dissatisfied
with his condition; if it be possible, however, I will
alleviate your sorrows; follow me.   I obeyed the old
man; he carried me to a corner of the cave; and, pulling
out of his pocket a book, wherein he read some cabalistic
prayers, I that moment saw a door open, and just at the
entrance perceived a black marble staircase adorned with
a baluster of gold.   A young infant, with a torch of
aloes wood in his hand, lighted us, while we went down
above three hundred steps.   We then came into a large
room all shining with rubies, and there found upon a
table of one entire piece of emerald, a little statue of
a woman holding a ring in her hand, which she seemed
to present to me.   Take that ring, Korkud, said the old
man; it is composed of six different metals, and was
made under such favourable constellations that everything succeeds well with him who is the possessor of it.
While you have it on your finger, misfortunes shall fly
from your house, and nobody shall be able to hurt you.
But it is on this one condition that all this good fortune
is annexed to it, that when you have chosen you a wife
you have no knowledge of any other woman as long as
she lives, unless you are willing that moment to lose your
ring.   So that your good fortune now depends upon
yourself; only take heed of this particular; and see that
you plunge not yourself again, by your own fault, into
the miseries from which you are now rescued.

I thanked the old man very heartily, took the ring,
and put it on my finger, as he bade me; and after I had

filled my basket with pieces of gold, which he took out of a large vessel of agate, and my pockets with several very beautiful diamonds, I was carried in an instant to Orixa, and set down at the door of my house. The day was far spent; I knocked hard at the door, and an old slave, whom I had left in the house, came and opened it to me. I went into a lower room, and while she was getting me something to eat emptied my basket, which was very heavy, and carefully locked up my new gotten treasures. The next day I got myself a suit of very good clothes, sold my diamonds, began to merchandise again, and in less than three years gained so considerably that I hardly knew the end of my riches. The young ladies who had despised me in my mean circumstances were now indefatigable in trying every allurement, but in my turn I slighted them all; and having made choice of one about fifteen years old, whose name was Zobayad, a mirror of beauty and a pattern of goodness, I made her my wife.

In all my acquaintance with other women, I never experienced half the charms that I found in my new wife. The enjoyment of my beautiful Zobayad did but augment my love, and I passed nineteen years with her in such perfect satisfaction that the condition so much insisted on by the little old man gave me no kind of uneasiness. I had four very beautiful sons by her, and saw them brought up in my house like so many young cedars that carry their heads to the clouds. The eldest was called Mammun; the second, Amru; the third, Karaguz, because he had large black eyes; and the fourth, Gadi, because he was very nimble. So happy an issue increased my fondness for my wife; and never did any of those illustrious lovers celebrated so much in Persian

romances for their fidelity and constancy (such as Maj-
num and Layla, Khosru and Shirin, Gamil and Shamba)
love with such ardour, as Zobayad and I felt for each
other. Nothing, in short, was so much talked of through
the whole kingdom as our perfect union; and I could
have sworn it would have lasted for ever, when my ill
stars led me one day by the gates of the public baths of
Orixa.

One evening, as I was passing by the baths, without
any idea of what was to befall me, I was stopped by an
old woman, who had formerly been my nurse, because
my mother was too frail a woman to suckle me herself.
Korkud no longer knows his beloved Mohiyar, said she to
me; he walks by without taking the least notice of me.—
Ah, my dear Mohiyar! said I, embracing her, how glad
am I to meet you! I did not see you at first. But why
do you not come to my house, for you must know I
have been this long while prodigiously rich?—I am persuaded, my dear child, said she, that you have still the
same love for me; but I am now settled in a way which
I would on no account quit. It is I who have the care
of all the women, both young and old, who come hither
to bathe, and since you know what a cheerful disposition
I possess, you cannot but think I am now in my proper
sphere. In short you do not imagine half the fooleries
which are committed in this house, for here it is that
the most reserved of the sex put off for some hours that
austere modesty they seem so attached to at home, and
enjoy themselves for most part of the time at their
husbands' expense, and then amuse them with some
fine story when they come home. No, nothing can be
pleasanter than these conversations!

This discourse of Mohiyar raised my curiosity; I expressed an earnest desire to be a witness of these curious particulars; and notwithstanding the danger of a discovery prevailed with the good woman so far that she promised to carry me into the bath if I would but disguise myself like a Jewess, and bring a box full of toys, and such curiosities as women usually buy. I did as she bade me, and the next day in this disguise was admitted into the place where the women bathe. I found everything Mohiyar had told me to be true, and was never in my life so highly delighted; but my curiosity cost me exceeding dear, the cursed old woman thought it not enough to give me this diversion, but must needs be procuring me another, which was the source of all my misfortunes. Amina, said she (for that was the name I took upon me), pray come and help me to attend this young woman, who is just come out of the bath. There was no refusing her request, so that I went into a little room, where she shewed me one of the most charming creatures that ever eyes beheld. I swear, madam, continued Korkud, by the camel which carries the book of glory to Meccah, that the daughters of the paradise of Eden cannot be more beautiful than the adorable Barud! She was scarce sixteen years old, and the sight of so many charms intoxicated my senses in such a manner that for some time I forgot my Zobayad, and thought no more of the wholesome advice which the old man in the cave of Gerahem had impressed upon me.

As soon as I quitted the bath I learned from Mohiyar the condition of this young woman; that she was a native of Kashmir, and belonged to a merchant who dealt in slaves. I therefore ran immediately to his

11

house, and giving him his own price for Barud immediately conveyed her to a small house without the gates of Orixa, where my wife never came and where I gratified my violent passion for this divine woman. But no sooner, madam, had I transgressed the old man's injunction than the ring fell off my finger and broke, and the pieces vanished; so that with all my searching I could not find the least bit of it.

This unlucky accident gave me some little uneasiness at first, but being then intent on my pleasures I took no further notice of it, and spent five entire months with Barud, drowned in pleasures, without once perceiving the effects of the old man's threats. Nay, I even smiled in secret at the strong faith I once had in his prediction; when my wife fell dangerously ill, and, as I was expressing all the grief imaginable for her, spoke to me in these words: You no longer love me, my dear husband! I have for some time perceived your indifference, and in vain endeavoured to discover by what means I have had the misfortune to displease you Heaven is my witness there has not a minute passed wherein you have not been equally dear to me; and it is this tenderness ill requited that now causes my death. Azrail is at my bolster; I now hear him call. Adieu, my dearest love! I wish that Barud may be happier than me, and less sensible of your infidelity. You see I am not unacquainted with your new amour, but I never mentioned it lest it should interrupt your happiness. You have it certainly in your power to make as many partners in your love as you please, I have nothing to say against the established customs of the East, but my heart is too much in love to bear such a partnership, and it is my delicacy in this respect which now costs me my life. These, madam, were the last sensible words that Zobayad spoke; she grew soon after very delirious, and sinking under the violence of her woes expired in my arms.

I had not, till this misfortune, made any serious reflection on my manner of living with Barud. How weak a creature is man! cried I, melting into tears. O Heavens! that ever my infidelity should cause the death of my dear Zobayad! a woman of such uncommon merit, worthy to be immortal. Unhappy man! this is the beginning of the afflictions that fortune is preparing for you, and which you draw down upon yourself by your own ill conduct. To be brief, madam, I did so many extravagant things I was obliged to be tied down for four days. But how great was the increase of my sorrow when, upon the recovery of my senses, I was informed that the ungrateful Barud during my wife's sickness had got another lover, and carried off a casket of jewels of very considerable value. This news nearly cost me my life; I became quite distracted, and had it not been for my friends, who never quitted me, should have stabbed myself a thousand times. From this period, madam, I found myself hourly sinking by a reverse of that fortune which before had been so propitious to me. My debtors became bankrupts, my vessels were shipwrecked, my stores and dwelling-house took fire, and in less than a year, of all the riches I had obtained with so much ease I had nothing left but the little house where I had kept Barud and my four children, the eldest of whom was not more than fourteen.

My sorrow had made so strong an impression upon me that I was perpetually weeping; when one day my children employed their eldest brother to speak to me in these words: We are, sir, said he, a very great expense to you, who have scarce enough to maintain yourself; let us go, then, and seek our fortunes; we will return in a year's time from this very day, and hope to make you the partaker of our acquisitions. I could not tell how to deny them what they requested, and embracing them, with tears in my eyes: Go, my dear children, said I, since you think there is a necessity for our parting. But whatever fortune betides you, fail not to have the fear of God continually before your eyes; let nothing alter your faith, and omit no opportunity of relieving the distressed. A good turn is never lost.

My sons, madam, departed, and every day during their absence I entreated the Holy Prophet to favour their undertakings, and not impute my iniquities to them. At length the time of their return drew near, and I was sadly tormented between hope and fear. Ah! said I several times, I shall not be so happy as to see my children again. They doubtless have perished through want, and I have been the cause of all their sufferings. O that I had followed the counsel of the old man in the Cave of Gerahem!—While I was thus tormenting myself, the day appointed for my sons' return came; and as soon as the morning began to appear I went into the street, sat me down on a stone bench at my gate, and ran to meet every soul I saw coming towards my house in hopes it was some of my sons. I waited all day to no purpose until the time of evening prayer. I then went into my house again, quite oppressed with grief, and was giving myself up to despair when I heard somebody knock at my door. I ran with all haste, and fancy to yourself, madam, how great was my joy when I beheld my four sons, perfectly well dressed and in good health.

The sight of my children renewed my faith, which was pretty nigh exhausted by the grief which their absence had occasioned ; I hung for above an hour about their necks, without power to speak a word, and several times fainted away. At length when I asked them if they had reason to be satisfied with their journey, Mammun was the first who spoke, and he answered me thus : For six months together, sir, I rambled about, without much caring which way I went ; when one day, on the bank of a river, I perceived a soldier pursuing a serpent, which seemed to implore my assistance. It was to no purpose that I opposed the man's intentions ; he cut it in four pieces with his sabre, and threw one of them into the river. But remembering your last words, that a good turn is never lost, Let me see, said I to myself, whether in this instance it will have its reward. So laying the three pieces of the serpent close to each other, I saw with great pleasure how they joined together. I then immediately undressed and plunged into the river, where, after many times diving, I found the tail of the animal, and joined it to the rest of its body. The serpent soon after this threw itself into the river, and in a moment's time I saw a beautiful woman rise out of the water. Mammun, said she to me, I owe my life to you, for without your assistance I should have been exposed to death ; I will therefore acknowledge the service, and demonstrate to you that a good turn is never lost. Just as you saw me when I was a serpent join again without the least sign of any division in my body, so may you, by merely pronouncing my name, join everything in nature that is broken or divided.   I am called the fairy Jiyalut, and whenever you want my assistance you shall always find me ready to serve you.   And in truth, sir, ever since that time, I have had daily experience of Jiyalut's good-ness ; all my desires are fulfilled, so long as they are but reasonable; and to convince you of this, here is a purse that every week supplies me with an hundred pieces of gold.

Mammun had no sooner finished his story than Amru spoke in his turn.   He told me that in crossing a forest he found a white bitch ready to die, with an arrow shot in her gullet: that he pulled out the arrow, and bound up the wound with a piece of the linen of his turband, and then carried her with much difficulty into a thicket, where he laid her upon a bed of leaves, and lay down by her himself all night ; but when he awoke was not a little surprised to find by his side an old fairy of a majestic countenance, and who, in gratitude for his com-passion for her, had given to him the nimbleness of a deer and the gift of divination besides.   So that with these talents wherever he came he had got whatever he pleased, and had turned his money into diamonds. With these words, he pulled out of his bosom a little leather bag, and shewed us a parcel of jewels worth above twenty thousand pieces of gold.

I was transported with joy at this strange relation, when Karaguz informed us that one night as he was going to lie in an old ruinous house in an open field he was surprised and affrighted with very doleful cries, and that as soon as it was day he perceived they came from an owl which had been caught in a snare ; that having compassion on the creature he set it at liberty ; but no sooner was the owl let loose than it called him by his name and bade him go down into a vault; that he did as he was ordered, and there found a trap, which he took away; that the owl and he afterwards went down into a grot, covered all over with gold, in the midst of which there stood a basin full of rose-water, into which the bird threw itself, and immediately there rose up a venerable old man, who called himself Morg; that this old man, by pronouncing certain cabalistical words, infused into his eyes such a brightness in the night time as would disperse all darkness for half a league round him, wherever he was; and that, over and above this, he had given him power to discover all hidden treasures, so that he was capable of enriching the most powerful monarchs upon earth.

Gadi heard his brothers with great admiration. I am not so powerful, said he, as you are; but as you will probably not let me want for anything, I content myself with only one talent which I have acquired in my journey. As I was returning home, much dissatisfied with my fortune, and without meeting with any remarkable adventure, I went one day into a poor peasant's house to beg a little water, which he not only gave me, but bade me go into his garden and eat some excellent figs. I did as he told me, and was taking my leave of him, when observing in the kitchen a trap-stand, wherein there was a vast great rat, I asked him what he intended to do with it?—I was just going to burn it alive, said he, when you came in; this devilish creature has for these eight days made such havoc among my figs that this is the least punishment I can inflict on it.—Let me beg of you, my good friend, said I, to give me this rat.—

Why, what will you do with it ? said he.—-I will spare
its life, answered I, for a good turn is never lost ; and
will take care to carry it so far off that it shall never
do you any more damage.—I will not deny you so small
a matter, said he ; take the rat and the rat-trap too, but
release it not until you have got far enough from this
place.   I did as the peasant desired me, carried the rat-
trap a day and a half, and then set the rat at liberty,
and went on my journey.   The night came upon me in
the fields, and I was going to lie down at the root of a
tree, when I perceived a light in a great house not above
a hundred yards from me.   I went and knocked at the
door, which was presently opened, and I was conducted
into a spacious hall, where supper was brought in.   A
young man, remarkably beautiful, then drew near, and
addressed me thus : Gadi, said he to me, a good turn is
never lost.   I am the sage Zulzul, whose life you saved
under the figure of a rat, when the country fellow would
have taken it from me.   Here are two daggers which
I present you with, by the help of which there is neither
tree so high, nor tower so steep, but what you may
easily climb ; I give you, moreover, the power of being
invulnerable for any two hours of the day you shall
choose.

I could hardly believe, madam, these strange
stories that my children told me ; only the purse and the
diamonds were a plain demonstration that they had met
with some extraordinary adventures.   I took, therefore,
three pieces of gold in order to make them a great
entertainment ; and after we had spent good part of the
night at table, and the conversation came to turn upon
their several talents, I seemed to be a little doubtful of

what they had told me unless I were convinced by my own eyes. To prove, sir, said Amru, that I have advanced nothing but what is true, I prophesy that a magpie, which has built its nest upon the great tree at the bottom of our garden, has this morning laid an egg, which she does now actually sit upon.—Well, then, said Gadi, if my brother Karaguz will but lend me the light, which he tells us proceeds from his eyes, I will this moment climb the tree, and bring you down the magpie's egg.

I took them at their words; we went into the garden, which Karaguz enlightened very wonderfully, and Gadi, by the help of his two daggers, climbed up the tree like a rat, to the very top of it, which was above a hundred feet high. He took the egg, and was bringing it down, when, unluckily treading upon a branch that was rotten, he fell to the ground with such violence that I thought he was dead. I gave a terrible shriek at his fall, and swooned away; but as he was invulnerable he immediately jumped upon his feet, and shewed me he had got no harm, which rejoiced me exceedingly. As for the egg, it was broken into more than twenty pieces; but as soon as Mammun pronounced the name of Jiyalut, the pieces of egg came together again. It was filled and joined without the least appearance of a crack; and Gadi, putting it into the nest again, at the end of the appointed time it was hatched. I must own, madam, I was not a little rejoiced at the sight of so many miracles; plenty was restored to my house again, and I no longer felt the misfortunes which had hitherto persecuted me. In this manner my sons and I lived for above a year together in all tranquillity, when there happened a most surprising accident at the Court of Orixa.

Our sultan, Mohadin, was one day a-hunting with his beautiful daughter Muwarrakh, and it was as fine weather as could be wished, when all on a sudden the air was darkened, and a frightful hurricane arose. The lightning dazzled all the huntsmen, and the thunder roared with such fury that the princess was sadly terrified; and alighting from her horse, in hopes of being safer near the sultan, went to throw herself into her father's arms (for the violence of the storm had dispersed all her attendants),·when she perceived, with the utmost horror and surprise, that she was in the arms of a little old man, almost naked and as hairy as a bear, who carried her through the air, in spite of her cries and her father's menaces, who in the same moment found himself bound fast to a tree with his hands tied behind him. The huntsmen, whom the storm had dispersed, returned at the voice of their sovereign; they found him in great tribulation, untied him, and carried him home in a condition sufficiently distressful to raise compassion in the most obdurate heart.

The Sultan Mohadin gave himself up to black despair, when his grand wazir advised him to make proclamation through the kingdom of Orixa and in Hind of the loss of his daughter, and to promise her in marriage to anyone who could rescue her out of the hands of a horrible magician, who had carried her away; and, in case the princess could not fulfil this promise, that he would give him half his kingdom. As soon as my son Amru heard of this news, continued Korkud, he was not a little rejoiced. Father, said he, I know where the princess is; and if my brothers will but assist me I will restore her to her father again. Gadi, Mammun,

and Karaguz all promised never to forsake him. Being
introduced to the sultan, Amru told him that Muwarrakh
was in the power of a magician called Marzuk; that
for a whole year he could make no attempt upon her
honour; but that she was to submit to his infamous
desires if she was not taken out of his hands before the
expiration of that time. He then assured the king that
he knew where the princess his daughter was confined,
and that he would bring her back in less than six months.

Mohadin, transported with joy at these tidings,
embraced Amru and his brothers, and furnished them
with everything they required. After they had travelled
a hundred and fifty leagues, they came to the Gulf of
Kambay, where they embarked in a vessel the sultan had
ordered to be prepared for them. The pilot, observing
Amru's directions, coasted along the Gulf of Indus;
and, sailing by Ormuz, entered the Sea of Bassorah, and
came to an anchor behind some frightful rocks that
surrounded a little island called the Blue Island. It
was not far from this island that the magician Marzuk
had by the force of his art built a tower of steel two
hundred feet high, which had neither door nor window
in it, except in the dungeon, which stood towards the
sea. There it was that he had shut up Muwarrakh;
and this fair princess spent her days and nights in
perpetual weeping, when my son's vessel drew towards
the shore.

They had a consultation for some time; and being
informed by Amru that Marzuk had not power to be
in the tower at night, they resolved upon that time for
the execution of their design. Accordingly, they came
to the prison where Muwarrakh lay, in the dead of the

night; and while it was very dark, without making any noise, Karaguz let Gadi have as much light as was necessary for him to climb up to the top of the tower, and he, by the help of his two daggers, having got to the dungeon, without any noise, surprised a dragon, which Amru had told him was asleep, set to guard the princess, and gave him such a terrible blow on the head with his sabre that he laid him flat on the ground. But as soon as the dragon was dead, it looked as if the destruction of the whole world depended upon its life. The heavens were all on fire, the flashes of lightning seemed as if they would set the universe in a flame, and a furious clap of thunder split the ship, wherein were my sons, into a thousand pieces, but without hurting any who were in it. It was now that Mammun's secret stood them in great stead; for he only pronounced the name of the fairy Jiyalut, and all the pieces of the ship came and joined themselves together again without the least fracture to be seen. The mariners found themselves at their respective posts, and my children, with infinite pleasure, saw the thunder and lightning end in a very still night. Gadi took this opportunity to go into the dungeon where the princess was enclosed, informed her in a few words of the execution of his designs, and, having drawn a rope and pulley from the ship by a cord, the end of which he carried in his hand to the top of the tower, let her down therewith in a rush basket into the ship, where she was received with exceeding great joy. But while others were paying the princess the honours that were due to her, Gadi was ransacking the apartments of the tower; and having found a little plate of gold, whereon were several unknown characters engraved, fixed up in the dungeon, supposing it to be the talisman by virtue of which the tower was built, he came down in all haste into the ship ; but being told by Amru that the life of the infamous Marzuk depended upon that plate of gold, he ascended the tower again, and having taken down the talisman waited for the break of day and until the ship was got behind the rocks, where it might come to an anchor. The morning had scarce begun to appear when the magician went into the dungeon ; but my son, who had hid himself outside the door, had no sooner pushed it to, broke the talisman, and thrown it into the sea, than the whole steel tower and the magician in it sunk down at once ; and Gadi, when he saw it was level with the water, threw himself in, and swam till he was taken up by the ship, which immediately set sail for Kambay, and from thence returned with the princess to Orixa without any manner of danger.

You cannot conceive, madam, how joyful the sultan Mohadin was to see the beloved Muwarrakh again. Amru, who is a very handsome man, had informed the princess of the offer her father had made, and as she seemed not averse to marry one she had so many obliga· tions to, our illustrious sultan has just performed his promise to my son, and it is in this place that his subjects are met to celebrate their joy by a thousand feats of gallantry for his daughter's return and marriage. Judge you, then, whether I have not abundant reason to be highly pleased with my good fortune. Amru is designed for the throne ; the sultan has given me the post of the prime wazir, who died about eight days ago, and my three sons have the chief employments in the Government.

Korkud had but just ended the adventures of his sons when we hear the shrill sounds of trumpets declaring the arrival of the Sultan Mohadin and the new married couple; all the soldiers put themselves under arms, whilst they passed through the camp, amidst the loud acclamations of the people of Orixa, who were come together to view this sight. Nothing was heard but expressions of gladness on every side, and the air rung with the names of the Sultan, of Amru, and of Muwarrakh, on whom the people bestowed a thousand benedictions. The bride and bridegroom were conducted to a pavilion of blue velvet, where the sultan himself placed them on a throne of massy gold, there they received the compliments of the chief nobility and officers of state, and afterwards passed into another contiguous tent where they were served with a very sumptuous entertainment. Korkud had recommended us to an officer of the sultan, to take care of us, and we were situated in a very commodious place to see the ceremony. As soon as the entertainment was over, the sultan's subjects began to shew their address and activity in a thousand different races both on foot and horseback; and at last this remarkable day ended in a play, which pleased the sultan and the princess wonderfully, as it represented to the life the adventures of the beautiful Muwarrakh with the magican Marzuk, and the manner of her deliverance by Korkud's sons.

After we had spent great part of the night in all these diversions, Takfur and Dardok retired to the tent which Korkud had ordered to be prepared for them. We stayed eight days to see all the magnificence of Amru and Muwarrakh's nuptials, and then proceeded on our way to Agra, where we arrived after a long and tedious journey. Not far from this city Takfur had a very stately house, where he usually resided. And at this happy place he enjoyed such tranquillity of mind, in the sprightly conversation of his beloved Dardok, as he had never known at Masulipatam. I, too, found my servitude so very easy with them that I was scarce sensible of it. The truth is I was not willing to leave them till my death, which happened to me about five or six years after we came into the Mogul's country.

  *   *   *   *   *   *

I must own, illustrious Fum-Hoam, said Gulchinraz, these adventures are very entertaining, nor am I in the least fatigued with hearing them.—If not, replied the mandarin, I will go on, and relate to your majesty what became of me afterwards.

ADVENTURES OF ALA-BADIN

AFTER I left the body of the slave I passed into that of one of the honestest men in Armenia. I was born at Erzerum, and son to a kadi of that city. My name was Ala-Badin. I had no great dependence on my father's high station, and therefore made it my endeavour by bravery and great exploits to advance my fortune, and was so successful therein that I became a favourite to the Sultan Uram, who then reigned in Armenia. But before I had the honour to be known to that monarch I used to spend some idle hours in hearing my father try causes.

One day there came an old woman who sold figs, holding a young man fast by the hand, all trembling. He seemed not above sixteen, but was extremely beautiful. Sir, said she to my father, I demand justice of you against this impudent young rascal; and judge if I have not sufficient reason. This morning he came to me to know how much money I would take for as many figs as he could eat. I began to make my computation: perhaps, said I to myself, he may be able to eat a hundred or a hundred and fifty at most. Well, my pretty youth, said I, you shall give me a silver sultanin. We struck the bargain, and he began, and swallowed in a trice fifty before my eyes. I trembled to see him; but what was more surprising, about two hours after, he came again and ate up a hundred of the finest I had. This made me almost mad; but thinking it would be his last time I was sitting quietly in my shop, when he came the third time, and gobbled up all I had in my pannier, ordering me to get him more, for that he would be there again in half an hour. I was so amazed that I could make him no answer, and had hardly recovered my surprise when behold my gentleman comes again, and insists positively that I shall supply him with more figs.

The kadi could hardly forbear laughing at the old woman's story. Why would you, said he to the young man, cheat this good woman? Is it not enough that you have emptied the whole pannier without desiring her to find you more? There is no justice in this procedure. The young man made no answer, but stood mute, like a criminal going to punishment, on which my father assumed a more lofty tone. I see, said he, by your not making any reply, that you are one of those vagabonds who go sharping about and disturb the public peace.

To teach you to live honestly for the future I order you to have fifty bastinadoes upon the soles of your feet.— Ah, sir! cried the young man, hearing him pronounce this sentence, I am not what you take me for; suspend, I beseech you, the execution of your orders, and permit me the favour to speak with you in private, and I am persuaded you will revoke this severe sentence.

My father, who only intended to frighten the youth, carried him into his closet, and took me along with him; but we were in the utmost surprise to find in man's clothes one of the most beautiful young ladies in all Erzerum, and whose father was a wazir. Sir, said she to the kadi, I am rightly served for my curiosity; I have two brothers, who are twins, exactly like one another, and though we were not all born at a birth, people tell me I have all their features. Now one of these, for a little pastime, and to teaze this old woman, made a bargain, as she has told you, and contriving to relieve each other in eating the figs, they thus alternately emptied her basket. I too had a mind to see the farce, and therefore desired one of my brothers to lend me his clothes, which he did; and I, coming to the fig-woman's shop, who took me for him, teazed her so long and carried the jest so far that at length she raised a mob, and has brought me to you, sir, to have satisfaction for the cheat she imagines I have put upon her. I hope, therefore, sir, you will not make me suffer the punishment you have imposed, but must entreat you to let me go home as soon as possible, lest my absence should be known in the family.—Fair young lady, said my father to her, I will not be so severe upon you, but let not your curiosity again put you on such rash adventures, which you may not always so

12

easily get rid of as at present. Do you not know it was
this cursed curiosity which ruined our mother Eve?
Go home, and for fear of any accident my son shall
attend you.

You cannot imagine, madam, continued the mandarin, what a joyful matter this adventure was to me.
The lady was so beautiful, so charming a creature,
that she captivated me in a moment; but as her
situation in life was far superior to mine, I thought
it improper for the present to discover my love to her
any otherwise than by my looks and respectful carriage.
In process of time the beautiful Zalig (for that was her
name) was not indifferent to my passion, but used sometimes to heave such sighs as convinced me of the
sensibility of her heart. This gave me courage to declare
my passion, and I had the pleasure to find she did not
disapprove of my love, but gave me leave to ʳemploy
all my interest in obtaining her father's consent, who
was then gone with a friend a small journey of about
thirty or forty leagues. But how great was my grief
to find at his return that he had disposed of his
daughter to his friend's son! Zalig, notwithstanding
the aversion she had to the person who was to be her
husband, was obliged to obey, and my loss of her made
me so uneasy that I was resolved to leave Erzerum.
The Sultan of Armenia happened then to be at war
with a very powerful neighbouring prince. I went,
therefore, and asked an employment of him, which he
had the goodness to give me, and in a short time my
superior officers reported so many advantageous things
in my favour that in two years he raised me to the
dignity of a wazir, and I had every reason to be con-

tented with my fortune. But all this while I had not forgotten Zalig, and was perpetually sighing to think she was in another man's arms. Having imparted my grief to a brave young Armenian in the army, who was one of my aide-de-camps, Sir, said he, since Zalig cannot be yours, you must endeavour to forget her. I have a sister at Erzerum, not above seventeen years old, who is a perfect beauty, and if you will do me the honour to be my relation, there is no doubt but my father will be very glad to consent. The young man told me so many advantageous things of his sister that he raised my curiosity, and as soon as the campaign was over, which ended to our sultan's honour, I returned to Erzerum, and went directly with my aide-de-camp to his father's house, but was informed, to my great sorrow, that about eight days before he had married his daughter to an infirm old man, but so very amorous that he had always three lawful wives and several concubines in his house.

I was so discouraged at being thus disappointed of two of the most beautiful women in Armenia that I resolved never to marry. Zinabi (for so was my aide-de-camp's sister called) understood with true concern the occasion of my journey. She doubtless would have thought herself much happier with me than with her aged husband, and as by her brother's means she had frequent opportunities of seeing me, she felt arising in her heart that sweet sympathy which grows up into love from the first sight. Her husband, who was very much in years, she foresaw could not live long. The excesses wherein the old dotard plunged himself every day soon made good her expectations, and the moment she was a widow her brother hastened to tell me the news. Notwithstanding the resolutions I had made never to engage myself in marriage, I could not refuse to pay Zinabi one visit ; and I found her then so very beautiful that all my protestations vanished. I would have married her that very moment for fear of being disappointed by some happy rival, but the custom of widowhood, which is limited to four months and ten days, made me wait with no small impatience till that term was expired. But this was not the only obstacle to my marriage. Zinabi set before me some other difficulties which had almost discouraged me. My spouse, said she to me, left three young widows of us, who have no inclination to part ; and, as you are both rich and handsome, you must marry us all three. One of them I love, because she comforted me in the sorrows of matrimony ; and the other I hate, because she sometimes exasperated my old husband against me. I should be glad, therefore, to have the pleasure of living with her I love, and of revenging myself on her I hate, who will have no objection to continue with me, because I have hitherto concealed my aversion.

The proposition of three wives at once almost turned my brain. Protest what I would to Zinabi, that she was the most beautiful woman in the world in my eyes, and that had I ten wives I would sacrifice them all to her, it availed nothing; she grew obstinate in her resolution. I will confound, said she, the haughtiness of my rival. One day she had the assurance to tell me every man living would leave me for her ; and I am very contemptible indeed if you do not think me deserving a thousand tokens of your love, even in her presence, purposely to upbraid her.—Her charms prevailed with me to comply with her desire, and I prepared myself to play the cruel part with this unknown widow, whom I did not desire to see any more than the other, before I came to marry them. The day came at last, and I was never more surprised in my life than to find that the object of Zinabi's hatred was the charming Zalig, who, being left a widow by her former husband, had been married again to Zinabi's old one. This incident was matter both of great pleasure and delight to me; cur former love was renewed with more eagerness than ever, and my first thoughts were how to avoid the designs of my aide-de-camp's vindictive sister. I took care, however, not to let Zalig know the snare her companion had laid for her, and praised our great Prophet both for defeating her malicious intentions and making her the instrument of putting into my hands so much good fortune at one time, for the third widow was likewise a very beautiful woman.

I proposed at first to have lodged them in three different apartments in my seraglio, for since I was become wazir and favourite I lived in great state, but the unjust Zinabi would not let me remove Zalig out of her sight, that she might have the pleasure of being an eye-witness of the slights I was to put upon her. I was, however, too sensible of my former love and too fond of my own ease to let Zalig perceive the least coldness towards her, nor had she any cause to complain on that account. My whole study and dexterity were, indeed, pretty well employed to make my wives live peaceably together; and I was one day almost at a loss to accommodate a small difference which happened between them. Zalig was always very curious in her dress; it was her passion to be fine, and accordingly she had made herself a suit of brocade so very rich and splendid that all Erzerum could not produce the like. This I easily foresaw would give the jealous Zinabi no small uneasiness; she always affected to be distinguished from her two companions; would bear no equality, but in everything expected the preference, and therefore, when she saw her rival dressed so splendidly, it vexed her to the heart, and she gave me some severe reproaches on the subject. It was in vain to tell her that Zalig's mother had sent her the clothes for a present; I was therefore obliged to have recourse to another expedient. Accordingly, I took Zalig aside and spoke to her in this manner: You cannot conceive the joy I feel to see the uneasiness your clothes have given Zinabi; I am displeased with her haughty behaviour, and if you pursue my advice there are ways enough to mortify her pride. If by a malicious generosity you wish to triumph still more over her, make her a present of those clothes she so much envies you, and see whether she has the meanness to wear your cast-offs. In the mean time, for your own honour and her disgrace, persuade yourself they are old things, which you have no farther occasion for, and therefore give them to her as a proof of the contemptuous light in which you behold her.

Zalig was quite delighted to hear me thus flatter her vanity, and offered the clothes with pleasure. After I had thus secured her, I went to Zinabi. I cannot bear, my dear sultana, said I, that so splendid a dress should increase the pride and haughtiness of your rival. It shews, however, that she has nothing very agreeable in herself, but borrows the little beauty she appears to have merely from the richness of her dress; and as I am resolved her fine clothes shall in future be yours, when she comes to see the admirable effect they have upon you she will be ready to die with vexation. Zinabi was pleased with this discourse, and believed I acted agreeably to the protestations I made of despising Zalig for 'the love of her. Another, perhaps, in her place would have been nicer about the matter; but in short, though Zalig sent the clothes that very evening as the despicable refuse of her wardrobe, Zinabi received them with an air of the greatest triumph.

I should tire your patience, madam, continued the mandarin, were I to relate the schemes I was obliged to make use of, in order to preserve any tolerable peace and civility between these fierce rivals. I found out the secret, however, of making them live quietly together, and continued this conduct between them till about seven or eight years after, when I was killed at the head of the King of Armenia's army.—It required no small skill and address, said the Queen of China, to maintain so long a union between two rivals in the same house.—I did it, however, replied Fum-Hoam, and was as much lamented by my three wives as if each of them had lost a particular husband.

ADVENTURES OF THE DARWAYSH ASSIRKAN

AFTER I had left the wazir's, I entered into the body of a young man whose name was Assirkan. Having spent my early years in a licentious course of life, I threw myself at last into a convent of darwayshes at Kandahar.

I had a hard time enough while I was a novice, but soon took care to make myself ample amends when I arrived to the dignity of the order. I applied myself incessantly to study, and attained a knowledge that distinguished me from the rest of my companions, and raised me to the honour of being superior of the convent; insomuch that nothing was done therein without my orders, which were looked upon with as much respect as if they had been the decrees of Heaven.

One day, as I was walking before the gate of the convent, there came a young man of a very good appearance, who addressed himself to me thus: Holy darwaysh, said he, with a very agreeable air, how happy and contented you appear!—And so I am, replied I; being free from those cares which attend the men of this world. Here we live in a state of tranquillity, undisturbed by tumultuous passions. We never go to court, have no lawsuits in our house, no women come near our convents, and we content ourselves with a little. What is there, then, that can possibly annoy our quiet? for these, if I mistake not, are the rocks whereon the generality of mankind suffer shipwreck.—Ah! how happy are you! said the young man, with a sigh. And are all darwyashes so?—I believe they are, replied I; at least I have not perceived, for these fifteen years which I have had the honour to preside over them, that anyone has repented his embracing this holy condition of life.—Ah! that I had been one of them! cried the stranger; my life had not then been dashed with all that bitterness which has so frequently interrupted my repose.—It is not yet too late, replied I; come and bury all your sorrows in this house; they dare not abide under the habit of our order.

Alas! said he, with tears in his eyes, a man should have his heart free to engage therein, whereas mine has been pierced with many a cruel dart for the space of thirty years in which I have been wandering about the world. —How! thirty years! said I, smiling; you seem not to exceed five-and-twenty at most.—My looks deceive you, then, answered the stranger; how young soever I appear, I can assure you I have lived above an age. But you will, perhaps, cease to be surprised when I inform you further who I am.—Ah! replied I, do not then keep me long in suspense; you raise my curiosity to such a degree that I would give the world to have it gratified. If you will please to go with me to the convent, we can be more at ease in my chamber, and I swear by the Holy Prophet that I will keep every secret inviolate with which you may be pleased to entrust me. The stranger then looked steadfastly upon me. Whatever danger, said he, may accrue to me by imparting to you the adventures of my life, yet I will venture, holy darwaysh, on the confidence of your oath, to satisfy your curiosity. He then went with me into the convent, and from thence into my chamber, where, seating himself on a cane sofa, he began, as near as I can remember, in these words:

STORY OF ABD AL-MOAL

It is something more than an age since I was born a subject of the King of Ormuz, and was an officer of his body-guard, when there came to his court a philosopher who had not only the secret of transmuting metals into gold, but had likewise an elixir which contained in it a

universal medicine, and had the same power and pro-
perty with the water of the Fountain of Elias. This
philosopher's name was as much a mystery as his elixir;
he called himself an inhabitant of the whole earth,
travelled everywhere without an interpreter, and was as
learned as the great Sultan Sulayman in the knowledge
of nature. With such talents as these this great man
had little occasion to make his court to kings; he was,
indeed, superior to them; and led by his destiny to
Ormuz, he so filled the town with his fame and wonderful cures that the sultan sent for him. Upon this he
.went to court, and having had the honour of being with
the king for two hours, he so pleased him with the
charms of his conversation and the marvellous things
he did in his presence that he presented him with a
diamond of inestimable value.

As courts are usually the residence of envy, the
prime wazir could not behold his master's liberality to
this philosopher without jealousy. Sir, said he, when he
had an opportunity of speaking to him in private, do not
confide too much in this mysterious man; there is not so
much of capacity as imposture, I am inclined to believe,
in what he does. Such men as he are commonly great
cheats, and the more your majesty confides in him the
more you expose yourself to dangers of the most alarm-
ing consequence; for who can assure you, sir, that this
pretended philosopher is not an emissary from some of
your enemies, and waits only an opportunity to poison or
stab you? Ah, sir! let not a person of whom you know
so little dare to approach your majesty, for what would
become of your wives and children if by any such horrid
attempt (the very idea of which makes me tremble) we

should have the misfortune to lose you? The King of Ormuz was moved with the discourse of this perfidious wazir, aided by the deceitful tears which he perceived running down his cheeks. You are in the right, said he; make, therefore, some enquiry into this man's proceedings, and if you find in them any shadow of suspicion, let him that moment be sent to the tower where prisoners of state are confined.

This was just what the wazir wanted; and in a few days he made the philosopher's conduct appear so very odious that I received an order from the king's own mouth to go and seize him. I executed his commands very punctually; but never was man more enraged than my prisoner when I told him whither I was to carry him. He imagined the king had caused him to be shut up on purpose to make him work at the grand secret; and was not surprised when the wazir came, and threatened him with the most severe punishments unless he would communicate to him the art of making gold. But his most cruel threats and torments did not shake the philosopher, who continued intrepid amidst such tortures as I could not bear to look upon without trembling. As I was appointed to be his guard, continued Abd al-Moal, I endeavoured by every consolation in my power to alleviate his sufferings, and for the most part did but badly execute the cruel wazir's orders, who had enjoined me not to let him have a moment's rest. Abd al-Moal, said the philosopher to me one day, I see that you compassionate my condition; my body is indeed but one wound, and my limbs are all disjointed. Perhaps it may be by the king's order that I am treated with this cruelty; but, ah! my dear friend, I rather impute my misfortunes to the wazir's insatiable avarice. It is in vain, however, for him to apply violence and torments, and I would rather cut my tongue out of my mouth than discover the least secret to that monster.—Sir, said I, to him immediately, though it is as much as my life is worth to speak to you in the manner I am now going to do, yet I am too sensible of your sufferings not to relieve them if I could; tell me only what I can do, and I am ready to execute it.—Abd al-Moal, said the philosopher, set me at liberty; it is in your power, and you may rest assured that I shall not prove ungrateful.—But how will you get away? replied I; you are not able to stand upon your legs.—No matter for that, replied he; I will find means to follow you.

In short, after we had concerted measures together, I made use of this expedient to set the philosopher at liberty. I had a slave much about his size who was fallen very dangerously ill, and when he came to die, mangled his body till it appeared like the philosopher's. I then made the guards drunk, and taking advantage of their situation carried in the night my slave's body into the prison; then, dressing it in the philosopher's clothes, took him on my shoulders and carried him to my own house without anyone perceiving the exchange I had made. As the guards had been in general intoxicated, I was presumed to have made one among them, and it was pretty late next morning before we went into the dungeon. When we entered I feigned to believe he was asleep, and gave him a severe kick with my foot as if to awake him; but seemed not a little surprised to find him dead. Immediately I sent to inform the wazir, who came that moment to the prison; and after he had beheld the body miserably disfigured and all over wounds, which he took for the philosopher's, he was not a little mortified to find that he had lost by his cruelty the possibility of ever knowing the prisoner's secrets ; but as there was now no remedy he treated it as lightly as he could, and hastened to the king with an account of his death, giving him to understand that he had split his skull against the prison walls in order to avoid the punishment of his crimes.

While the wazir was regretting the loss of the philosopher I concealed him in a secret apartment in my house, where he ceased not to thank me for having saved his life. At the end of eight or ten days, when he had a little recovered his strength, Abd al-Moal, said he to me, embracing me very tenderly, what I would never have granted to the wazir in the most cruel tortures, I am willing to give you in return for your kindness. In a short time you shall be among the number of the adepts; but take warning by the fault I have committed in shewing myself too openly at the Court of Ormuz. And as neither of us will be long safe in this place, buy a camel on which you may carry me in a covered cradle, such as women have when they travel; I will put on their dress, and you may pretend that we are both going together on a pilgrimage to Meccah.

I did as the philosopher desired me. At the end of eight days all things were ready, and after I had obtained the king's leave to go and visit the tomb of the Holy Prophet, it was not long before we departed. We had scarce got out of the kingdom of Ormuz before the philosopher began to teach me his secret. He ordered me to bring him all the drugs he wanted for the preparation of what was his grand masterpiece ; and after he had

wrought several days in my presence on the real matter,
which so few people understand, he convinced me at last
that in the mercury of the philosophers are enclosed all
the four elements, though itself be no element ; that it is
a spirit, but invested nevertheless with a body ; that it
is a male, and yet does the office of a female ; that it is
an infant, and yet has the arms of a man ; that it is the
most subtle poison, and yet cures the most stubborn
leprosy ; that it is life, and yet kills everything ; that it
is a king, though another possesses its kingdom ; shuns
fire, though fire be drawn from it ; is water, but water
that wets not ; and in short, is air, but nevertheless .
lives upon water.

This, continued Abd al-Moal, was what the philosopher so plainly demonstrated, that in a few hours I
comprehended the whole secret of the grand work, and did
such miraculous things as I myself could hardly credit.
The transmutation of metals was the least of my
wonderful performances ; the universal medicine and the
elixir of life (that is, the water of youth), whose com-
position he taught me, was of a much greater value. To
be short, my good darwaysh, I never left this great man
so long as he lived. For though the elixir of health had
restored him to the bloom and vigour of a young man,
yet he was so crippled in all his limbs by the cruel
tortures which the wazir had inflicted upon him that he
was soon weary of the uncomfortable life he led ; and
taking no more of the salutary balsam, in about ten or
twelve years he ceased to live because he was determined
not to live any longer, and left me overwhelmed in the
utmost sorrow.

Notwithstanding the natural manner and the air of

truth and sincerity with which Abd al-Moal recounted
to me this part of his adventures, continued the Mandarin
Fum-Hoam, I had some difficulty in believing him.
Although it be not impossible, said I, that by the help of
your elixir you may have lived a whole age, yet I own
I should like to see the experiment tried.—It is easy to
do that, answered Abd al-Moal, if you have any creature
in the convent worn out with old age.—We have, continued I, an ass which can hardly stand upon its legs,
and which for these two years we have kept without
labour, merely from a principle of charity, because it has
belonged to the house more than twenty years, if you will
please to make this wonderful experiment upon it.—With
all my heart, replied he.—Whereupon we went down into
the stable, where he made the ass swallow ten or twelve
drops of his elixir in a glass of water.　I locked the door
close, took the key with me, and we returned to my
chamber, where, after a light collation, I desired Abd al-
Moal to continue the relation of his adventures, which he
did in the following manner ;

　　After I had lost my dear philosopher I spent a great
number of days in sorrow, and then proposed to travel,
having first made myself a sufficient quantity of gold
to defray my expenses.　I went through several countries
till at length I came to Damascus, where I found the
people in the utmost consternation.　The sultan was just
dead, without issue, of a malignant fever ; and his spouse,
the queen, to whom the throne belonged, was at the
point of death by the same distemper.　The physicians
had applied all their remedies in vain, and the angel of
death was making his advances to seize upon her soul
when I desired permission to see her majesty.　It was

the general opinion that there were no further hopes of her life; and therefore they made no scruple to introduce me into her apartment. Having obtained leave to give her some drops of my elixir, it had so quick an effect that the queen, who was before surrounded with the horrors of death, saw in a moment the mist which had hung over her disperse; her looks, which were wild before, became composed; she began to know her women and physicians; and having been informed that I was the person to whom she was indebted for her life, she gave me her hand to kiss—a favour never heard of before, and which gave some room to think she would not stop there with her acknowledgments. In an hour after I gave her a second dose of my remedy, and it was with extreme joy I soon found that it quite expelled the malignity of the fever; her pulse came to be regular again, and in four days she was restored to perfect health.

I was looked upon with admiration in the city of Damascus; and the queen having engaged me with the most endearing kindnesses to tell her who I was and the nature of my remedy, I could not refuse to satisfy her curiosity, though I had always before my eyes the adventure of the philosopher. But very fortunately for me, the thing happened quite otherwise, for as soon as she was informed of my wondrous talents she resolved not to lose the opportunity of making her kingdom one of the most flourishing in all Syria. She was young and perfectly beautiful, and therefore doubted not but she could secure my affection at her pleasure; and in truth I was so overcome with her goodness, and her charms had made such an impression on my soul, that it was not long before she perceived my situation. To

be short with you, then, my good darwaysh, she made
me King of Damascus; and notwithstanding the male-
volence of some of the grandees of her kingdom, I knew
how to maintain myself on the throne, and to gain the
love of my subjects. As I was master of all the treasures
in the world (for gold grew under my hands, and I could
make as much of it as I pleased every day without fear
of any law to punish me), I presently eased my people
of their taxes, heaped presents upon the nobility, enriched the poor, adorned the city with edifices and stately
mosques, and became as formidable to the enemies of
the state as I was beloved by my own people, who had
never experienced so much happiness as under my
reign.

I lived with the queen in a state of the most perfect
felicity, without either of us growing older, by means of
my elixir, and saw all the subjects of my kingdom continue young, without any apprehension from old age or
from sickness. The queen was extremely beautiful, and
for above fourscore years I loved her, without having
been once guilty of infidelity to her bed; when losing
my way one day, as I was hunting some leagues from
Damascus, I found myself alone at the foot of the
Mountain Libanus, and almost choked with thirst. I
perceived not far off a neat little house, whither
I hastened, and alighting from my horse tied it to the
gate, which I pushed open, and saw the master of the
house, with his wife and three children, sitting under the
shadow of a large tree in the courtyard. The two sons
were about twenty years old, and the daughter near
fifteen. As soon as they saw me the mother and
daughter ran and hid themselves in the private apart-

ments of the house, and while I was asking for a little
fresh water to quench my violent thirst, one of the
young men looking steadfastly on me fell with his
face to the ground, and kissing it with much reverence.
God is great! cried he; we are now under the shadow of
the king of kings. Let us humble ourselves before the
Sultan of Damascus, who honours us with his presence!
At the name of sultan, the father, who was a man of
quick parts, immediately conceived great hopes for the
advancement of his fortune.—The sultan here! cried he;
thanks be, then, to our Prophet! We shall soon know
whether it be in reality our illustrious monarch, since he
will not, I am persuaded, refuse my daughter his pardon.
—What crime, then, has your daughter committed?
said I, in some astonishment.—She has been audacious
enough, replied her father, to love the august sultan,
whom God preserve! and yet she has now power to fly
from his presence. Some few days since, she beheld in
these plains the supporter of the world, and the heart of
this young aspiring creature had boldness enough to raise
itself to the majesty of the king of kings.

I had in my disposition a great deal of clemency for
crimes of this nature, continued Abd al-Moal, and could
not therefore forbear smiling. I ordered him, however,
to call his wife and daughter; and as they approached
was dazzled with the charms of the beautiful Dulzagar
(for that was the name of this young peasant). Happy
slaves! cried the father, now is your poor cottage become
the magnificent pavilion of the king of nations. Here is
he who is as high as heaven, and this poor cottage now
equals the proudest and most stately palace. Let
Dulzagar shew the most private apartments of the house

to the support of monarchs.—The mother and daughter stood trembling, and, out of veneration and modesty hung down their heads. The charming Dulzagar, in particular, seemed to be filled with the great ideas her father had given her, and was in the utmost confusion at finding herself in my presence. It appeared as if she was asking herself, What is become of that austere virtue of the Eastern damsels, who, always secluded from the commerce of men, cannot forbear trembling when anyone approaches them? She stood immoveable, without once thinking to withdraw her fair hand from mine; and, my thirst still continuing, I went with her into the cherry orchard, and there refreshed myself very agreeably with the fruit which offered, while the rest of the family remained in the court.

The branches of the trees hung down so exceeding low that we wanted nobody to help us to gather the fruit. In this delicious place I satisfied the old man's intentions, and if I quenched my thirst by eating the cherries, I kindled, on the other hand, so strong a flame in my heart for the fair Dulzagar that I had not power to leave her, though I had already spent more than two hours in her company alone. In the mean time, night came on, and hearing the noise of some of the huntsmen, who were in quest of me, I called two of my most favourite eunuchs and gave them charge of this charming creature. I then presented her mother with a large purse of gold, which I usually carried in my saddle-bow, and wrote an order to my grand treasurer to tell out for her father a hundred thousand pieces of gold, which I put into his hands.

The old man, transported with joy, threw himself

13—2

that moment at my feet. This day, said he, is doubtless our jubilee; since my king, whom Heaven preserve in health, and make victorious over his enemies! the invincible Sultan of Damascus, undoubtedly leaves me a grandson, who will one day become the felicity of the nation of the Prophet; may the Lord of the Koran confirm and give a blessing to my hopes!—I embraced him with a smile, and having charged him, as well as the rest of the family, to keep this adventure secret, I ordered the two eunuchs who had the sole custody of Dulzagar to change her lodgings every day that the queen might not discover my new amour. Sometimes this beautiful creature was by my order kept in a peasant's cottage; at other times in a grove, whose shade defended us from the heat of the sun; but most commonly, in some cave or other, at the bottom of Mount Libanus; and this intrigue was carried on for above three months without the queen's having the least suspicion. I knew the delicate sensibility of her heart, which had never been accustomed to any division of my love, and that a discovery of this kind would kill her with grief, the rather as we had never had any children. My going so frequently a-hunting gave her, however, some uneasy apprehensions, which made her place spies in the country; by which means she obtained the knowledge of my secrets, and wounded herself with a most tormenting jealousy. I saw in her countenance all the anguish of her heart, without seeming to perceive it; and as I was going one day to caress her, in order to dissipate the gloomy thoughts which continued to prey upon her mind, she pushed me from her with some disdain. You mistake yourself, sir, said she; you

certainly imagine yourself with your new mistress. She
has now the entire possession of your thoughts; and
that you may know I am not unacquainted with your
amours, to-morrow you will meet her in the suburbs of
Damascus. Perhaps there are few women in my
situation who would not have kept this to themselves,
that they might have surprised you together; but, as
such a discovery would pain me too much, I chose
rather to acquaint the king with my own lips that
I am not ignorant of the measures he pursues for the
destruction of my peace, thereby hoping to prevail on
his prudence to forsake them in time, and spare me by
that means the anguish which I must experience from a
fuller conviction of his infidelity. Then, lifting up her
eyes to heaven, O Holy Prophet, continued she, great
ambassador of God, preserve my honoured sultan from
the malice of men! Perhaps it is not his own inclination
which leads him to violate the faith he once gave me, for
he is of the number of the just; but some base slave
has wrought upon his heart and excited his resentment
against me. If then there be any such traitor, O make
thou their bed in hell, and let the fire thereof be their
covering!

I was sensibly affected with these remonstrances,
continued Abd al-Moal; and had it been in my power
to relinquish Dulzagar, and make the queen easy, I
certainly should then have done it; but this amour had
got too much dominion over my soul. I did, however,
all I could to soothe her, and changing the place of
meeting, ordered Azuf, one of the eunuchs who attended
my mistress, to bring her the third day after this conversation to a very hollow cave in the forest of

cedars. I had myself arrived at the place appointed, and impatiently waited for Dulzagar, when the queen, changing her resolution of going elsewhere, and perhaps instructed by her spies, came with a design to surprise me. She was followed by her eunuchs, and made towards the place which I had appointed for the rendezvous of the huntsmen and dogs; but when she was got about half-way, the sky grew prodigious dark, and the thunder and lightning raised such a tempest as had ˙not been seen for a long time. This obliged the eunuchs to carry the litter just under the broad trees that grew at the entrance of the cave, where I was waiting for Dulzagar, and where, being fatigued with hunting, I had fallen asleep upon a kind of seat that nature had formed in the rock, and which one of my eunuchs who attended me had covered with leaves.

When the queen was informed by some of her eunuchs sent out for that purpose, that I could not be found, her grief was redoubled. Where can the sultan be? said she to her women. Alas! if the bare pleasure of hunting is enough to make him despise the badness of the weather, the rapture he promises himself with my rival will make him, no doubt, venture his life, without once considering how dear that life is to me. But alas! while I am thus idly complaining, he is perhaps rioting in the arms of his beloved mistress. The day, however, will probably arrive when I shall there surprise him; that happy day, alas! which seems at present so remote, when, oh when will it arrive!

While the queen was thus lamenting, the faithful Azuf, both to save Dulzagar from the storm, and to relieve my impatience, brought her behind him on horseback,

and made the best of his way to the cave; but his horse
chancing to be unshod, it stumbled and fell lame, when
he perceived a company of the queen's eunuchs about
five hundred paces from the cave before he could reach
it. In these sad circumstances nothing could be more
unlucky than to be found in such a place as this with
a strange young woman so beautiful as Dulzagar. He
therefore advised her to conceal herself beneath a thicket
of bushes, and giving her a lesson in case she should
fall into the queen's hands, he made off from the place,
when my mistress was unfortunately discovered by the
ʻeunuchs, who carried her immediately to the queen. The
queen, who was surprised at Dulzagar's extraordinary
beauty and at the extreme neatness of her dress, and who
was not a little uneasy to find her in such a suspicious
place, began to have a thousand jealous thoughts, and
haughtily asked her who she was, and what she did there
alone?—Alas, madam! said she, pretending not to know
her, I was going to Damascus to implore the queen's
protection against certain Guebres, who shelter themselves in these mountains, and among whom I was
brought up, though I am by extraction a Mohammedan.
They carried me away when I was about six years old,
into a little village about three leagues off, and I could
never yet find my parents, having forgotten their names;
but, shocked at their religion, I have now made my
escape from these idolaters, to return to the law of our
Holy Prophet, well knowing there is but one God. Save
me, therefore, madam, from these worshippers of fire,
who will doubtless sacrifice me to their idol if I should
have the misfortune to fall into their hands. Grant me,
therefore, your protection and favour with the queen,

that I may be again reckoned among the number of those who seek for the true light. A secret voice has reached my heart; it tells me, that the sultana is the supporter of religion, that she will deliver me from the persecution of my ravishers, and restore a pure and innocent soul to the lost ways of Heaven!

.   The queen, though she piqued herself on her piety, and was thus artfully attacked on her weak side, did not yet banish all her suspicion. She was grieved that the interest of religion thwarted and controlled her jealousy, and had determined nothing either for or against Dulzagar, when Azuf, who had at a distance ˙ beheld the queen's eunuchs carrying off that amiable person, and for my interest or my mistress's safety was resolved to run all hazards, came up, and called to them either to retire or to put themselves in a posture of reverence, for that the invincible Sultan of Damascus was coming. The queen at these words, fearing to let me see this new proselyte, ordered one of her most faithful slaves to take her up behind him, and to carry her to the old seraglio of Damascus, while she advanced to meet me.

This order Dulzagar had reason to dread was upon the point of being executed, when as they were passing by the cave where she knew I was, she let herself slide from the horse, and pretending to have hurt her leg, cried out with so much vehemence, and in a voice so pitiable, that I ordered the eunuch who attended me immediately to run out. But how great was his astonishment on seeing the beautiful Dulzagar in the hands of one of the queen's slaves, and accompanied by Azuf! Without the least hesitation, however, he drew his sabre, and threatened to take off the slave's head if he made the least opposition, telling him that I was in the cave, that what he did was by my direction, and that the least resistance would cost him his life. The queen's eunuch obeyed, and after they had brought me my dear mistress, they both retired with the horse in their hand to a corner of the cave, and left me to my liberty. Ravished with the enjoyment of my adorable Dulzagar, I gave myself no concern about any other person, and was reflecting how I should exert my authority over the queen in case she attempted to disturb my pleasures; but alas! how short were their duration!

Abd al-Moal, continued the mandarin, could not restrain his tears; but after a short pause he went on again with his adventures in this manner. The queen was not a little pleased with her good fortune in having the fair Dulzagar in her power; but while Azuf conducted her away from the cave, under pretence of meeting me, another violent storm bursting just over her head, she was obliged to return to the shelter of those trees she had just before quitted; and as the thunder was very dreadful, she was going to step into the cave, when one of her women, pulling her by the robe, represented the danger she might expose herself to in a place that might be a retreat for wild beasts, and advised her at least to send some of her slaves to visit the cave before she ventured in. You are in the right, said the queen; but without giving themselves that trouble, they need only discharge their arrows in every part of the cave. This order was no sooner given than executed; above sixty slaves all let fly at once on every side, and I was in the utmost surprise to find myself wounded with three arrows, and to hear Dulzagar crying out, embracing me, Ah! my dear prince, I am murdered!

The cries of this beautiful dying person and myself, continued Abd al-Moal, made the queen order her people to retire; and her slave and mine, who were both like-wise wounded, calling out to tell them that the Sultan of Damascus was in the cave, a dead coldness seized her, and she fell down in a swoon while she was ordering some-body to run immediately to my succour. They found me, alas! holy darwaysh, all weltering in my blood; but would to Heaven, that Dulzagar's wounds had been no more dangerous than my own! That adorable creature had received one arrow, among many others, that pierced her heart; and the condition wherein I saw her almost distracted me. Wounded as I was, I drew my sabre, and made a horrible slaughter among those unhappy slaves who were no otherwise culpable than by executing the queen's commands; and in the first transports of my passion was about to cut off her head and afterwards to stab myself. But I had not strength to execute this cruel design; instead of which I fell down with weakness, and my eunuchs put me in the queen's litter, and carried me back to Damascus. My surgeons drew the arrows out of my body, and the wounds were not mortal. I permitted them, however, to dress them just as they thought fit, not thinking it worth while to make use of any of my infallible remedies, so much had my life become a burden to me.

The queen durst not appear in my sight for some time, but when she had allowed my grief as much time as she thought was proper, at the end of fifteen

days she came to my bedside. I could not bear her
looks without trembling. Ah, madam! said I, this is
what your destructive jealousy has exposed me to;
but I wish to God I had shared the same fate as Dulzagar! I should then have thought myself much happier
than at present. You have raised me to a throne, indeed,
but I have put your kingdom in such a flourishing condition as acquits me in a great measure of the obligation
I have to you upon that account. You had it not, I
suppose, in your intention to destroy your rival, but she
is not the less dead; nor can I impute the loss of her to
anything but your jealousy.—It is true, sir, replied the
queen, melting into tears, I deserve these just reproaches;
but being accustomed for so many years to possess your
heart alone, I could not bring myself to share it with
another. But why did you not exert your authority?
why did you not plainly tell me your intentions? I
should then have sighed in private but submitted to your
will, and Dulzagar might have still been alive. Forget,
my lord, that I am the cause of her death, being innocent,
and pardon an involuntary crime, which I would willingly
expiate with my own blood if I could thereby restore the
person who was so extremely dear to you. Look no
longer on me with those angry eyes, which embitter
all the pleasure of my life! I made the queen no
answer, continued Abd al-Moal, but by the tears I
shed in memory of my mistress, for whom I erected a
most stately monument. Poor relief of my lasting
sorrow, and what will never be able to diminish it!
From that time I have been the prey of the blackest
melancholy, and can find pleasure in nothing. The
queen, too, was so grieved to see my indifference to

her, that without suffering her life to be prolonged, she sank under her affliction.

After all these losses, my life in the possession of a throne became a burden to me. I envied a thousand times the condition of every private person, and after I had taken a firm resolution, I assembled the grandees of Damascus, abdicated the throne in their presence, and desired them to choose for themselves a monarch worthier of them. But they would not readily consent. You, said they, bursting into tears, are our common father; why will you forsake us ?—I would not, however, suffer myself to be shaken by their prayers and tears, though I was sensibly affected with them. At length I agreed to nominate a viceroy for six years, who should then become their lawful monarch if in the mean time they heard nothing of me. It is now, alas! above seven-and-twenty years since I left them, during which time I have been wandering about the world without any fixed place of residence; and though I have learned, by a kind of philosophy which enables me to bear all the bitter afflictions of life, to despise the grandeur of a throne, yet I have nevertheless but too much weakness at the bottom of my heart. And thus, holy darwaysh, I think I have reason to say that your quiet life is preferable to that which I have hitherto led; and that I find I have not virtue enough to embrace it, since above thirty years have not been able to wear off the loss of my dear Dulzagar, whom I shall always lament to the hour of my death.

CONTINUATION OF THE ADVENTURES OF THE DARWAYSH ASSIRKAN

SCARCELY had Abd al-Moal finished the history of his adventures, continued the Mandarin Fum - Hoam, when we heard my ass bray in such a manner as gave me reason to believe the elixir had performed its operation.   We went, therefore, instantly into the stable, and I was in the most astonishing surprise to see the creature so much changed that I could not have known him again.   For whereas his skin was before as bare as a drum-head, it was now covered with hair as fine as silk ; and his eyes, which but some hours before seemed almost extinct, had now a surprising vivacity.   In short, there was no room to doubt but that the ass was in reality made young again.   Well, then, said Abd al-Moal to me, is this enough to satisfy your incredulity ?—Ah, sir ! replied I, I am sufficiently convinced of the efficacy of your secret ; nor was there any need for this trial to confirm my faith, the bare recital of your adventures, which are as affecting as they are singular, was sufficient.—That is too complaisant, replied Abd al-Moal ; but I knew from your looks that you were a person whose secrecy might be relied on ; and indeed you are the only one except the Queen of Damascus in whom I have had this confidence, the example of the philosopher having taught me not to put myself inconsiderately in the power of men ; but that you may be still better assured of the facts I have related to you, take this paper, wherein is a powder to make gold, and these two phials ; this phial restores health to sick

persons who are deemed incurable, and the other may
properly be called the elixir of immortality, since by a
prudent management of it you may live more than an
age, provided you be not surprised by any of those
unforeseen accidents against which there is no remedy.
— After Abd al-Moal had made me these valuable
presents, notwithstanding all the persuasion I could use,
I could keep him no longer ; and therefore, having
conducted him to the gate of the convent, I saw him
mix among a crowd of people which was pretty common
before our house, and so lost sight of him for ever.

The paper and two bottles that Abd al-Moal left
me made me think myself richer than the King of
Kandahar. To make an experiment of his elixir of
immortality I took a few drops of it on going to bed; and
rising at break of day next morning, found myself as
young as a person of twenty, though I was near fifty
years old. But if I was pleased with this change, I was,
on the other hand, under some apprehensions that my
youthful appearance might be noticed and disapproved of
by our darwayshes, who would thereupon deprive me of my
superiority in the convent, and make known the circumstance to the king himself. Perhaps I shall have the
same fate as Abd al-Moal's master, said I, and therefore
let me depart from hence. As soon as I had taken this
resolution, I put up some pieces of the convent's plate,
and going into the stable, mounted my ass, who was in
full vigour, and with the keys which were every night
brought up to my chamber, I got out of the convent, and
travelled almost all day, very little concerned about what
they would think of my departure. I put up at the first
inn I came to, and there bought provisions for myself

and for my ass. I passed the night very quietly, and the next day, having quitted the habit of a darwaysh, pursued my journey without apprehension.

It is to no purpose, madam, continued the mandarin, to enter upon a detail of my journey; I will only relate to you the principal passages thereof. One day among others, then, as I came to a pleasure-house belonging to the King of Zamorin, and was going to take up my lodging in one of the outer galleries, the king returned from hunting, and seeing with what tranquillity I was settling my abode for that night in a place which was not designed for public reception, was somewhat surprised, and ordered me to be brought before him. How comes it that you have so little discernment, said he to me, as not to distinguish such a palace as mine from a common inn?—Sir, replied I, will your majesty vouchsafe to permit that I ask you one question? Who lodged first in this house after it was finished?—Some of my ancestors, answered the king.— After them, who inhabited it?—It was my father.—And after your father, said I, who was the possessor of it?—Myself, replied the king; and after my decease I hope it will descend to my posterity.—Ah, sir! cried I, a house that changes so often its inhabitants is certainly an inn, and no palace! And it is for this reason that the Persians have no term to shew the difference; intimating thereby that men are travellers upon earth, and that they all arrive, some sooner and some later, at the same common end, which is death.

The king, with whom I had this discourse, was satisfied with the truth of it. You are in the right, said he to me; and it is with very great justice that one of our poets has elegantly compared all kinds of men to the pieces wherewith we play at chess ; some act the kings, the queens, the knights, the fools, and simple pawns. There is a vast difference between them while they are in motion, but when once the game is over and the chessboard shut, they are all thrown promiscuously together into the same box without any sort of distinction. Death does the very same thing ; kings, emperors, merchants, slaves, warriors, men of the robe and of the revenue, all then become equal; and there is nothing but our good works and charity towards our neighbours that will give us the superiority. Let us, therefore, always be doing commendable actions ; for they bring with them an inward satisfaction which the wicked never enjoy. The king at these words returned into his palace, and ordering me to stay where I was, sent me likewise a plentiful repast and clothes convenient to cover me during the night. Next morning I went to thank him for his kindness, and departed. After several days' journey upon my ass, I came one night to Nagapatam, where I went to lodge with a good old woman. I took care of my ass, and put him in the stable ; and as there were still some hours before night, I proposed to take a turn about the city. However, my roving thoughts carried me into the suburbs, and thence I wandered so far that night came upon me while I was yet in the country. There was no doubt but that the city gates were shut ; I therefore endeavoured to find some place where I might retreat with security, and after searching for some time came at length to the bottom of a hill where I found a kind of cave, and by the light of the moon perceived at the entrance of it a sort of niche into which I got, and was settling myself to pass the night quietly therein when I saw a young damsel of exquisite beauty entering the place seemingly with the utmost dread.   Behind her came an old woman, bending under the weight of years, who took her by the hand and encouraged her to advance farther.

As soon as the old woman, who had in her hand a kind of dark lantern, had got about to the middle of the cave, she took out of her bosom a little horn, which she blew ; and immediately there spread towards the mouth of the cave such a smoke, or rather such a thick cloud, as quite intercepted all human sight ; nay, as even hindered the light of the moon, which then shone very brightly, from entering therein.   At this instant a horrid dread seized all my senses, and the young woman who accompanied her was so terrified that she could scarcely keep her feet.   What are you afraid of ? said the old woman ; since I have been overcome by your persuasions to endeavour to grant that to you which I have refused to so many others, ought you to be thus terrified ?   Be as courageous now, since this is only done to obtain what you desire, as you were before to request it of me. In a short time, that ungrateful man who now despises you shall be in this place, and you shall soon see him at your feet, begging you to grant him but one favourable look to ease his aching heart.—After these agreeable promises the young woman seemed in some measure to recover her spirits.   But, good mother, said she, can nobody know what passes here?—Do not you see, said the old woman, the bar I have put upon the door ?   The earth shall sooner open before us, and shew us the bottom of its abyss than any person

14

enter here against my will.   After this she bound her
temples with vervain and rue; and stooping down to
the ground, wrote thereon certain characters with the
point of a dagger; then she bound the young woman's
thumb with a red thread, and pricked it with the point
of a needle till it bled; and at last, pronouncing aloud
certain imprecations which made me tremble, summoned
her infernal correspondent before her.

I expected no other, continued the mandarin, than
to see some frightful spirit appear, and my fear redoubled
with every fresh conjuration the old woman made, when
I beheld coming out of the earth a monster much like a
bear, who at first fell to licking his mistress's feet with
great submission, and then rearing himself on his hinder
paws, muttered some ill-articulated words in her ear,
and so vanished suddenly away in smoke as did also the
vapour which filled the cave's mouth.   Ah! I am be-
trayed! cries the old woman; there is somebody hid in
this place, but it shall not be long before he shall bear
the punishment of his curiosity!   Then coming straight
towards me she touched me with a hazel wand which
she had in her hand, and I was that moment transformed
into an ape.   But how much was I astonished at this
extraordinary change!   I threw myself at her feet, and
embraced them with respect, shewing by my gestures
that my fault was involuntary; but when I found nothing
would avail me, I fell into such a violent fury that,
without considering what she might further add to my
punishment, I flew in her face, tore out both her eyes,
and then made my escape into the country.

In the first transports of my grief I fell into the
utmost despair, and was a thousand times going to beat

out my brains against a stone; but at length, putting
my hopes in our Holy Prophet, I made to a tree which
stood nearest the city, and hid myself under its branches
till break of day. As soon as the morning began to
appear I clambered over the walls of Nagapatam, and
without being noticed by anyone came to the old
woman's house, where I had left my ass and a pair of
little bags, containing the valuable presents which
Abd al-Moal had given me. I then found means from
the top of the house to get into the chamber which
was designed for me, and throwing myself on the bed,
waited till the people had got up. Some hours after,
the woman who was to have lodged me came into the
chamber, and was not a little surprised to see a fine ape
sleeping very quietly. She made much of me, and I
returning her kindness in the best manner I could, took
up my bags before her and carried them to a little press,
where I locked them up; and giving her the key, inti-
mated by my gestures that she was to take great care
of it. Her surprise every moment increased; and as I
afterwards carried her to the stable to let her know that
I recommended the care of my ass to her likewise, she
began to be afraid, and imagined that I was some wizard;
but observing the tears gush from my eyes she doubted
whether I might not be her guest who was some way
transformed by witchcraft, and thereupon testified all
possible concern for the lamentable condition in which
she beheld me.

This good woman had but one daughter, who was a
widow about thirty-five years old, and dwelt in a house
next adjoining. Her husband had left her with many
young children; and among the rest she had a daughter

of uncommon beauty, hardly fifteen, to whom my landlady carried me and gave me as a present, hoping by
this means to dissipate the extreme melancholy I was in.
But during the first days of my metamorphosis I was so
little sensible of the care that good woman took of me
that I scarce made any return to the fondnesses which
the amiable Gahun (for that was the name of her grand-
daughter) shewed me.   Besides I was uneasy about my
bags ; and therefore in a few days went back again to
the old woman's house, and gave her to understand that
she would do me singular pleasure in returning them, and
that she might sell my ass if she pleased.   My bags I took
with me to my new habitation, and, having locked them up
in a garret where no one came, was resolved to bear my
misfortune with patience, and to wait till Providence
should think fit to deliver me out of my wretched state.
I have already told you, madam, continued the mandarin,
that Gahun was a perfect beauty.   As she was every
moment giving me a thousand innocent caresses, it would
have been difficult for me not to have conceived an
extreme tenderness for her.   In this manner I passed
away a whole year ; nor did I perceive the violence of
my love until I was on the point of losing this beautiful
creature for ever by a most dangerous fit of sickness.
I was so sensibly afflicted to see her become a prey to
such acute pain that I dissolved into tears at her bedside,
and was perpetually feeling her pulse as if I had been an
able physician.   But perceiving that in spite of all the
remedies they gave her she still grew worse and worse,
I bethought myself at last of my elixir, whereupon I
ran up into the garret, and soon returning to my amiable
mistress took a cup full of water, poured some drops of

the elixir therein, and presented it to her, who made no
scruple to receive it at my hands.   Gahun soon felt the
effects of this wonderful remedy which reduced the
humours to a just equilibrium, and diffused through her
whole mass of blood such a balsamic unction that at
the end of three days she found herself perfectly recovered, and looked more beautiful and healthy than
before her illness.   Never was greater surprise than
what the mother and grandmother of my charming mistress experienced; she, too, every moment gave me
fresh proofs of her acknowledgments, though sometimes
she could not but wonder with herself how she came to
feel such a tender esteem for an ape without being able
to understand the cause and original of it.

One day, however, as she was looking very steadfastly at my nails, she observed that they were covered
with a thin skin, which was unusual in creatures of my
species, whereupon she acquainted her mother with this
discovery, and (my old hostess having never disclosed the
suspicions she had of my metamorphosis) her mother told
it, next market day, together with the wonderful cure I
had done upon her daughter, to an old negro-woman, who
expressed upon this occasion an earnest desire to see me.
She had no sooner examined me thoroughly, but she
confirmed Gahun and her mother in their idea of my
being a man, who she supposed had felt the displeasure
of some great magician, and she promised to restore me
to my former shape.   The day after to-morrow, said she,
is the new moon; be sure, then, that you provide against
that time a large tub full of black goat's milk, and leave
the rest to me.   I will answer for our success in this affair.
I thanked her in the best manner I could, continued the

mandarin, and made signs that I would requite her pains ; and Gahun´ and I both waited with the utmost impatience for the appearance of the new moon. The negro-woman's orders were punctually executed ; the tub and black goat's milk were ready at the appointed hour ; and after the woman had put into the bath such herbs and powders as we knew not, and plunged me thrice over head in it, pronouncing over me certain barbarous words, I that moment resumed my former appearance. Gahun's modesty would not permit her to be present at this operation, but she was in the mean time making ready her father's clothes for me. When I came out of the bath I threw myself at the negro-woman's feet, desiring her to return in three days, and promised her a reward answerable to the service she had done me.

Gahun came in as soon as decency would permit ; and what joy did I see sparkle in her eyes when she perceived that I seemed not above twenty, and tolerably handsome too ! Beautiful Gahun, said I to her, in the presence of her mother and grandmother, will you now refuse the offer of a heart that adores you ? You who have had some esteem for me while I was under the form of an ape, will you not confirm it now I am in a condition to answer you ? I restored you to life by a wonderful liquor which few people possess, and have riches enough to content the most ambitious minds ; but ۔I should be still much concerned to owe your heart to gratitude or interest, I would only be indebted to love for that valuable possession.—Sir, said Gahun's mother, embracing me, have compassion on my daughter's modesty ; the declaration you desire would cost a young person too much. The generous blush which at present overspreads her face is a sufficient indication of the love she feels for you, and her silence is the best proof that she accepts your proposals of marriage ; but not longer to delay two lovers whose union is so dear I will myself run to the kadi's house and bid him get ready the contract ; and within an hour at furthest will be here with an iman, who shall join your hands.

I could not well tell how to express my joy and gratitude to the mother of my dear Gahun ; she left us, and at the appointed time returned with the kadi. We signed the contract, and soon after the iman came and performed his office ; so that after a great repast they left me alone with my new spouse, in whose arms I met with more pleasures than ever I had known while a darwaysh. The next morning I purchased thirty pounds' weight of lead which I immediately changed into gold. I made a present of an ingot of gold that weighed three pounds to the negro-woman who restored me to my true shape ; the rest I sold to the Jews, and put my beloved Gahun in a condition to vie with the richest women in Nagapatam, where I lived with her many happy days without anything to disturb our serenity. We had a numerous family, which I intended to have established by the means of my elixir ; but it was written in the book of fate that we should both die on one day ; for there happened at Nagapatam a terrible earthquake when we least of all expected it, which buried us both in the ruins of a magnificent mosque which joined to our house.

*   *   *   *   *   *

These, certainly, said the Queen of China, are very odd and whimsical adventures ; they have, however, given me extreme satisfaction. But what became of you afterwards ?

STORY OF PRINCE KADIR-BILAH

I WENT, madam, answered Fum-Hoam, into the body of a young child, in the kingdom of Delhi; and though I was born in the cottage of a poor labourer, yet I was nevertheless descended from illustrious blood, for my father, who was reduced to this deplorable condition, was the son of the deceased King of Tigris. But to make this history intelligible to you we must trace it a little higher.

My grandfather, who was called the Sultan Alfumi Garbachi, died suddenly about sixty years old, without naming his successor as usual. My father, who was called Abadaraman, was the eldest of forty-six sons and twelve daughters whom he had by different women, and was also the best beloved; but as he was abroad in the wars against our enemies when the king died, four of his brothers confederated together. They seized on the throne, filled the kingdom with blood and slaughter, massacred all the rest of their brothers, and after many battles with my father reduced him to the necessity of avoiding by flight a similar fate. My father had only with him the wife he had most affection for, and with her he retired into the kingdom of Delhi, where, as he was resolved to live a private and retired life, he bought a small piece of ground which, by the help of slaves whom he likewise purchased, might serve to maintain his family. I was in this place born to that prince, who named me Kadir-Bilah, and by the time I was ten years old I began to take prodigious delight in hunting, and this violent exercise rendered my body so strong and so well inured to fatigue that at eighteen years of age I was able to encounter lions, bears, tigers, or any other wild beasts.

One night as I sat dozing by the fireside I heard my father and mother, who imagined me asleep, discoursing of their misfortunes. It was then I first understood, with no small surprise, that my blood was answerable to the greatness of my spirit, and that my uncles' cruelty had made my father leave his country. This was sufficient to make me determine to take my way towards the kingdom of Tigris. I departed, therefore, without saying anything to my father, and after I had passed the sea, and undergone a thousand perils in my journey, I arrived at last at the Court of the King of Dafila, who, as I understood, was at war with Abgaru, the only surviving uncle of the four, and who then reigned, having poisoned the other three that he might have no competitors.

On a certain day when there was to be an engagement, I entered myself a volunteer in the Sultan of Dafila's troops, and performed such gallant actions that the king distinguished me among those brave men who had contributed to gain him the victory, and soon after gave me the command of a body of troops. I formed them all by my example, to be so many heroes, and became the terror of my enemies for the whole three years during which the war continued, and wherever I fought was sure to draw victory after me. Nay, I did more, for I killed Prince Abgaru with my own hand ; and having thus put an end to the war, which had lasted a long while between him and the Sultan of Dafila, I thought it then a proper time to declare myself.

In short, I had no sooner caused the chief lords of
Tigris to be assembled and notified to them that I was
the son of Prince Abadaraman, than they immediately
proclaimed me king. Not at all exalted with this title,
however, which was no more than my due, I went
immediately to wait on the Sultan of Dafila, and having
acquainted him with my origin he not only approved my
ascending the throne of my ancestors, but offered me
likewise his only daughter in marriage; and as I had
heard great encomiums both of the beauty and merit
of that princess I gladly accepted his offer, and married
her at the head of the camp with a magnificence proportioned to our condition. Having thus established
myself in the empire, I deputed two of my principal
officers of state to my father with a letter, wherein I
informed him of all my adventures, the news of which
was the more agreeable to him as my absence had
caused him much grief of heart, and had given him reason
to believe that I had been devoured by wild beasts.
Upon his return to his kingdom I obliged him to
assume the throne notwithstanding his resistance, and
became myself his first subject.

While the Sultan Abadaraman, my father, who was
the model of an accomplished monarch, expended all
his time and pains in the government of his kingdom,
I went with my spouse through the principal cities
of Abyssinia to restore that justice which had been
banished by Abgaru and his three brothers; and one
day as I was in a castle not many leagues from Tigris,
I went into a closet wherein were some books, and
having opened one I found it to contain a very remarkable passage. I read in this book that near Ispahan

there was a building (according to the tradition of the country), called the Tower of the Forty Virgins, because it is haunted with spirits resembling young girls, and is therefore uninhabited. I could not forbear smiling at so ridiculous a fancy, but reading further in the same book I found that for above a hundred and fifty years several gallant Persians who went to stay all night in the place were never after heard of. And the origin of this tradition, whether true or false, was thus related, viz :—

About two hundred years ago the people of Ispahan were sadly tormented with a prodigious quantity of rats, insomuch that they had not a grain of corn but what was damaged by them. And when several people were endeavouring to find out an expedient to deliver themselves from this scourge, there appeared all on a sudden a little dwarf not above two feet high and frightfully deformed, who on the payment of a large sum of money, which he contracted for, undertook to drive away all these vermin in an hour's time.[1] No sooner had Jiyuf (for so the dwarf was called) made the agreement than he took out of his budget a tabor and pipe, and by whistling and drumming about the streets of Ispahan there was not a rat or mouse in the town which did not come out of its hole and follow him as far as the River Zandarou, where they all went into the water and were drowned.

As Jiyuf disappeared with the rats they imagined they should hear no more of him, but the next day he came again to demand the money he had agreed for. They paid him indeed the sum, but the people were so base and covetous as to give him several pieces

---

[1] Cf. the "Pied Piper of Hamelin."

deficient in weight. This he soon discovered, and upbraiding them with ingratitude threatened to be revenged on them if they did not perform their bargain. They, however, treated his threats with disdain; but next morning the whole city was in a ˙terrible consternation to find on a sudden an old black woman, above fifty feet high, standing in the market-place, with a whip in her hand. Ungrateful people of Ispahan, said she, know that I am the Jinniyah Mirjihan Banu! You have falsified your word to my son, and I have come to punish you; and to convince you of my power observe, therefore, what I am about to do. No sooner had the jinniyah cracked her whip than the thunder began to roar enough to terrify the most undaunted, the air grew black, and a thick darkness overspread the city for six hours, at the end of which time, and when scarce anyone was recovered from his fright, Mirjihan Banu appeared in the same place again. People of Ispahan, said she, with a most terrible voice, if you wish to appease my wrath bring me hither forty of your most beautiful daughters under fifteen, otherwise they shall die this night.

Though the prodigies which this jinniyah and her son had performed were enough to have taught these ungrateful people more wisdom, yet they made no haste to obey her; but on the next morning how great was the grief of the principal men of the city to find their daughters strangled! Nothing was heard among them but sighs and bitter groans. Mirjihan Banu, however, not in the least moved to pity them, for four days successively made the same demand, and four times punished them for their disobedience. At length on the fifth day they were resolved to resist her will no longer, but brought out all the young women in Ispahan that were under fifteen, and when she had chosen out forty of them, these unhappy victims of their fathers' perfidy, at the sound of a large leather-trumpet which she began to blow, were obliged to follow the jinniyah as far as this tower, which no one had ever perceived before, and which was apparently raised that moment by magic art. Thither they all went in with her, and were never seen any more; only every night there was a frightful noise heard in the tower.

Though this history seemed somewhat singular to me at that time, yet I paid no further attention to it, and several years passed without my once thinking about the book. But when the Princess of Dafila, my wife, by an unavoidable fatality died in child-bed without leaving me any issue, I was so full of grief on the occasion that for six weeks together I shut myself up in the palace without seeing any person whatsoever. After which time, in some measure to dissipate my sorrow, I retired into the castle where I read the " History of the Tower of the Forty Virgins "; and calling for the book, found the circumstances of this strange story attested by so many contemporary authors of undoubted authority that I began to be a little less incredulous of the facts contained in it. I read it over again, therefore, with attention, and having found at the end of the book a prophecy, which people assured me was legible not above twenty years before, on a plate of gold fastened to the bottom of the tower, and which had a good deal of reference to me, I was resolved to make a journey into Persia, and go in search of this adventure at the risk of my life, as many a brave Persian had done before me. The words, madam, continued the mandarin, that were written upon the golden plate, were these:

"The sun, under whose shade and influence all nature moves, is but a faint ray of the brightness of the girdle of the master of this place. If Kordat keeps in the bowels of the earth forty virgins more beautiful than the houri, Isfandir shall preserve their chastity until a prince descended from the blood of Malilak arrives, and to whom the words which one of our poets puts in the mouth of a discontented father cannot be applied:

> " ' My tender heart's upon my son,
>   But my son's heart is on a stone.'

Prince, whoever thou art, who hast the great Sulayman for the head of thy family, enter this tower without fear, where thou wilt find a charming object who shall replace in thy heart the princess whom thou lamentest. He that would fish for pearls should throw himself into the sea."

The prophecy surprised me the more because it seemed addressed to me alone, for I was descended from the Sultan Sulayman and the Queen of Sheba; I had lately placed my father on the throne, and was sadly afflicted for the loss of the Princess of Dafila. All which reasons confirmed my resolution of going to try the adventure of the Tower of the Forty Virgins. Accordingly I acquainted the king my father with it, and notwithstanding his remonstrances to the contrary, set forward on my journey, and arrived in Persia without the least accident befalling me.

When I had rested myself some days at Ispahan

after the fatigue of my journey, I left my officers in a house which I had engaged for my use, and went alone to the bottom of the tower, where I read on the golden plate the same words as I had found in the book. Without the least hesitation I went directly into a porch which had no light but from one skylight, and where I could see a little door that seemed to lead into some subterraneous place, whose darkness startled me not a little. And just as I was about to enter, casting my eye upon the porch wall, I perceived in a niche a sword and buckler, to which was hung a roll of parchment, whereon were these words: "The place where thou art going to descend is so dreadful that it would frighten a lion into a lioness, but this sword and buckler of Jiyan-ibn-Jiyan, which hath passed through the hands of thy ancestors, will enable thee to do exploits equally marvellous with theirs, who have gained themselves fame over the whole earth. Go down, therefore, without fear into these dark and gloomy recesses, putting thy whole confidence in him, who only with these words, 'there is no other God but God,' overthrew Lat and Holizi."

This was encouragement enough for me to pursue my design. I therefore took down the sword and enchanted buckler, which, as soon as I had put upon my arm, and was entering upon the stairs that were to lead me to the deliverance of the forty virgins, I found gave a bright and shining light sufficient to dispel all the darkness of the place. After I had gone down a thousand steps I came into a large marble hall, the roof and sides of which were all beset with diamonds of a prodigious size. The chief door of this hall opened into a delicious garden ; but the only way into it was over a foot-bridge, where a monstrous giant held two crocodiles in a leash to hinder any one from passing ; so that I saw it was time for me to prepare myself for the combat. I advanced, therefore, with all imaginable intrepidity, but had I not received on my buckler a blow which the giant made at me with his club, I must have certainly been crushed into a thousand pieces. Having happily, however, evaded it, I gave him such a terrible back-blow with my enchanted sword that I cut off both his legs ; and his body, in falling into the water that ran under the bridge, dragged one of the crocodiles along with it. All that I had then to do was to encounter the other, which I attacked with great courage ; but as its skin was harder than any diamond, I was obliged to make several powerful strokes at it before I could send it after its companion.

As soon as I saw the passage clear, I went immediately into the garden, and walked along a parterre adorned with white marble statues fixed upon pedestals, I took notice of only one pedestal without one. After I had ranged over the garden almost twelve hours, fighting and conquering new monsters, and destroying all enchantments that I met with, I came at last to a little mosque into which I entered, and was struck with the most profound veneration at the sight of a Persian, who was reading aloud in the Koran, and after he had shut the book, cried out—O great Prophet, friend of God ! the commendation of thy glory is perfect in the verse Toulax, and of thy great goodness in the chapters Faha and Jasim.

Prince, dearly beloved by Mohammed, said the

venerable person, turning towards me, praise the Sovereign Creator of the world, because it is He alone who has opened to thee a way unknown to all mankind besides. You see in me Mohammed-Mahdi, the twelfth and last iman of the great Prophet, though my enemies falsely report me to be dead; because in the battle which I fought with the Caliph of Babylon for the support of the true religion, God was pleased to take me from the midst of it and to translate me to this enchanted place, where I am to continue until the time appointed for my return upon earth, not only to restore the race of imans to the imperial throne, but likewise to kill Dijal, who by his impostures would destroy the wise precepts of the book which God by an angel dictated to his ambassador. —Is it possible, cried I, in a transport of joy, that I should live to behold the ornament of the servants of God—that great iman, who, to the end of the world, is to illustrate those truths which his cruel enemies in vain endeavour to obscure? — Yes, without doubt, answered the iman, it is I who am reserved for these wonders; and after several ages expect the great day in which God is to be glorified by my means.—But when will that day arrive, said I to the inman; that day of consolation to true Mohammedans, and of confusion to their enemies?—I am going to shew you, answered he, how far distant we are from it. Then taking me by the hand he carried me to the top of a quadrangular tower, from whence he shewed me a city which he told me was twelve thousand parazanges[1] in circumference, in which were twelve thousand gates, over which were as many

---

1 A parazange contains four thousand geometrical feet.

granaries full of mustard seed for the sustenance of one single bird, which was to eat no more than one grain a day.

The world will not end, my dear child, said he, until this seed be entirely consumed ; but when that day will be, no one knoweth but God.—And how do you call that fine city ? said I.—It is called Jihawhar-Abad, replied he, and very justly, because it has immense treasures in it. All Persian historians sing its praise ; but few people have the honour to see it, even at a distance, as you do, and none ever entered into it without passing the Pul-Sirrah[1] and giving an account of their good actions. It is to this stately city, continued Mohammed-Mahdi, that true Mohammedans after their death go and choose for themselves the women who are for ever to continue virgins, which Mohammed promised them, and carry them thence into the Garden of Eden. When a person is once convinced of this truth, can he give himself up to the world ? Consider what the world is, O man ! and you will find it to be nothing but a phantom and a dream ; and since it is only able to yield you sorrow and affliction, why are you so earnest after goods that perish and so very negligent of what are immortal ? How deplorable is your condition when you forsake the voice of justice and the laws of our Holy Prophet ! Make not yourself, said he, tents upon earth that can only be fixed for awhile ; and encumber not yourself, to no purpose, with baggage that must always be packed up and ready for a march.

I was extremely ravished, continued the mandarin,

---

1 Pul-Sirrah signifies the half-way bridge.

to hear this sublime discourse of the iman, when we heard the most delightful music at the bottom of the tower. Prepare yourself, said he, for the last combat you are to engage in. This is the Jinniyah Mirjihan-Banu, the old woman who, to pleasure her son, brought into the gardens belonging to this place forty of the chief lords' daughters of Ispahan, and there turned them into stone.—Oh, Heavens! cried I, are the figures which I took to be marble as I passed by them, the beautiful virgins of Ispahan?—Yes, said Mohammed-Mahdi, and those which represent the men are so many gallant persons who have attempted to rescue them out of the tower.—But why is there one pedestal, cried I, which has no statue upon it?—That is designed for you, said he, if you suffer yourself (as other heroes have done before you) to be seduced by the artful impostures of the jinniyah; for then both you and those you attempt to deliver shall continue in this state of insensibility until the end of the world. Nor must you think that you can attain your end without Jiyan-ibn-Jiyan's puissant buckler, which will shew you the enchantress such as she really is; that is to say, ugly, and in the same figure wherein she appeared at Ispahan; whereas your fascinated senses will represent her as the model of all perfection. Be sure you fall upon her, then, with your sword and buckler, pursue her to the bottomless pit, and when she and Jiyuf and all her retinue retreat thither, cover the top of it with the wonderful buckler the Prophet has sent you, and leave it there as a trophy of your victory, which all the elementary powers will never be able to remove without the permission of Him who with one breath created the world, and can with the same dissolve it into nothing.

15—2

I did very readily what the iman ordered me, continued the mandarin; I went down to the bottom of the
tower, where I beheld one of the most beautiful persons I
had ever seen.   But when I was a little more than ten
paces from her, and held up my buckler against her, both
she and all her company seemed so exceedingly hideous
that I made no hesitation but fell immediately upon her,
sword in hand.   When she perceived that her wiles and
stratagems were of no avail, she cried out most lament-
ably and betook herself to flight.   I pursued her close,
drove her across the parterre, where the white statues
stood, and when she had endeavoured to escape me,
but in vain, she and all her jinnis were forced to throw
themselves into a kind of pit, and I covered the top of it
with my buckler.

Immediately hereupon proceeded from the bottom of
the pit horrible groans, and the violent tossings of the
evil jinnis so shook the earth that I could not stand upon
my feet, but fell down, holding still my sword in my hand,
and after a short swoon found myself in the open field
not far from Ispahan, surrounded with forty young
damsels more beautiful than the moon when at full, and
nine-and-thirty fine gentlemen who fell at my feet to
thank me for the liberty I had procured them.   Sir, said
one of these brave Persians to me, some one of these
beautiful young ladies is designed for your spouse ; when
you shall have cast your eye upon her whom you are
pleased to honour with your favours, we will entreat the
others to choose whom they like best among us, and will
each be content with his lot.   I knew perfectly well it
was the intention of the Prophet that I should comfort
myself for the loss of the Princess Dafila, and therefore,

after I had surveyed all these fair persons with attention, I gave my hand to one among them whose sweet looks and shining beauty were not inferior to those of our first mother, the wife of the Sultan Adam.

After all the rest had chosen them husbands, we were preparing to make our entrance into Ispahan when a vast crowd of people who came out of the gates informed us that the Sultan of Persia and all his court were coming to admire an event so extraordinary that had happened not far from the gate of his palace. The violence of the earthquake and the fall of some part of the Tower of the Forty Virgins had made too great a noise in the neighbourhood not to have been carried to his ears. I therefore put myself at the head of my little company, and went to meet a monarch whose personal merit was renowned over all the East. After I had paid him the civilities that were due, while my Persians and their new wives lay prostrate at his feet, I acquainted him who I was and in what manner I had accomplished so extraordinary an adventure. The prince heard my story with admiration, hugged and caressed me very tenderly, and desired that I and all my retinue would lodge in his palace.

There was nothing after this but feasting and sporting for above a month together; in which time the king conferred great wealth and benefits upon the thirty-nine Persians whom I had restored to their liberty. As to myself, I was sensible that my absence would make my father very uneasy, and therefore made preparation to return into his kingdom. Wherefore, after I had received all the civilities which it was proper for me to accept from the King of Persia, I took my leave, and having a very prosperous journey soon arrived in the kingdom of Tigris. Abadaraman, highly satisfied to see me return after so long an absence, and the more so because I brought with me a spouse fit to be the queen of the whole earth, conjured me to leave him no more. I fulfilled his request; and at his death succeeded to the throne, and governed the people with so much equity that I make no doubt they lamented my loss when I came to pay the common tribute to nature in extreme old age; and continued to my children the same love which they had shewn to me in my lifetime.

  *   *   *   *   *   *

These events, said the Queen of China, are very curious; the moral they include pleases me much, nor can you do me a greater favour than to continue them.— With all my heart, madam, answered the mandarin; but they begin now to draw to a conclusion; for after I had left the body of Kadir-Bilah I entered that of a young infant, who was born at Gannan in the house of a mandarin of letters, learned in the law, and was called Fum-Hoam, the name which I now actually bear. My father, who was a man well skilled in all sciences, spared no pains for my promotion, and in a short time so far improved me in the study of our law and religion that at twenty years old, or something more, the sultan who reigned before our august monarch (whom Allah preserve!) made me a mandarin of the first order; and by a particular privilege I administered justice at Gannan, the place of my nativity.

I applied myself very diligently to the most sublime sciences, and had the good fortune to contract an acquaintance with a philosopher of profound erudition, who communicated to me the power he had over jinnis; and it was by their help that I restored the Sultan Malik al-Salim to the throne of Georgia.—I will always remember that service, answered Gulchinraz, and must conjure you to continue to my father your protection, which is so necessary for his return to Tiflis; and do not fail coming to-morrow at this time, because I am desirous to reason with you about the different adventures of your life, which instead of persuading me that your religion is better than mine have only confirmed me still stronger in the belief of the laws of Mohammed.—We shall see that to-morrow, answered the mandarin, smiling. I hope, however, that the Sultan of Georgia, the King of China, your majesty, and myself, will agree about that point.—I doubt it very much, replied the queen.—But I am pretty certain of it, answered the mandarin with a smile.

CONTINUATION OF THE HISTORY OF MALIK AL-SALIM, OF TONGLUCK, AND OF GUL-CHINRAZ GUNDOGDI

THE two monarchs and Gulchinraz had a great deal of discourse about the different adventures of Fum-Hoam, and after supper each retired to his own apartment, where they passed the night very quietly. As soon as the morning appeared, Malik al-Salim went into the Sultan of China's chamber, which was parted from his only by a rich closet, where the shutters and curtains were not yet open. Are you asleep, sir? said he.—No, answered Tongluck. Gulchinraz, whose head is filled with Fum-Hoam's

stories, has awakened me to tell me a pleasant dream.
She told me that she dreamed we three were last night
carried into Georgia, and that your wazirs accompanied
by the mandarin were waiting with impatience until it
was time for them to come and testify their joy for your
happy return.—That is very strange, replied the Sultan
of Georgia. I have had exactly the same dream which
made me awake so suddenly, and what is very astonishing I protest I find a change in the palace; my chamber
as I was getting up appeared to be the very same as
that in which I used to sleep at Tiflis; the closet that
parts us seemed in the dark of a different figure than
usual, and I think much fault may be found with the
situation of things even in this room.—It is an easy
matter to convince you of your error, cried Tongluck,
laughing and running to the window. But how great
was his surprise to find himself in a place he knew
nothing of! and how great the joy of Malik al-Salim
and his daughter, on finding themselves in their palace
at Tiflis! Scarcely could they believe their own eyes.

Gulchinraz got up with the utmost expedition, and
going with her father and husband into an ante-chamber
that led into the guard-room, heard a confused noise.—
As she opened the door Fum-Hoam appeared at the head
of the wazirs of Georgia, who threw themselves at their
sultan's feet, and expressed more by their tears than they
could in words. Malik al-Salim was moved with tenderness and compassion; he embraced each of them
separately, and ordered them to distribute a hundred
thousand pieces of gold among the people. The return
of this good king spread in a few hours an exceeding
great gladness over all Tiflis; nothing was heard but

acclamations of joy, and the people who were doubtful of their happiness begged the sultan to shew himself in public. He was too well pleased with their zeal to deny them that small token of his love; he appeared for above an hour upon a terrace that looked into the square, and shewed them at the same time the Princess Gulchinraz and the deserving husband which Heaven had provided for her.

After the first transports of joy were over, and the two monarchs were at liberty, they embraced the mandarin a thousand times. Is all this that we see real? said Malik al-Salim to him. Is it possible that we can be at Tiflis? Is it not rather an illusion and the result of a dream which my daughter and I both had last night?—No, sir, replied Fum-Hoam; you are really in Georgia. The jinnis who are under my direction have executed their orders punctually. They carried us into this country in fewer than three hours; and you are not, I hope, fatigued with the expedition.—No, indeed, said Gulchinraz, I never slept better in my life, and had such pleasant dreams that I was not desirous to awake.—You have not told the king, your husband, all, then, added the mandarin.—That is true, continued the queen, with a blush; but since you can enter into the bottom of my thoughts I will tell him. I fancied, sir, said she to the Sultan of China, that I was with child and delivered of a most beautiful prince. As soon as he was born, your majesty was for having him carried to the pagoda-royal, to return thanks to the gods for giving you a successor. I was sadly concerned to see that you refused, even though I requested it with tears, to have him brought up in the religion of our Holy Prophet, when, somehow or other, the Mandarin Fum-Hoam was in my chamber. Mighty monarch, said he to you, our gods are nothing but monsters, to which the fear and credulity of the Chinese have built temples. There is but one God in the universe ; He is the first mover of all things, and His great Prophet is Mohammed.—Whereupon you looked upon the mandarin in the strangest confusion, and said— What ! is it you who talk at this rate to me ? You, who have always been the support of the religion of your fathers ; you, whom our gods account one of their chief sacrificers ; you, in short, who have promised to engage my wife to live with me in the same faith.—I once made you that promise, answered Fum-Hoam ; but I must now discover to you my real sentiments, and cast off the mask which conceals a true friend of the great Prophet.

After that, by a train of extravagant imaginations such as sleep usually produces, this illustrious philosopher seemed in a moment stripped of his old skin ; the wrinkles which were indented on his face and made it so venerable were all smoothed, and instead of him I thought I beheld a young man much about two-and-twenty years old, dressed in a Persian habit. I embraced him with much tenderness, nor could I tell why, only my father and you, sir, did the same. It is time to depart to Tiflis, said he to us, and then giving us his girdle to take hold of, we flew through the air with incredible swiftness and arrived at this palace.

This, sir, was my dream, and Fum-Hoam must give us the explication of it.—That, madam, I will gladly do, said the mandarin, and I hope that you will all be soon satisfied ; but I must first of all ask pardon for the imposture I have made. I never really was, nor am I at present, the Mandarin Fum-Hoam; he is actually at Gannan, and I only assumed his shape as often as I had occasion for it.—Not Fum-Hoam! cried the King of China; who are you, then?—I am a Persian, sir; I was born at Tiflis, and in this palace, even in this very chamber first saw the light. — In this chamber! replied Malik al-Salim; ah! how is that possible?—It is easy to conceive, sir, since I am Prince Al-Rohamat, your son, who at two years old was taken away by corsairs; but to convince you of this I will presently appear to you in my own natural form. Upon this, some part of Gulchinraz's dream being accomplished, the old man disappeared, and in his place came a person like him she had seen in her dream; and now they beheld a beautiful young Persian, who had in his face all the lines and features of the King of Georgia.

This surprising adventure put the two kings and Gulchinraz into an inexpressible astonishment. What! cried out Malik al-Salim, embracing the young Persian, do I see again my dear Al-Rohamat, that beloved son, whose loss cost me so many tears? Is it he who has restored me to my throne? Is it he whose life has been such a chain of wonders?—Ah, it is Al-Rohamat! I am convinced by the emotions of nature, my heart tells me it is he, and his extreme likeness to my daughter is a certain confirmation of the voice of nature. He was taken from me on the coast of Guriyal; I made every possible enquiry after him, but in vain; I could hear no tidings of him, and alas! believed he was buried in the sea; but now I have met with him again, invested with more power than all the kings upon earth put together. What consolation is this to my old age! what extravagance of joy! The good father then renewed his embraces ; Tongluck and his spouse almost smothered him with their caresses, which, after he had returned with a great deal of tenderness, I will now, said he, acquaint you with my adventures without any manner of disguise.

STORY OF AL-ROHAMAT, AND THE CONCLUSION OF THE HISTORY OF MALIK AL-SALIM, KING OF GEORGIA, OF SULTAN TONGLUCK, AND OF GULCHINRAZ GUNDOGDI

I WAS brought up in a castle by the seaside not far from Guriyal, where the sultan, my father, at that time resided, when a fancy took my nurse one day that she would go out a walking, and as the weather was fine she had strayed half a league from home, without ever minding where she was ; in her return, however, she was intercepted by six corsairs. Her cries made the slaves who followed us come up, but as none of them was armed they soon ran away, and the corsairs carried me and Sa'adi (for that was my nurse's name) into a small boat, that soon ran us aboard a vessel, which immediately put to sea. The wind, which was favourable at first, presently changed, and there arose so furious a tempest that we thought a thousand times we should have been lost. However, after we had borne the violence of the sea, and been tossed about for some time, the storm at last ceased, and we arrived at Kafa, the place where the corsairs who took me away usually live. They sold me,

as they did the others they had taken, and I fell to a
rich jeweller named Naddhan, who designed me for a
companion to his only son, much about my age. As the
richness of my clothes gave him reason to believe I was
a person of no mean condition, which my nurse confirmed, without discovering what blood I was descended
from, he took all imaginable care of me, and the little
Alazizi, his son, was not treated with more tenderness
than myself. Sa'adi was in the utmost grief at not
having an opportunity to acquaint the sultan, my father,
where I was, and thereupon she. fell into so deep a
melancholy that at the end of six months she died, and
left me alone, abandoned and ignorant of my parentage.

Alazizi and myself began soon to have the use of
our reason, and the young man was so charmingly good-
humoured that I loved him with the utmost tenderness,
which he was not backward in returning. This friendship increased with our years, and we were become
inseparable ; when Alazizi unfortunately conceived a
passion for a jeweller's daughter of Kafa, named Zahir,
who, to his great sorrow, he soon understood was
promised to a kadi's son, for whom she had an invincible
aversion. Okilan, the kadi's son, was not only very
ugly and insolent, but a mere brute in his temper ; and
so confident of the agreement he had made with her
father that he gave himself no trouble to gain the young
lady's consent. Alazizi was informed of Zahir's sentiments, and, having found means to bribe one of her
slaves, was introduced into the house, and declared his
passion to her in such affectionate terms that she was
charmed with his merit, and even entreated him to
rescue her from Okilan's tyranny, and prevail with her

father to break off the match. Alazizi made me the confidant of his love, and we imparted it to his father Naddhan. The honest jeweller, who loved his son very tenderly, went immediately to confer with the father of Zahir.

My dear friend, said he, I understand that you design your daughter for the kadi's son; but have you thoroughly considered the matter? for, to say nothing of the young man's ill qualities, reflect a little on the engagement into which you are about to enter. The kadi will despise you; his son, who is a mere debauchee, will soon be weary of Zahir, and return her on your hands again, to your great disconsolation. Now I have an expedient to avoid all these inconveniences; you know Alazizi, nor is it proper for me to remind you of his merit; he adores your daughter; I have no other child but him. I have above fifty thousand pieces of gold, and as much or more in jewels; my house is my own; and few people have a greater number of valuable slaves than myself; all these I offer you, if you will break off your engagement with the kadi. Consider, therefore, of my proposal.

Zahir's father was a little startled at this proposition, but as he could not promise himself near the advantage in matching his daughter to Okilan, he readily accepted Naddhan's offer; desiring, however, that the engagement might be secret until he should find an opportunity to get quit of the kadi's son, which was no very difficult matter to accomplish, for he scarcely ever opened his mouth without uttering some rudeness or other—nay, that very night he made use of several, which Zahir, in pursuance of her father's order, sharply resented; so that the quarrel grew high, and the jeweller coming in, took his daughter's part with some warmth, and desired Okilan to go home about his business. The young brute who valued himself on his quality, took this affront in very great disdain, and went out in a violent rage.

The jeweller went immediately to Naddhan, and after they had agreed together they determined to have Alazizi and Zahir married the day following. When Okilan understood this he was in a great fury, and vowed to revenge himself; and it was not long before he put his design in execution. As Alazizi and myself were one evening coming from his mistress's house, we were attacked by the kadi's son at the head of eight ruffians. We had happily time to put ourselves on our defence, and had killed three of them before we received the least wound; but as my young master was no very expert swordsman, he received from Okilan a blow with his sabre which cleft his head asunder. I was now left alone against the six assassins, and, growing mad and furious at the sight of Alazizi's death, resolved to perish or revenge his fall. I forced my way through the villains who kept me from Okilan, and at length stabbed him to the heart with a dagger which I held in my left hand, while I defended my life with my sabre in the right. After this I fought only to secure my retreat; for I was wounded in five or six places, and it was with much difficulty that I reached Naddhan's house. His grief for the murder of his son was inexpressible; and the surgeon whom he instantly sent for was about to dress my wounds, when about forty officers, with the kadi at the head of them, broke open the door, and tore me from the arms of that unhappy father. They then beat me most unmercifully, and carried me to a frightful dungeon, where they threatened me with the most infamous punishment. It was to no purpose for me to protest my innocence or remonstrate against the kadi, who ought not to be both judge and party. I had certainly been condemned to the most cruel death, if Naddhan, notwithstanding the weight of his affliction, had not instantly applied to the Governor of Kafa, and related to him, with floods of tears, the murder of his son and the revenge I had taken of the murderer. But all the natural eloquence which sorrow dictates availed nothing. It was not in the power of words to move the heart of that governor. His greedy eyes were fixed on a very fine diamond which the jeweller had on his finger, and Naddhan, perceiving the object which engrossed all his attention, offered to give it him, provided he would save my life. I accept of your present, said he, for the love I bear you ; for you know I have always esteemed you, though it is not in my power to determine this affair. Your best way will be to present your petition to me, wherein you appeal to the Sultan of Azak. I will then order your slave to be removed into some of the prisons of this castle, but I cannot dispense with his being in a dungeon. I will be responsible, however, for his life, till your return from Azak, whither I would advise you immediately to hasten if you would defeat the kadi's violence : this, my dear friend, is all I can do for you.

Naddhan did as the governor advised him. I was removed by virtue of his petition ; he went over to Azak, and at length obtained, but not without warm solicitations and a present of two thousand pieces of gold to the prime wazir, my liberty and the kadi's recall. After about four months' absence, during all which time I was languishing in prison, Naddhan returned from Kafa with a new kadi, who had the sultan's orders executed relating to me. I was therefore released out of prison; but oh! in what a sad condition did my master find me! So little care had been taken of my wounds that some of the wounded sinews were quite shrunk, my face was bent down to the ground, and the dampness of the dungeon had given me the rheumatism all over my body.

In this deplorable condition I was carried to my master's house, who could not forbear weeping at the sight of me. The ablest physicians with all their medicines were unable to restore me; and thus I continued until my master's death, which happened about three years after, when he bequeathed me his whole estate. The first thing I did was to give freedom to the slaves who had served along with me, and to purchase others; and as my life, considering the lamentable condition I was in, was very irksome to me I passed my time in reading good books; and meeting with one among the rest, which treated of the great Sulayman's excellence by means of a ring that enabled him to do everything, I read with great eagerness the principles of that noble science, which, by a way unknown to the vulgar, conveys to us the knowledge of the most sublime truths.

I was grievously vexed that I could not readily enter into the sense of this science, which seemed to be concealed under a too mysterious cover. I saw with admiration, that by pronouncing certain words after a peculiar manner one might move the heavens and the earth as easily as one's lips; that at the pronounciation

16

242 Transmigrations of the Mandarin Fum-Hoam

of these words, the jinnis, both good and evil, stood aghast, and enquired of one another why the world was in such disorder ; that other words made them come round the person who pronounced them, just like soldiers about their general ; and that, by the force and combination of particular letters, all the powers of the air and earth might be bound up in the same manner as they were once subjected to the will of that sage, who was such a favourite with Heaven as to attain this profound knowledge.

The more I perused this book the more I lost myself in deep meditations ; and one day, as I was musing on these things, and pronouncing all manner of ways the different words which the Sultan Sulayman made use of to command the jinnis, I was not a little surprised to see before me, on a sudden, a young man, who seemed not more than fifteen, and of a more than mortal beauty. A part of thy vows is heard, said he ; I am one of the jinnis of the air, whom thou hast invoked in terms of which thou dost not as yet thoroughly comprehend the force ; but as thou possessest the qualities requisite to be initiated into mysteries which are above the comprehension of the vulgar, see that thou go—how great soever the expense may be—into the province of Kistag, to a little village called Sargultzar, because of the great plenty of roses which grow there. Thou wilt there find a famous physician named Koda-Bandi, whom thou must address in the words which make all the wicked intelligences tremble in their profound caverns, " Allah-Illah Iha, Akhbar-Allah " [1] (for this is the

---

[1] God is great, God is great.

manner of salutation among the sages), and tell him that Aralim desires him to fill thy brain with the dew of a rose that is white and as clear as crystal. And no sooner had Aralim uttered these few words than he immediately disappeared.

You cannot imagine, my dear sister, continued Al-Rohamat, turning to the Queen of China, what satisfaction I felt at the apparition of this jinni. I lost not one of his words, but wrote them down for fear of forgetting them; and so preparing for my departure, caused a palanquin to be made, and bought me two camels to carry me to Sargultzar, where I arrived after a very tedious journey. My first care was to inform myself where Koda-Bandi lived; and they told me, not far from a fountain that wrought every day the most extraordinary cures. In short, I was informed that people from all parts of the world came thither for their health; that the paralytic recovered the use of their limbs, and those of a bad digestion stomachic heat enough to concoct their food; that old people seemed there to grow young again, and women to add new charms to their beauty and comeliness; in a word, there was no malady so old and obstinate but it might be washed away in this fountain, and that Koda-Bandi, who had the direction of the waters, ordered them to be taken different ways according to the age and constitution of the patient.

As soon as I had rested myself a little, I was carried to this famous physician's house. I saluted him as the jinni commanded me, and no sooner had he heard these divine words, than repeating them with a marvellous transport, Praise and magnify God, said he, young man, for vouchsafing to make choice of you to be instructed in so sublime a science as that of which the great Sulayman was master; and to deliver you from the misery which man is ordinarily subject to, by giving you the command over all intelligences. For, indeed, what is man? And how does he enter upon this scene of life? May not one properly enough say that he is a poor mariner whom the sea has cast· ashore after it has made him the sport of its waves and fury? Nature, when she looses him from the bands of his mother's womb, only exposes him upon the earth destitute of those succours which she usually affords to other creatures. He cannot sustain himself; he is born naked, and fills the place of his nativity with his cries, which indeed are the most just and natural of all his actions, for how can he too much bewail that almost unavoidable train of infelicity which seldom fails to attend him !

This is the condition of a common man, but the true philosopher and the sage is. of quite a different nature. His knowledge raises him as much above the ordinary level of mankind as the heavens are above the earth. He suffers not his passions to govern him; he is greater than all kings and princes; he commands the elements; all nature is subject to him; the jinnis obey him; and nothing but what is unjust is too difficult for him to accomplish; this is what you are about to become. Your patience under your afflictions, your continual application to the study of virtue, and your constant inclination to do that which is good, have obtained you that favour which is granted but to few. Take, then, especial care that the many benefits which the goodness of Heaven bestows make you not proud, and be sure to conceal all the knowledge I am going to communicate, under a plain and modest appearance, and such as may not draw upon you the envy of the wicked : this is the method which I take to be perfectly happy. There are few sick people who come here that do not return in good health ; but think you it is the water which they drink, or bathe in, that has this operation upon them ? No, no, my dear friend ; I have a sovereign remedy of a very different kind for all their maladies, and to convince you of this, smell only the elixir enclosed in this small phial.—I opened it, continued Al-Rohamat, and put it to my nose ; but no sooner had I smelt the vapour that issued from it than I felt a strange disorder in every part of my body ; and instead of being crooked, as I was before, I raised myself as upright as it was possible to be.

This, said Koda-Bandi, is what I could easily do to all who come to Sargultzar, but then these miracles would soon draw upon me the envy of the physicians. I choose, therefore, to heal my patients gradually, and to make them believe they owe their respective cures to the waters of this fountain. Nay, I must even desire you not to seem as if you were healed till some few days are past, during which time I will thoroughly instruct you in our mysteries. Assume, therefore, the posture you just now used, and call your slaves, and desire them to go to the place where you first alighted, and there wait till they are sent for.—I did as Koda-Bandi desired me ; and in five days' time, wherein I pretended to be drinking the waters of Sargultzar, that famous philosopher disclosed to me all the secrets of nature, so that I became as able a proficient as himself in a science which may be

justly esteemed divine. At the expiration of that time
I left Koda-Bandi, and my slaves were astonished to
see me as straight and upright as if I had never been
otherwise, and at my return to Kafa everyone looked
upon my cure as a miracle.

As soon as I got home, I ordered the Jinni Aralim
to attend me, and according to Koda-Bandi's instructions
consulted him about my birth. He surprised me very
agreeably by informing me that I was the son of Malik
al-Salim, and that my name was Al-Rohamat. He
informed me likewise of the manner in which I was
stolen away by the pirates, and of the death of my
nurse. It was with the most inconceivable grief I
learned that the Sultan of Georgia was banished from
his kingdom by the usurper Dilsinghin, and after having
for a considerable time wandered about the East, was
at length obliged to seek for protection under one of
the King of China's subjects.

On receiving this information I immediately passed
over into the dominions of Tongluck, where I saw Malik
al-Salim and Gulchinraz, without being in the least known
by them. I then took upon me the form of Fum-Hoam,
whom I conveyed to my house in Kafa, where I caused
him to remain in a deep sleep while I personated his
appearance. With the rest, sir, you are perfectly
acquainted. It was by my means Tongluck was informed that Holonjah had in his house a lady of Georgia,
who excelled the very houri in beauty; that this monarch
resolved to see her under an assumed name; that he fell
in love with her; that he cut off the traitor Dilsinghin's
head; and, in short, that he was joined to my dear sister
by bands which will continue sacred and inviolable as

long as they both shall live. Only, sir, continued
Al-Rohamat, addressing his discourse to the Sultan of
China, if I have pretended to be a zealous follower
of the religion of your ancestors, it has been to engage
you by an irrevocable oath to live with the queen your
spouse in the religion she professes; and a little reflection, I hope, will determine you. For, in truth, is there
anything more contrary to good sense than the transmigration of the soul from one body to another? To
accommodate myself in some measure to the extravagant
accounts of your mandarins of the law, I have told you
some histories much to the taste of what they are every
moment relating, and some of which have really happened
in the world, but not to me, who never was any other
than what I am now, except when I thought proper to
make myself appear to your eyes under another figure
by virtue of some cabalistic words with which I am
acquainted. How can they, according to their own
principles, remember in one body what was transacted
in another? But suppose they could, upon the sup-
position of the soul's passing from body to body, how
miserable must it needs be to be always subject to
the prevailing inclinations of the form it inhabits? For
in short, all wild beasts have a sad and cruel tincture
of their own species; fraud and malice are hereditary to
the fox and monkey; flight and timidity belong to does
and harts; and it is greatly, indeed, vilifying the soul to
imagine it has not sufficient power to alter the habitude
of any body in which it resides.

According to the accounts propagated by some of
your mandarins, men are often irrational, while the most
savage and ferocious animals are frequently endowed

with the most exalted understandings. Ah, my dear
lord! you have surely too much good sense to be a dupe
of such ridiculous fables; but seduced by the prejudices of
education, have never once reasoned about the religion
of your forefathers. Is it possible that you can persuade
yourself, as the vulgar believe, that the immortal nature
of our souls is subject to a body which is only the
nourishment of worms; and that among an innumerable
multitude of souls there should be so fierce an emulation
who should first enter into the body that is lately formed,
and not rather agree among themselves that the first
comer be the first received into the body which wants it?

According to this way of reasoning death will be
nothing more than a frightful name. All its methods of
approach will be indifferent to us, and it will be the same
thing whether we do good or evil actions, which is a
position abhorrent to nature. You will tell me, perhaps,
according to the system of your mandarins and of Hindu
Brahmins, that in proportion to their merit or demerit
souls pass into baser or nobler bodies; but what sort
of bodies do your doctors and the Brahmins account
superior to the rest? A cow, they say, is a superior
animal, because this creature has something divine in
it. The soul which resides in that creature hopes
shortly to be purified of all the sins wherewith it was
polluted in the world by being presented to their gods.
And what are these gods themselves but monsters or
imaginary beings, invented by the knavery of your
first sacrificers, and supported by the licentiousness
and independence of those who have succeeded to
their places? A cow, one of the clumsiest animals
next to a hog, which you make your finest dishes

of, and which we hold in abomination! And do you really believe such idle stories? No, sir, no; I am persuaded to the contrary, and that my sister has already shewn you the difference between so ridiculous a religion and that of Mohammed, whose great truths, as they are contained in the Koran, deserve admiration. This venerable work, extracted out of the great book of the Divine decrees, was set aside at the creation of the world, to be deposited in one of the seven heavens under the firmament, and was thence brought, verse by verse, to our sovereign Prophet, by an angel of the first hierarchy, in the space of three-and-twenty years, according to the exigencies of mankind. So that none but persons of the purest hearts dare touch this book, which was sent him from the King of all ages — Allah, who, with the breath of His mouth, made the heavens and earth, and every living creature! And of this truth, both wise men and angels are fully persuaded—viz., that there is no other God but He, and that Mohammed is His ambassador.

This precious book contains the history of all that is past, infallible predictions of what is to come, and just and righteous laws for the time present. It enjoins us to do good actions, not to fail repeating five prayers every day, and to make the legal ablutions regularly. What can be more beautiful than this verse in the chapter of Araf? " Be ready to forgive," says he; " do good to all men, and have no contest with the ignorant."—What can be more eloquent than what is couched in the chapter Houd, where, to assuage the deluge, God is brought in, saying these sublime words? " Earth, drink up thy waters; and heaven, draw up those which

17

thou hast poured out! whereupon the water immediately retired, the rainbow rested upon the mountain, and these words were heard—" Woe to the wicked ! "

This, sir, is the religion which we profess, these are the laws which it imposes ; it consists not, like yours, in the adoration of monsters and of rebel angels; we worship God only, whose power is infinite, and who, as our Prophet teaches us, needs but a few grains of dust to overthrow His adversaries and to punish the wicked in a terrible manner.   For was it not He who to chastise the pride of Kaykahus sent a gnat to penetrate his very brain, and to give him such exquisite torments that he was obliged to be destroyed ?   Was it not He who made the body of Farrayum float upon the sea with his iron breast-plate on; to let His people see how He had delivered them from so formidable an enemy, with whose death they were unacquainted ?   Was it not in favour of Mohammed, and to preserve him from the fury of the Gorayshites, that while he was reposing himself in a cave on the Mountain Thur an acacia tree grew in one night at the mouth of the grotto, wherein a pair of wild pigeons built their nest and the rest of the entrance was covered over by a spider's web, which made his pursuers believe that no person had lately entered there ?   Does he not tell you further, in the chapter of Elephants, that God sent against His enemies flying squadrons, who pelted them with stones that were marked with every man's name, and scattered them like corn in the field which the birds ate up ?   Do not pretend, then, sir, to compare your religion with ours.   You have promised Gulchinraz, that if I prevail not with her to embrace the worship of your gods you would trample under foot the idols you have now the weakness to adore. That time is happily come, and I have an incredible satisfaction to perceive that my discourse has made some impression upon you. Yes, sir, you are already a Mohammedan in your heart, and by your example your whole people will embrace the religion of Mohammed, and not eat of the fruit of the tree Zakon, which grows only in hell. You and your posterity shall in that great day, which shall make the stoutest tremble, hold the book containing an account of your actions in your right hand, be placed in a new-planted apple orchard, refresh yourselves with the fruit of the tree of Muza, and our Prophet's virgins of Paradise will all strive who shall please you the most.—Yes, my dear Al-Rohamat, said the Sultan of China, this instant I am a Mohammedan, nor can I too soon perform the exercises of that religion. I shall therefore have an infinite obligation to you if you will acquaint my subjects with my resolution.—I will engage for my success in this affair, answered Al-Rohamat, and for the blessings which our Prophet will bestow upon the precious infant which Gulchinraz now bears in her womb. He shall in his generation be as illustrious in the cabalistic sciences as the most renowned philosophers, and to the end of your days be a consolation to you both.

Tongluk kept his word with Al-Rohamat. He abjured his errors, and became a good Mohammedan; and by the marvellous assistance of Al-Rohamat, returned with Gulchinraz into China, where, under the figure of Fum-Hoam, Al-Rohamat destroyed the various idols, and established the religion of Mohammed; and the queen was soon after delivered of a son, who fulfilled all his uncle's predictions and became his worthy successor.   As for Al-Rohamat, after his father's decease he reigned in Georgia with so much wisdom that his memory is to this day held in equal respect with that of the first heroes of Persia ; and performed things in general so far above the ordinary course of nature as will for ever be thought incredible by all those who are not instructed in the profound mysteries of the Cabala.

END OF THE TRANSMIGRATIONS OF THE MANDARIN
FUM-HOAM

Printed and Published by H. S. Nichols & Co., 3, Soho Square, London, W.

A LIST OF

CHOICE AND INTERESTING

PUBLICATIONS

Beautifully Printed and Issued

BY

H. S. NICHOLS & CO.

BOOKSELLERS PUBLISHERS & LITERARY AGENTS
PRINTERS & BOOKBINDERS

3 SOHO SQUARE

·LONDON W

And at 41 Quai des Grands Augustins PARIS

18

It is respectfully though particularly requested that all Recipients of this Catalogue will read the following :—

PUBLISHERS' NOTE.

WE desire to call the attention of Book Collectors and the Public to the following interesting particulars with regard to the Publications enumerated in this Catalogue, viz. :—

All Books published by us are printed on our own Presses, on our own premises, and under our own personal supervision ; and we are proud to say that the books printed and issued by us cannot be surpassed for beauty of type, paper, general " get-up," and the thousand-and-one other important trifles and details which are so necessary to make up what is now-a-days described by the term " choice."

All the founts of Type used by us in the printing of our books are most carefully chosen for their beauty of design and quaintness of style, and by using only new type, the best inks, the most skilled craftsmanship, the latest and best machinery, joined with the earnest desire to surpass what we have hitherto done, following our Motto of " Nunquam Satis," we are enabled to produce books of the very highest typographical excellence, and we have the satisfaction of feeling that the works issued and printed by us are worthy of being placed side by side with the books printed by the great Masters of the Craft of bye-gone days, and are books which all true Biblio-philes will appreciate, covet, and hoard.

With regard to the literary merit attached to our Publications they will speak for themselves, and our intention is to supply books which will become rare within the very near future, for we, as Bibliophiles, as well as Bibliopoles, know the entrancing interest and enthusiasm attaching to Desiderata.

It is not merely with the intention of making our books become scarce that we produce small and strictly limited numbers, for greater appreciation is given to books of which only small editions exist, very little interest and value being attached to those works which can be purchased everywhere ; we are content to serve the select few and to serve that select few well.

.The " Daily News " of 28th December, 1893, in reviewing " The Thousand and One Quarters of an Hour," in a leading article, says :—

" Mr. Smithers has edited, and Messrs. Nichols publish the "Contes Tartares," " The Thousand and One Quarters of an Hour," translated from the French of Gueulette, an imitator of the " Arabian Nights." But " six hundred and eighty only " of this edition are produced, the publishers probably calculating that, while there are scores of thousands of readers for the dainty reveries of M. Zola, there are only seven hundred, or so, of just men left who like an Oriental tale. . . . . The ingenious reader now surmises that this discovery leads up to the story of the Sultana, and so tale gives birth to tale, much rejoicing the six hundred and eighty who have not bowed the knee to Baalzola."—*Daily News.*

Reviewing the same book, Mr. Richard Le Gallienne in the *Star* says :—

" It would be dangerous to take up his book for the odd quarter of an hour—say, before an engagement—without being led on for a hundred or two if not the whole thousand. Those who still think that the best 'novels' yet written come from the East, or are to be found in Boccaccio, will welcome this addition to the not too well stocked shelves of fantastic romance. Many of the stories are what we euphemistically term 'hearty' in character, and for good honest fun 'The Story of Al-Kuz, Tahar, and the Miller' is especially to be recommended. How is it that millers should so often be *dramatis personæ* in stories of gallantry? The book is well printed and bound, and many thanks are due to the editor, Mr. Leonard C. Smithers, and the publishers, Messrs. H. S. Nichols and Co., for the happy thought of the translation."—*Star*.

And the same Writer says of Sir Richard F. Burton's "Kasîdah,"

" Yet for all that it is a distinct enrichment of our literature, and it should not be allowed to remain in the inaccessible form of a hundred-copy guinea edition—fine book as Messrs. Nichols have made of it."—*Star*.

These quotations, and the constant receipt by us of unstinted praise from Subscribers, stimulate us to continue our efforts, and in issuing this Catalogue (which itself is an original production in its form) we beg to assure our Subscribers of our unfailing industry, care, and judgment as regards our future issues, and we call upon intending Subscribers to send us their Names without delay, for of those books which as yet are not out of print, very few copies remain unsubscribed for, and prompt application is necessary.

N.B.—All books issued by us are intended to be sold at the net advertised price, without deduction, and are supplied to Booksellers on terms which will not allow of any discount being given by them.

THE

THOUSAND AND ONE
QUARTERS OF AN HOUR

(TARTARIAN TALES)

EDITED BY

LEONARD C. SMITHERS

LONDON

H. S. NICHOLS and CO.

3 SOHO SQUARE W

MDCCCXCIIII

19

THE THOUSAND AND ONE QUARTERS OF AN HOUR

IS IN

One volume of 316 pages, demy octavo, appropriately bound in black cloth, with specially-designed ornaments in gold on the sides, gilt tops, edges untrimmed.

600 small-paper copies, price 6s. net.

75 large-paper copies, beautifully printed on Arnold's un-bleached hand-made paper, royal octavo, bound in white vegetable parchment wrapper, with the same specially-designed ornaments in gold on the sides as in the demy octavo edition, gilt tops, edges untrimmed.   Price £1 1s. net.

There are also Five Special Copies on Japanese vellum, which are not for sale.

No further copies of any of the above-described editions will ever be printed.

· THE

GASTRONOMIST

AN

ALPHABETICAL LIST OF THE PRINCIPAL

DISHES, COURSES, WINES,

AND

SERVICE,

IN

𝔉𝔯𝔢𝔫𝔠𝔥, 𝔈𝔫𝔤𝔩𝔦𝔰𝔥, 𝔊𝔢𝔯𝔪𝔞𝔫, 𝔞𝔫𝔡 𝔖𝔴𝔢𝔡𝔦𝔰𝔥,

BY

THEODOR BENGTSON.

LONDON:

H. S. NICHOLS AND CO.,

3, SOHO SQUARE, W.

1893.

19—2

Square 8vo.; pp. 93; bound in cloth, gilt;
Price 2s. 6d., net; post free, 2s. 8d.

The

Carmina
of

Caius Valerius Catullus
Now first completely Englished into Verse
and Prose, the Metrical Part by Capt.
Sir Richard F. Burton, K.C.M.G.,
F.R.G.S., etc., etc., etc., and the
Prose Portion, Introduction,
and Notes Explanatory
and Illustrative by
Leonard C.
Smithers

LONDON : MDCCCXCIIII : PRINTED FCR THE TRANS-
LATORS : IN ONE VOLUME : FOR PRIVATE SUB-
SCRIBERS ONLY

THE CARMINA OF CAIUS VALERIUS CATULLUS

One volume of about 320 pages, the small-paper edition, medium octavo, 1,000 copies only, printed on fine hand-made paper. Handsomely half bound in vellum, with gilt design. Price £3 3s. net.

Large-paper edition, 50 copies only, royal 8vo, printed on Arnold's unbleached hand-made paper, with proofs before letters of the frontispiece in two states, on Japanese vellum and India paper. In similar binding to the small-paper edition. Price £6 6s. net.

There are also four copies on Japanese vellum, which are not offered for sale.

The frontispiece of the volume is William Blake's celebrated portrait of Catullus, printed on India paper.

No further copies of any of the above-described editions will ever be printed.

عبدو

حاجي

القصيده

THE KASÎDAH

BY

SIR RICHARD F. BURTON

M ESSRS. H. S. NICHOLS and CO. have pleasure in
announcing the issue of an *édition de luxe* of the
above Work.

"THE KASÎDAH" is a Mystical Oriental Poem of
extraordinary power and beauty on the Nature and Destiny
of Man, and is Anti-Christian and Pantheistic.

So much wealth of Oriental learning has rarely been
compressed into so small a compass, and it is a great
revelation of the strange phases of Eastern thought and
speculation.

The edition is strictly limited to ONE HUNDRED numbered
copies, large post quarto in size, is beautifully printed (on
one side of the paper only) on Arnold's unbleached hand-
made paper, and is elegantly bound in black cloth, with
Arabic inscription in gold on the sides, gilt tops, other edges
untrimmed.

The price per copy is ONE GUINEA net.

There are also five special copies on Japanese vellum
which are not for sale.

H. M. the Queen has been pleased to accept one of
the copies on Japanese Vellum.

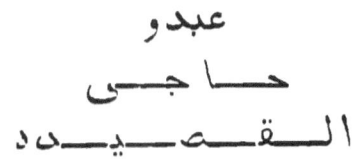

Ex otio Negotium.

OR,

MARTIALL

HIS

EPIGRAMS

TRANSLATED.

—— *vivere Chartæ*
Incipiant, Cineri gloria sera venit.
MART. lib. 1. Epig. 26.

BY

R. FLETCHER.

LONDON : PRINTED FOR DISTRIBUTION AMONGST
PRIVATE SUBSCRIBERS ONLY : MDCCCXCIII

Edition limited to one hundred and five copies, printed on Arnold's unbleached hand-made paper, large post 8vo., pp. 112, bound in blue cloth gilt, art design.

OUT OF PRINT.

CRAZY
TALES.

Σκηνη πας ὅ Βιος και παιγνιον. η μαθε παιζειν
Την σπουδην μεταθεις, η φερε τας οδυνας.

Life is a Farce, mere Children's play,
  Go learn to model thine by theirs,
Go learn to trifle Life away,
  Or learn to bear a Life of Cares

J'abandonne l'exactitude
  Aux gens qui riment par métier ;
D'autres font des vers par étude,
  J'en fais pour me desennuïer.
                GRESSET.

LONDON : PRINTED FOR DISTRIBUTION AMONGST
PRIVATE SUBSCRIBERS ONLY : MDCCCXCIIII

Edition : 210 Copies, large post 8vo., printed on Arnold's un-bleached hand-made paper, and bound in sage green cloth, the sides and back of which are covered with blind tooling of an antique design, with gilt top, front and bottom edges untrimmed. Price 10s. 6d. net.

5 Copies printed on Japanese vellum, large post 8vo., in similar binding. £2 2s. net.

MEMOIRS

OF THE

EMPRESS JOSEPHINE

WITH

ANECDOTES OF THE COURTS

OF

NAVARRE AND MALMAISON

IN TWO VOLUMES

VOLUME I

H. S. NICHOLS AND CO.
LONDON

3 SOHO SQUARE W

MDCCCXCIIII

Ready in July.

Edition strictly limited to 500 copies in two volumes, demy 8vo., well printed on fine paper, and bound in blue cloth, with edges untrimmed, illustrated with portraits of the Empress Josephine (after Isabey), and of her first husband.

The Subscription price per copy will be ONE GUINEA net.

Five extra copies will be printed on Japanese vellum, price FOUR GUINEAS net per copy.